THE WILD MOON

Soulbound Shifters (Book One)

A Soulbound Shifters Novel

Riley Storm

COPYRIGHT

The Wild Moon

Edited by Olivia Kalb

Cover Designs by Jacqueline Sweet

CONTENTS

CHAPTER ONE

The full moon is supposed to be a time of new beginnings. Of starting over. Finding yourself.

In my experience, that's been a load of shit.

The full moon brought me plenty of things. Embarrassment. Humiliation. Discomfort. Pain. Confusion. Anguish. Loss.

That last one really hurt. They all did, of course, and every month I had the unbelievable luxury of being forced to relive them. Each and every one. Over and over again.

I'm not bitter, though. Nor do I hold a grudge. Not against the moon. It waxes and wanes, without thought, without care. It's not sentient. It didn't pick me. It wasn't the moon that fucked my life up.

No, that honor belonged to one Johnathan Aldridge.

Now there's someone I hold a grudge against. It's only natural when he destroyed my entire world, isn't it? That's how I justified it, at least.

Muttering angrily to myself as I dredged up old memories, I strode along the sidewalk through my hometown of Seguin, trying hard not to make eye contact with anyone I passed.

Home.

That word had a different ring to it now, and I'd prefer not to dwell on it.

"Dani?"

I looked up at a familiar voice. "Hey, Fran," I said, trying my best to feign politeness as I took stock of my surroundings.

Apparently, my brain had been auto-piloting me across town without thinking. Usually, I avoided the post office and my old boss.

"How are you?"

I stared, momentarily unsure how to answer such a simple question when my answer was anything but.

Telling the truth was an option, of course. I could tell her all about the shitty, fucked-up life I was living in the big city. Then there was the trauma I experienced every month on my return to this dying hellhole. Or the trauma about my family. Or. Or. Or. The list went on and on some days until it felt like I had a damn CVS receipt worth of issues. Which wasn't entirely fair. There were only like three. Or four.

I didn't go into detail, though. Frannie was a

nice woman, and she didn't deserve to be unloaded upon like that. I should be polite.

"I'm back here," I said instead, letting my face do the explaining. "That should tell you everything."

The other woman smiled sadly, shaking her head at me. Her hair, long, brown, and locked into a simple braid, bounced easily from the motion. "The Wild Moon."

I nodded. "The Wild Moon."

It was the only thing that brought me back. Sort of.

Technically, it was the Alpha's rule. All shifters must be with their pack on the Wild Moon, or they would be deemed Wild and hunted down. So, I came back to avoid being hunted and killed by Lars Aldridge and his enforcers.

Yes. *That* Aldridge. I really do have great taste in men.

"See you tonight, then," Frannie said, accurately recognizing that I didn't really want to talk. My return to Seguin wasn't social, nor even of my own choice.

I had to be here.

Nodding, grateful for the excuse not to continue the conversation, I moved past my old boss and old workplace at the post office and continued along Seguin's sole main street.

Half the places I passed were boarded up, businesses and houses alike. I wish I could say that the place had gone to shit since I left, as people left in protest of my treatment, but in reality, it had been this way for years, slowly shrinking as people died and weren't replaced.

Our population was shrinking. Nobody wanted to talk about it, at least not with me, but it was obvious if someone took thirty seconds to pay attention. I'd wondered why that was when I was younger and not so cynical. Now I just attributed it to the long-ruling Aldridge family being a bunch of assholes and nobody wanting to be in their pack.

It probably wasn't the truth, but it fit my hateful little fantasy of them, and that was what mattered to me.

I purposefully took the long route to my destination. The shortcut would take me past a dark, abandoned house. In that sense, it was just one of dozens in the tiny little town, but this one hadn't always been that way. Up until eight months ago, it had been very, *very* different. Alive. Vibrant. Full of love and energy. Hope.

Now it lay dormant, absent those things, just like it was absent the family that once lived there.

Like my parents, I would never return to it.

CHAPTER TWO

I hesitated.

Not because I was scared. No, how could I be? The house in front of me was my best friend's. She and her family lived there, and I had been coming since I was a young kid. I knew it inside and out, from every nick on the giant wooden porch to the hidden crayon stains behind the old couch where we'd colored as kids. It was as much my home as hers.

And it didn't come with the bad memories of that darkened, abandoned place I'd passed by earlier.

No, I wasn't scared. I was hesitating because I needed to build up my energy. This was about to be the most close contact I'd had in twenty-eight days. Since the last time. Normally, I could suck it up, but tonight was different. This Wild Moon was going to be a special one, and I wasn't going to let my usual dour mood affect my best friend in the entire world.

Moment taken, I strode up the three rickety steps attached to the wrap-around front porch and went straight to the storm door, pulling it open and rapping firmly on the old wooden door behind. The knocks echoed on both sides of the door, followed seconds later by the hammering of footsteps.

I braced myself.

A short bundle of blonde in a teal sports bra and black athletic shorts came flying out the front door in a squeal of excitement, picking me up and spinning me around.

"Dan!" she cried, squeezing me tight.

I grinned and bore it like a good friend, ignoring the unusual short form of my name. Joanna Alustria was the only person who could call me that and still make it sound feminine, so I let her get away with it.

"Hey, Jo," I half-grunted through her squeeze. "You're feeling strong today."

The diminutive blonde dropped me. I landed easily, legs bending just a hair to absorb the landing.

"I know, right?" Jo said eagerly. "I feel *strong* today. Maybe it's just me imagining it. I don't know. Did you feel stronger the night of *your* Soulshift?"

I shuddered internally, trying not to think about that night. "No, not really," I said quickly.

"Other senses, yes. But not strength. That only came after."

"Weird," Jo said giddily, acting as if we hadn't seen each other in hours instead of a month. "My other senses are fine, but I feel like I'm stronger today. So maybe that's my thing."

"Maybe," I said with a shrug. "I really don't know."

Jo smiled up at me. While she was short and thicker, I was the opposite. Tall and without a curve to my body. We were the perfect counterparts, which had probably helped fuel our friendship.

She was also the only reason I was back in town.

"I take it you're excited about your Soulshift?" I teased.

"Are you kidding?" Jo said with a long exhale. "I've been waiting eight whole months to catch up to you! I can't wait for it. My wolf and I, united. Oh, hey, you changed your hair!"

Laughing at her mile-a-minute mind track, I flicked my hair forward, showing off the newly dyed chunky blue highlights. I'd done it on a whim a few weeks earlier, feeling the need to change something. The plain black tresses had simply become too boring.

"Yeah," I said. "I wanted to change it up. What do you think?"

"I'm digging it!" Jo said, playing with a lock of blue. "It suits the new you."

The new me. She wasn't wrong there. A lot had changed in the past eight months. A lot. Except for Jo. She hadn't changed a bit. She'd never judged me before, and she never judged me now. If I needed to become a new person, she accepted that immediately. After all, to her, I was just Dan, and that was all she needed.

And it was all I needed. Our childhood innocence was an eternity ago, but our friendship was something I held onto with more than a bit of desperation.

"Well, are you going to come in already?" Jo said, pulling the storm door open and holding it for me. "No bag, I see."

"As usual," I said with a laugh, playing out our familiar byplay about my monthly visits.

"How's life in the big city?" she asked, following me inside and closing the door behind her. "Are you still loving it there?"

"It's great," I said. "Wonderful. I'm really starting to find my place there, actually."

I didn't want Jo to worry about me.

"By Vir's Oath," Jo said, uttering a familiar shifter curse. "You have got to be the *worst* fucking liar I have ever met, Dan. Seriously. How do you expect me to believe that?"

"Blind hope and faith?" I replied deadpan.

Okay, maybe I should have expected better of Jo.

"Tell me the truth," she said in a more serious tone. "How are you doing? I know these visits aren't enjoyable for you. But I care about you, Dan."

"Thanks, Jo," I said, flopping down on the old wooden couch covering the crayon marks, my usual lounging spot when I crashed at the Alustria household. "And the truth is, it's been hard. Really hard. Making ends meet is tough. Some of my jobs have been rough."

That was an understatement, I thought to myself, thankful that my shifter healing meant Jo would never know the truth. I didn't want her to worry about me more than she already did.

"You know you can come back," Jo said quietly. "You can stay here. With Dad and me."

She didn't mention her mother. We never did. It was easier that way.

"You know I can't," I said quietly. "Not here. I can't be here anymore, Jo. It's too painful. The memories. Ever since they disappeared, Jo, I ... I can't stop thinking about them. I can't stop blaming myself."

"Dan," my best friend protested gently, telling me with that one word that I shouldn't hate myself for what had happened. She didn't need to say more to get the point across.

"I know," I said. "But still. I have to try and find

them."

Jo nodded silently. She didn't press me for more information. Like I said, BFF. She knew I didn't want to talk about my search for my missing parents. After all, there was nothing *to* talk about. They were gone, and there wasn't a single clue about what had happened to them. I'd spent thousands of dollars over the past eight months trying to track them down to no avail.

I bit my lip as everything started to come back. Not now. I couldn't handle the thoughts right now. I needed a new subject. Something that wouldn't threaten to overwhelm me and send me into a spiral of depression and sadness.

"I'm excited to see you tonight," I said, switching back to the big topic. "Finally, both of us will have shifted."

"Yes!" Jo cried. "Me, too. Being eight months younger than you has never mattered more until now. I've been *dying* to shift. To run with you under the moonlight, Dan."

"And maybe find your Soulbound mate?" I teased.

"Maybe," Jo admitted sheepishly. "You're going to be there, though, right?"

"The entire way," I promised.

Unlike me, Jo would not go through her Soulshift alone. No shifter should. That first meeting of wolf and human, transforming into the animal form, it was scary. Terrifying even. But I couldn't speak to the part after. The forming of a Soulbond with another shifter.

After all, I'd been denied that particular pleasure. Eight months running now. Unheard of for a female shifter. They never went Unbound past their Soulshift. Only the males did that.

Not me.

I was determined that Jo would have someone there for her. Her Soulshift would not be traumatic.

Unlike my own.

"Thank you," Jo said a bit sheepishly, clearly embarrassed but appreciative of my support.

"That's what best friends are for," I said. "Now, tell me what you've been up to since I last saw you!"

It would be best to distract her for the last few hours until the sun fell. At which point, we, and every other shifter in Seguin, would head to one location.

The Alpha's house.

Isn't life grand sometimes? Once a month, I get to come back to the place I hate and spend it in the company of the people who destroyed it.

CHAPTER THREE

"Out with it," I grumbled as we made our way up the graveled laneway to Aldridge Manor.

"What do you mean?" Jo asked, keeping step with me easily, though she needed nearly two steps for every one of mine. Normally, I slowed down to meet her halfway, but today I was distracted.

I did so now, however, and tried my best not to look around. There wasn't much to see yet anyway, though I knew what was to come.

"I can see you staring around, and I can all but hear the disbelief in your step, Jo," I accused. "You're my best friend, loser. You can't hide shit from me. What is it?"

"Nothing," she said as we walked past the line of trees that ran level-straight parallel to the road, blocking all view onto the property.

"Liar," I muttered.

Jo shrugged, the movement visible in my right

peripheral. I didn't look at her, instead keeping my attention focused outward, away from us. We shouldn't be in danger here at the heart of Seguin pack territory, but I was still uneasy.

Part of that would be my wolf. She knew the Wild Moon was almost here, and she longed to be set free. It had been a month since the last time. Living in a city didn't give me much in the way of freedom to shift on my own and let her bleed off some energy.

Probably yet another reason the Wild Moon shifts are always so, well, wild. A captive freed at last is going to go wild. Why should my wolf be any different?

"Wow," Jo said, taking in the house in front of us. "It's beautiful."

I lifted my eyebrows. Beautiful isn't quite the word I would use to describe the Aldridge place, but unlike Jo, I'd been here before.

"I keep forgetting this is your first time here," I said. "To me, it's just a big building full of bad memories."

"You gave all this up?"

Now I did turn to stare at my best friend. Maybe I should say I glared at her. Harshly.

"Gave it up?" I repeated. "Seriously, Jo? He was a huge asshole. Besides, we were just dating until he had his Soulshift. I made that clear from the start. I don't know what changed in him, but he knew that going in."

"Maybe," Jo said with a shrug, glancing at the lamps that flanked the driveway every so often, leading all the way up to the house itself.

Mansion would probably be the more accurate term. Lars Aldridge was the latest in a long line of Aldridges to rule the Seguin pack, and somewhere back in the line, one of his ancestors had decided that a giant mansion was a necessary part of that.

"I couldn't have kept seeing him even if I'd wanted to," I reminded Jo. "Lars wouldn't have let anyone do that if they were Soulbound. Not even his son."

"I guess," Jo said, though I could feel her soft disagreement. She had always lusted after the finer things in life more than I, so it made sense, I suppose, that she would want this sort of life.

Not me, though. No fucking way. The grand lifestyle the Aldridges tried to lead was tiring and boring. Not to mention fake as fuck. They all pretended to be polite and gracious, but in reality, they were just a bunch of assholes.

As I'd found out when I'd dated the youngest of them, who proceeded to ruin my life when I wouldn't give him what he wanted.

We passed along the side of the house, where several darkened rooms were barely visible through the windows even with the clear skies overhead. Though the sun had set hours ago, the moon hadn't come out. Not yet. Soon though, very soon.

I trembled at the reminder that my wolf would soon be free, and once more, we would fight for control. A battle of the minds to see who would control the body. I had thought it only happened that first night, the Soulshift, but it seemed my wolf was hellbent on escaping from me every Wild Moon.

Just something else that wants nothing to do with me. My wolf, my family, my mate, whoever they are.

I was a reject on multiple levels, and it was growing harder by the day to keep it all categorized.

But today wasn't about me. Today I had to keep my shit together. For Jo.

"What are we doing?" Jo asked as I led her toward the back of the crowd forming at the base of a rock formation.

"Hanging out back here, away from our dear leader's altar of bullshit," I muttered, earning me more than a few looks from other members of our pack.

Most of them looked at me, realized who I was, and then looked away. They didn't care about me, and I didn't care about them. A few stared longer, however, and I fixed one of them, Derek, with a vicious glare.

"What's his deal?" Jo asked as Derek grinned and turned away, unfazed by my look.

"He's just one of Johnathan's ass-kissers," I muttered. "They take great pride in seeing how much I hate coming back here. It's like an ongoing victory for them. I don't know."

"What a bunch of assholes," Jo said.

"Forget 'em," I said as the crowd stilled, the low mumble of whispered conversations coming to an end.

They could feel it. As could I. The time was almost here. Soon the pale white orb would rise in the sky, and the Wild Moon would overcome us all. I inhaled sharply, feeling the groundswell of excitement rise up all around us. Three hundred different sets of pheromones filled the air.

There was something about the full moon that set a shifter free, and even now, in my eighth time through it, I was still caught off guard by the fierce exultation of eroticism that flowed through the pack.

"What's going on?" Jo asked as the people around us began to strip.

"Lars is going to climb up there," I said, nodding my head at the rock formation. "He'll stand on his very own Pride Rock, make some arrogant little speech to remind us that we're all part of the pack, then we'll shift."

"Oh. Okay. But why is everyone getting

naked?"

"Do you really want your wolf getting stuck in your sports bra?" I said, the heady scent of sex warming my body. There were so many gorgeous people around me.

Men. Women. Couples. Blood was swirling through my veins, filling my body with warmth. I longed to join them. Skin gleamed in the light of the house, illuminating soft, supple curves and thick, powerful arms. My breath was growing shallower.

Keep it together. For Jo!

"It's always uncomfortable the first time," I said as Jo started to strip, looking to me for confirmation. "But it gets easier."

"Dan? Are you okay?" Jo asked, staring at me.

"Just ... a lot," I said, trying not to stare at all the flesh around me.

Some of the pack were like me, doing their best to restrain the baser desires the Wild Moon brought to the surface. Others were far less caring and stared openly, drinking in the veritable buffet of sights in front of them.

"We are the Seguin pack," a voice intoned over the group of nearly four hundred shifters gathered in the back of the Aldridge house.

I looked up to see Lars Aldridge, naked and strong, standing on top of his three-tiered Pride Rock formation, lording his Alpha status down over the rest of us.

My wolf basked in the Alpha's presence.

I wanted to tear his throat out.

"*We are the Seguin pack,*" I repeated back, along with everyone else, even Jo, who joined in at an elbow from me.

"We look after our own," Lars said, spreading his arms wide.

Who does this fucker think he is? Jesus? What an arrogant prick.

"*We look after our own.*"

I repeated it back, same as the others. Sometimes I hate myself. Why couldn't I manage even that little bit of resistance? It's not like Lars was using his Alpha command to force us to repeat after him. Yet here I was, swept up in the heat of the Wild Moon anyway and doing as I was told.

"We have one Soulshifter among us tonight," Lars said, pointing to where Jo stood at my side, naked and doing her best to hide her nudity.

I stood beside her and panted like a dog in heat, ignoring the rest of Lars' little speech about looking out for Jo. I'd never given in to the feelings before, never lowered my inhibitions enough to take part in the reckless mating that came with the Wild Moon, but that didn't mean it wasn't easy.

"Dan," Jo whispered as attention turned away from her. "I'm afraid."

"The Wild Moon is upon us," Lars intoned. "Prepare."

I looked down at my friend and smiled. "Me, too," I whispered as the moon came over the horizon. "Be strong."

Inside me, the she-bitch wolf from hell howled with sweet, sweet victory as it broke free of my grasp, the last of my mental bonds shattering as the full strength of the Wild Moon came over us.

CHAPTER FOUR

We fought for an eternity, battling in the corners of my mind.

After eight months of repeating the experience under every full moon, some might say that it had become a ritual at this point. A dance with rehearsed steps, each party knowing their role and playing it to the hilt until time wore out. For many of the pack, I'm sure that's the case.

Not for my she-bitch. The wolf half of me hated that I never let her out, except when the Wild Moon dictated that I had no choice. She fought me with every ounce of her not-inconsiderable power, and what's more, she was smart. She learned.

The first time we met, she put up a barrier between us. A simple flat wall. When I fought back, she came at me, trying to straight-up kill and eliminate me. I trapped her by letting her push on the center of the barrier, stretching it until I could tie the corners of it around her, turning her own wall against her.

At least, that's the easiest way to describe what the absolute insanity going on in my mind felt like. I'm not sure there's a literal way to express it. Not unless you've had a second soul inhabit your body and given enough power to overwhelm you if you aren't strong enough.

This time, though, as our wolf body ran, we battled in silence within my mind. Feints and traps. I never knew what was her and what wasn't. We were one and yet two. In the background, our body ran with the pack under the moonlight. Occasionally, a male would close in, but that at least was something we agreed upon.

They always quickly learned that we weren't to be touched. Our bond was different, special. Around us, the pack ran, confident and free, the two halves of their souls unified. At peace.

We waged war.

Eventually, I turned the game on my wolf. I sent my own illusions and falsities out into our mind, and she didn't know how to react. Didn't know where to try and stop me. And so, I slipped past her and took control of everything, locking down my mind.

I was the master here, and she would learn to submit to me. Even under a Wild Moon. She wasn't happy about it, but once I was back in control, there was no way she would win. She sensed that and once more settled into her submissive role. Though, I could sense her anger. She would be ready next month, and we would go over it all again.

And again.

Lucky me.

As we settled down, however, I let some of her trickle back in. Merging our instincts and knowledge. We trotted along with the pack, breathing a sigh of relief. Now we had to find Jo to ensure that *she* was okay. Unlike us, she'd never bonded before. She'd never met her wolf. It would be a whole new fight for her.

In our efforts to track her, we diverged from the pack, something calling us to the northwest. We didn't care. The pack wasn't home. It wasn't ours. We were here only because we had to be. Not because we wanted to.

That was the human part of us speaking. Our wolf felt differently. We wanted to stay. To bask in the presence of our Alpha and enjoy the pack. To become one with the pack. But we didn't. We always left, and that made us sad.

Overhead, the moon was setting, and the power of it began to fade. We had to find Jo, and soon, before the call of the Alpha. Before he summoned us back. If Jo hadn't bonded with her wolf, then she would be hunted. Wild wolves were not allowed to exist. The Alpha would kill her the second he found her.

Unless we did something first.

Where are you, Jo?

We trotted across a strange meadow. A lone tree, its branches devoid of life, jutted up at the top of a hill. It was dead. Our eyes picked out the sight of a lightning burn, a jagged black scar down one side of the tree. At the tree's base was a large hole in the ground, and the scar seemed to continue into the hole.

Our instincts took us toward it, but before we could reach it, a lone howl drifted across the night sky. The Alpha was calling.

Instantly, we veered back, heading toward the south side of the lands where the Alpha and the pack would be waiting for us. We fought against it briefly, and for a tantalizing second, almost won. In the end, however, we knew it was pointless. When the Alpha called during a Wild Moon, we obeyed. Some battles our human side was simply not strong enough to win on its own. Both sides would have to fight, and the wolf in us obeyed the Alpha.

Paws digging in deeper into the ground, we ran faster, knowing we would likely have the farthest to go to reach the Alpha. It wouldn't do to be late. That would call undue attention upon us. We hated attention.

The manor came into view, and we wandered to the front, our head swinging around, scanning the pack. Where was Jo? Why wasn't she up front already?

It was customary that the newly shifted wolves would come to the front of the pack at the end of the Soulshift. Then the entire pack would stream by like a military unit on parade. That way, a newly shifted wolf could review the entire pack to try and bring their Soulbond into existence, linking them with their mate for life.

Being that this was our eighth time going through it, we knew to go straight to the front and plunk our ass down on the grass and wait in boredom for the pack to go past us. We longed for the Soulbond to find us. It was lonely.

Two Wild Moons ago, we'd watched Kyler find his Soulbond. We remembered it fondly, the mating of two wolves who had instantly fallen in love with one another. The joyous howls of the pack that had gone up to celebrate the new mating left chills on our spine even now. We wanted that. We wanted our mate.

Behind us, the Alpha climbed the ascent to his Pride Rock, looming over the pack like one of the ancient shifter deities from legends of old. The human in us scoffed at that idea. The gods of old, like Amunlea, Empress of all Shifters, had been written as regal, elegant, and kind.

The Alpha was an asshole. Even our wolf could agree on that, regardless of her preference to obey his calls. Obedience and fondness did not go hand in hand. Still, we found ourselves looking at him, waiting for him to command the pack to proceed.

Behind the Alpha strode another figure. A little smaller than the Alpha, the wolf was still as pitch-black, blending neatly into the night in a way our silver-white fur never could. It was dark to our light.

At that thought, our world exploded.

Warm sunlight rushed through us, shoving our human half into the backseat, once more giving full power to our wolf. It surged out from us and into the night, a long golden link that plunged into that darkness.

A wave of something we'd never felt before filled us, buoying us up. Lifting us high on its wonderous touch. For the first time since we'd shifted, we were *complete*.

We howled. The pack howled with us.

Happy. Joyous. A Soulbond had been formed this night. After eight long months, we knew on some level that our search was over. That it was in the past.

We surged forward, eager to meet our mate.

Inside, our human side rebelled in horror as it realized who we were running toward.

The Alpha's son.

Our ex.

CHAPTER FIVE

Fuck this.

The wolf in me wanted to run toward him. To link with Johnathan. It was tired of being alone, tired of feeling unwanted.

So am I, sister, but this is not the way we're doing it.

We took a step forward as I fought for control, beating aside all the wonder and joy that filled our body from the feeling of being Soulbound at long last.

I fueled my fight with all the anger and hatred I felt for Johnathan and what he'd done to my life. To *our* life. I reminded my wolf how he had destroyed it.

She didn't care. She whined, straining against my control, eager to go and nudge noses with Johnathan, to rejoice in our pairing. All she saw was the Alpha's son. A powerful mate indeed to any wolf shifter. We would produce excellent babies. Sleek, swift, strong. Perfect for ruling and continuing our line.

The animal brain instincts were strong. I could even feel parts of the human in me straining toward him, toward that pairing. He was stepping closer, likely as shocked as I was about the pairing. Why had it taken so long to blossom? It made no sense.

Yet here we were.

My wolf wanted him. Wanted it all. *We could rule the pack*, she thinks. *At his side, we would eventually be the queen of the pack.*

I don't want any of that, I snarled, fighting it with everything. *I want none of him. I reject him.*

I reject the Soulbond. It's wrong, I told my wolf. *It must be. It has chosen wrong. We are not mating with him!*

Around us, the pack stirred in confusion even as Johnathan came closer, his long legs easily carrying the powerful form of his wolf to us. He was larger than us. Just the way we liked it.

Not larger where it counts, I reminded my wolf, our body literally shaking in place as we struggled, our second fight of the night. The closer the black-furred wolf got, the stronger the bond became. My wolf's insistence was strong.

But my hatred was stronger.

This man had destroyed my family. He'd dug up information no one else had seemed to know and dropped it so casually into my life in a way he'd *known* would end the way it had. Part of me wondered if he knew my parents were about to disappear as well. That would have just been the cherry on top for the pathetic asshole. All of that simply because I dumped him.

And now he expected us to just stroll off into the sunrise together, a happy couple? I was supposed to just forget all the trauma he'd inflicted on me like I was some sort of flaky Stockholm syndrome case study?

Yeah, fuck that shit.

My anger snatched control of our body away from the wolf. Fury gave me strength I normally couldn't have accessed, and I shoved my other half aside with a vengeance. I practically forced my bones to reshape themselves, tearing the wolf away from the Wild Moon.

Johnathan had hurt me. Embarrassed me. Done everything he could to hurt me without caring who knew or who it affected. It was time he had a dose of his own medicine, I decided. Time someone made *him* feel a fraction of the pain I'd felt.

"Stop," I snarled as I stood up, naked and unafraid in front of the entire pack, the single word cracking out like a whip, freezing my Soulbound mate in his tracks. "This isn't happening."

I ignored the rumbles from the pack behind me. Their opinions did not matter to me. Not one of them. Not even dear old Alpha daddy, who I could sense was watching the goings-on with great interest from above me on his stupid Altar of Arrogance. This was *my* choice, and I was going to make it. I was not going to let some magical bond force me to take this asshole as my mate. No way.

"You ruined my life, you piece of shit," I spat at Johnathan. "Your pathetic, fragile ego couldn't handle being dumped, and so you had to lash out to defend your stupid masculinity. You destroyed my family, all to make yourself feel better. Well, guess what, asshole? I reject you. Right here, right now, in front of everyone. I will *never* be your mate. Do you understand?"

The black-furred wolf growled threateningly at me. As if I should just shut up and do as he said. I lifted my eyebrows, staring down at the beast. My wolf urged me to let her back out, howling wildly inside my mind as I denied it the happiness it so desperately wanted.

This is for the best, I told it. *I want to be happy and to find my family. I can't be locked down to this asshole or this dying town if I want to do that! I just can't.*

I turned and ran without another thought. There was nothing left for me here. Nothing left in this town. I had to go. I had to run and be free.

My wolf understood that, at least. Although she resented me for denying her the Soulbond, there was one thing she longed for more: running free under the Wild Moon. What little of it remained.

She lent me her power. We shifted again and ran onward, four legs faster than two, sending us racing across town. Somewhere. Anywhere but the Aldridge house and the rest of the pack. I could never go back there.

It was time I left Seguin forever.

CHAPTER SIX

At some point, my wolf's energy faded.

We slowed our run to a trot and eventually came to a halt, staring as one at the eastern sky. Red rays of light were shooting up through the horizon, piercing the wispy clouds with their brilliant glow. It was going to be a sunrise to remember.

Just like it had been a night to forget.

Gritting my teeth at the unpleasant, painful sensations of my fourth shift of the night–double the amount I'd ever attempted before–I eventually got to my feet. To my *human* feet. My wolf was exhausted, and she retreated into the corners of my mind to rest. This had been the most energetic Wild Moon yet that we had experienced, and a part of me couldn't blame her for feeling that way. I, too, wanted to keel over and sleep for days.

But I couldn't. We had to get out of town, and soon. It wouldn't be long before Johnathan came looking for me, and I wanted to get a good head start on him. Of course, I'd never be able to truly lose him. We were Soulbound now. Linked forever, a pull that I would have to fight for my entire life to deny.

Now there's some high-level irony, I thought unhappily.

For eight months, I had returned to Seguin in hopes of finding my mate. Someone who I could be myself with, who would understand me and make me feel whole again.

Eight Wild Moons of waiting at the front of the pack for my Soulbond to kick in.

Eight Wild Moons of continual humiliation.

All the while, I spent my time searching for my family, trying to find any trace of my parents.

And when it came down to it, fate saw to it that I ended up mated to the *one* person I hated more than anyone else. I'd wished so hard for something I didn't deserve that I'd been granted something even *worse*.

How was this *fair*? I raged against it inside, wanting nothing more than to sever the bond, to be free once more. It had never occurred to me that, although I'd been without a mate, I had been *free*. Unencumbered and able to do as I pleased, outside of returning for the Wild Moons. There had been nothing else to worry about. Now, however...

A cool breeze picked up, and I shivered, reminded of my nudity as the wind swept over my form, causing goosebumps across my skin. I'd learned to give myself over to the Wild Moon, but outside of that, I was still self-conscious about wandering around naked. I needed to find clothes somewhere, since returning to the Aldridges' to retrieve what I'd worn the night before was out of the question.

Looking around to survey my options, I inhaled sharply as I realized where I was. Somehow, in my flight, I had come to the one place I spent eight months avoiding. My parents' house. My childhood home.

It wasn't boarded up yet, unlike half the houses in town, but I figured it was only time before that happened. Nobody had set foot in there since the night of my parents' disappearance on my Soulshift night. The first time I'd come back to Seguin, I'd come to the house, with plans of staying there simply for the night. But I'd found myself standing almost in the same spot, unable to go inside.

But back then, I'd had clothes.

"You can do this," I told myself, wishing I felt as confident as I sounded.

It's amazing how one bad memory can outweigh a lifetime of positive ones. How my guilt has prevented me from returning even when I didn't do anything wrong.

The breeze picked up again, oddly cold for an early May morning. Usually, I could shrug off the breeze. Perhaps I'd overdone it last night. I wasn't sure.

I approached the house, my guilt weighing me down with each step. My feet began to drag across the gravel driveway as I approached, unwilling to fully pick themselves up. They would prefer to stay still, or better yet, turn and head elsewhere.

Can't do it, I told myself. *Need clothes. Can't go strolling around town with your titties bouncing around like some hussy. Not to mention, it's not comfortable. And it's cold.*

With so many factors in favor of going inside and getting some clothes, I convinced my body to keep obeying my commands.

You aren't at fault. They didn't disappear because of you.

I blinked back sudden tears. The thing was, I could say that all I wanted. Tell myself every platitude, about how I was the innocent one. However, the *truth* was, I didn't know why my parents disappeared.

There was a lot I didn't know. A lot I should have asked them that night instead of running out of the house. Then again, finding out at twenty-one you're adopted and your so-called parents have lied to you your entire life would mess with anyone. I don't think I reacted *that* strongly, all things considered. I didn't say anything I couldn't take back, which was my one saving grace.

But I also never had the opportunity to ask them *why*, and the not-knowing ate at me every day. Even now, I could feel it inside me. Swollen, a low pulse pulling me toward it.

I frowned. That wasn't right. What the hell *was* that? I looked inward to the source of the feeling. It wasn't painful or agonizing. It wasn't the guilt or darkness that followed it everywhere. It was warm and fuzzy, and–

"Oh, hell no," I growled, anger overcoming everything else.

I walked up to the house and went inside without a second thought, doing my best to shove aside the call of my Soulbond. I could tell now that's what I felt inside. Drawing me to Johnathan. Even as I thought it, I could tell he was out and about, using our new connection to try and track me down.

Well, tough luck, asshole. I would be long gone by the time he arrived at the house. I'd never held out any real hope that he would respect my decision, but it was nice to have proof he really was that much of a douche. If he couldn't respect me now, why would he ever do so later?

I shot that thought at my wolf, trying to instill in her *why* we had to avoid him, but all I got back was a tired whine and desire to sleep in the presence of our mate.

Not gonna happen.

I didn't bother apologizing. She wouldn't get it.

My room was just the way I'd left it: a disaster. It was easy for me to find the clothes I needed because it was an *organized* disaster, as I'd told my mom many times. She didn't approve. I smiled briefly at a memory of her frown each time she walked past my open door. She didn't accept mess anywhere outside of my bedroom.

The rest of the house was immaculate because that was just the way my mother liked it. I'd long since stopped referring to her as "the woman who raised me" or my "adopto-mom" as I'd done for a brief period. Until I knew for sure one way or another whether they had loved me or simply faked it, I was willing to give them the benefit of the doubt that they *had* loved me and raised me because they cared. I *had* to give it to them. I didn't want to deal with the other side.

I paused outside my parents' bedroom, trying not to look inside. I failed. I could see nothing out of place. Nothing except for the unmade bed. Even calling it "unmade" was generous. It simply wasn't pulled taut to the corners. That little distinction, that sole piece of the house out of place, had been my *only* clue that something had happened to my parents. My mother never left the bed unmade. Ever. Yet this time, it was. Why?

It was a question that had driven me insane for months. I didn't dwell on it much anymore because I finally convinced myself I wasn't going to glean anything from it, but I knew it was like that for a reason.

Shaking my head, I pushed past the room and went downstairs. I needed to get moving. My father's truck was still parked over at Jo's, where I'd left it. I had to get there and say my goodbyes to her before Johnathan tracked me down.

If I was lucky, he went there first, only continuing to my old house when he found I wasn't at Jo's. Hopefully, I would lose him by going back to Jo's. If so, there should be just enough time for me to hear about her night–and where she'd gone. Had she found her mate early in the night? Had they gone off to be together, perhaps?

I smiled, happy for my friend.

"What the fuck is that smile for?"

The sudden intrusion into the silence that had been my companion all morning sent me scrambling back from the door. I'd been so absorbed in my own world that I hadn't even noticed Johnathan waiting for me at the entrance.

So much for avoiding him.

"Go away, Johnathan," I said, using his full name. Maybe if I didn't antagonize him, I could escape from here and be on my way without having to fight.

"How *dare* you treat me like that in front of everyone?" he snarled.

"*Enough*," I shouted, surprising us both with the force of my voice.

Johnathan hesitated as he approached, but I only managed to slow him down, not stop him entirely. He bulled his way through the command until he was leaning over me, practically face to face. Although, given my height, he couldn't truly impose his full size over me. I stared into his dull blue eyes. What had I ever seen in him?

"You will come back to me," he rumbled icily. "You will accept our bond and pair with me. Publicly and privately."

Even now, I could feel the bond. In such proximity to him, it was all but hammering at my skull, urging me to turn myself over to it and give in. Life would be so *good* if I did. We would be happy and content. For life.

And I would also be abandoning who I am and where I came from. I will not submit to this small-dicked egotistical bag of gas. Absolutely not.

"No," I said. "I will not. I'd rather be so single my fingers are perma-pruned than ever consider sleeping with you again. Got it?"

Apparently, he didn't understand. Figures, he wouldn't know the first thing about making a woman wet. Coming closer, his square face now inches from mine, he spoke again in a completely new tone.

"Submit to me."

I flinched back at the blatant use of his Alpha command. My wolf whimpered and tried to drag me to my knees as Johnathan worked to overpower us. I'd never been subject to such a focused dose of an Alpha call before, and it nearly worked. My knees were wobbly and made of jelly, practically forcing me to drop into a submissive pose.

The thing is, it didn't work. Oh, he came close all right, but Johnathan was only the heir to the pack. He wasn't in command, not yet. He and his jet-black hair, tight clothes, and arrogant wannabe-Alpha mode could take their uppity sense of self-importance and piss off.

When my wolf realized I wasn't about to submit, she surged back to the surface, absolutely *pissed* that our mate would try and force us to submit. Even though she wanted to be with him, it seemed even my other half felt it had to be by *choice*. An Alpha should *never* use their power over their mate. And so, we did perhaps the second-stupidest thing we could have done.

We attacked.

CHAPTER SEVEN

Our jaws went for Johnathan's neck as we launched our self at him.

My wolf and I were united in our anger, and we slammed into Johnathan, taking him to the ground even as the change came over us again. Our fangs grazed his neck, but before they could penetrate flesh, a fist made of steel slammed into our ribs, flinging us off him.

We yelped in pain, scrambling to our feet, even as Johnathan shredded his clothing and shifted.

Idiot, we thought, charging at him. This wasn't about playing fair or respecting any honor of the fight. This piece of trash had tried to *command* us to obey him. He didn't deserve our respect.

So, we slammed into him mid-change, taking him out at the knees. The half-human half-wolf form went to the ground. We found his neck and sunk in our teeth. He froze.

Holy shit.

Somehow, we had beaten him.

Part of us wanted to rip his neck out. To tear great chunks of flesh and watch him bleed to death, ridding us of the Soulbond forever. Setting us free. Permanently. We almost did. Our teeth tightened imperceptibly around his neck.

But that didn't seem like enough punishment for him. He would never atone for all the pain he had caused us. So, instead, we backed away, shifting back to human form.

I smiled at him as I got to my feet, tugging the sports bra back into place. Somehow it hadn't shredded during the transformation, and in my rage, I hadn't even noticed it. I was still nude from the waist down and would have to get *more* clothes from upstairs, but it didn't matter. Nothing did.

A laugh bubbled up through my lips as I continued to stare smugly at Johnathan. He knew what had just happened, and he knew as well as I did that word of it would never stay between us. The pack would find out, and he would be humiliated. Beaten by a nobody. Some Alpha *he* was.

"You're going to regret that," he snapped.

"No, I'm not," I said. "You know why? Because you will never see me again. We will never be together. So, it doesn't matter. I reject you, Johnathan Aldridge. I deny you. Whatever the fuck I have to say. Let it get through your thick skull that I will *never* be your mate. That *this*," I pointed back and forth between us, "will never happen. *Ever.*"

His eyes burned with anger. "You can't reject a Soulbond," he said. "It doesn't work that way."

"*Watch me,*" I snarled, feeling stronger than I ever had.

"It will grow stronger," he said, standing now, the tattered remains of his clothes hanging from his muscular frame.

"Then I'll grow stronger, too."

"You'll come for me eventually."

I laughed. "You arrogant prick. I've never come for you before, and I certainly won't in the future no matter what meaning you want to interpret. It's all fake. That would be the only way. I'd fake it like I faked any pleasure we had while dating."

He shook with fury, but I just didn't care. I'd beaten him once, and I could do it again.

"You will suffer," he warned me.

I rolled my eyes. "I suffered while I was with you. I'd rather suffer this way on my own than waste perfectly good batteries trying to satisfy myself for the rest of my life just for *your* ego. I'm done with you. Now get out."

"This isn't over!" he snarled as if I was supposed to be scared.

I laughed again in his face, uncaring. "You just got beaten by a *nobody*, John. Some Alpha heir *you* are. Once word of this gets around..." I shook my head. "Just go. Get out of my face."

He started to go. Walking away, beaten. Finally, I was paying him back for the comment he'd made that day outside of the post office. The comment that had ruined my life.

"How did you know?" I asked sharply as he reached the door.

He turned at the waist to look back at me, muscles stretching tightly over his stomach. "Know what?" he asked, frowning.

"That I was adopted," I managed to spit out without losing control. I fought hard to keep myself calm and cool. Maybe I could use this time to find out what was going on. To find out the truth from him. My need to know was all-consuming as I waited for an answer.

To my surprise, Johnathan's face softened. I had expected mockery. Cruel laughter, perhaps. Outright denial. Instead, he smiled at me sadly. Like he cared about me.

Was this the Soulbond already changing our perceptions of one another? Encouraging us to accept it? Or was this something else?

"Come with me," he said quietly. "Accept the bond, and I'll tell you everything you want to know."

I stared, speechless. Utterly and totally speechless at this sudden transformation. So unexpected was it that I found myself leaning toward him to do just that. I wanted to know who

I was and where I'd come from *so badly* that I almost gave in right then and there.

"Think of all the positives of being mated to the future Alpha," he continued. "How that will help you."

And just like that, I was back.

"I don't *need* your help," I said harshly, hate filling me once more. "I don't want it either. Either tell me what you know or get out of my life!"

"I'm sorry," he said, shaking his head at me. "I can't."

He went out the door, and I walked over to it and slammed it on his retreating back before he had a chance to look back.

"Bastard," I said, throwing my hatred at him.

Through the door, I felt an answering pulse of frustration. John was just as irritated at my unwillingness to accept as I was at the fact that I was bonded to him in the first place.

"Fuck the Soulbond," I snarled. "There has to be some way to deny this thing. To sever it. I can't *actually* be stuck with him for the rest of my life, can I? Life isn't *that* unfair."

Of course, for that to be the case, there would have to be other examples in our history of shifters being paired up with people they disliked. My father had been a huge history buff. In fact, he'd been the Alpha's right-hand man, searching out hints of our ancient past. He'd educated me about all sorts of lore, from the old gods to the lost shifter city of Shuldar.

But he'd never once mentioned any tales about rejected Soulbonds.

I contemplated all the stories he'd told me over the years as I grabbed fresh clothes, but I couldn't come up with *anything*. Nothing helpful. Even if it were only a legend from a time when our species was united as one pack under the gods, I would have taken that and ran with it.

"Sheer stubborn willpower it is," I decided, heading down the stairs again.

"Sheer stubborn willpower *what* is?" a new, decidedly more feminine voice asked from the bottom of the stairs.

"God dammit!" I yelped, slamming myself back against the wall in surprise. "Will you people quit doing that!"

Jo stared up at me, tears in the corner of her eyes. "I'm sorry, Dan. I didn't mean to."

I gaped at my best friend. I'd never seen her look so distraught before. She looked horrible. She was wearing the same clothes from the night before, only now they were filthy and torn in a few places. Her hands were covered in dirt, and she had giant bags under her eyes, which were red and puffy from crying.

"Jo!" I cried, rushing down the stairs. "Jo, what happened?"

CHAPTER EIGHT

The instant my arms went around her, my best friend broke.

I got an arm under her and guided her to the nearby couch, trying to figure out what the hell could have gone wrong. Was it her Soulbond? Had it failed to materialize as mine had? Since it had happened to me, it was no longer unheard of. But even I hadn't had a reaction like this. No, I decided, something else was going on. Something worse. But I couldn't get a word out of Jo to figure out what it was!

Powerless to help, I did what I could. I sat next to her and held her while she cried. I was going to have to change my shirt. Again. At this rate, I'd go through my entire wardrobe before I left town. On the plus side, shopping spree? Though I'd have to come up with the money somehow. That was a bit of a bummer.

As my mind wandered, Jo sobbed into my shoulder. The poor girl was absolutely distraught. Had someone died? She needed something to calm her down. I gently eased my way out from under her arm and settled her into the corner of the couch. I grabbed a box of tissues from the coffee table and shoved it at her.

"Here," I said gently. "I'm going to make us some tea. I feel like we could both use it. I'll be right here, though, okay? I'm not leaving."

Jo didn't have the composure to speak, but she managed a nod before burying her face in her arms again.

I got off the couch, trying desperately not to note that it was my mother's favorite couch. I'd somehow sunk into her spot, as if now that she was gone, someone else had to take up her mantle of matron of the house.

She's not gone. Just missing. She might still be alive.

The supplies for tea hadn't been touched while I'd been gone, but it was my mother's go-to drink, and I soon had bags hanging over the lips of a pair of mugs and water well on its way to boiling so they could steep.

"You got her this one," I said softly, looking at the mugs. "We were what, ten?"

I held up the white mug that said "World's Best Teacher" on it. My mom hadn't been a teacher, but she was like the mother Jo had never really had, and to a ten-year-old, anything that said

"World's Best" on it was worthy. My mom had cherished that mug.

Jo glanced up, and for a moment, a smile graced her face. I smiled back at her, trying to put as much empathy and care into that one look as I could. I was dying to ask questions and pry answers from my friend, but the words had to come from her. She had to be ready to talk about her experience.

"Have you been back here?" Jo asked suddenly. "You know...since?"

I shook my head. "No," I told her. "Not until today. It was always too painful. Too many bad memories that I couldn't seem to shake. The unknowns are the worst part. Not knowing the truth."

"Yeah," Jo said quietly. "I get that. Not knowing is...It can tear you up inside."

There was something there. I frowned. "Are you okay, Jo?"

I couldn't help it. She was my best friend, and I had to know.

"I'm fine," she said. "Physically, I guess."

"What do you mean by that?" I asked, pouring the water into the mugs. "Something wrong with your mind?"

"I don't know," Jo said flatly.

I considered her answer while I brought the mugs over and set them on a pair of coasters in front of us. "You don't know?"

"I mean. I think I'm okay. Maybe. I don't know. That's a lie," she said with a cry-hiccup. "If I were fine, I wouldn't be a mess like this."

"Perhaps," I agreed, not sure what else to say. "What went wrong?"

"Ha. More like what went right?" Jo said bitterly. "The answer to which is absolutely nothing. How could it when on the night of your Soulshift, you can't do the one thing you're supposed to do?"

My frown deepened. I knew I should probably ease up on it lest I give myself some permawrinkles. Which, of course, was bullshit. But hey, media influence at its best, right? Still, I relaxed my face.

"Your Soulbond didn't form either?" I asked gently, feeling horrified for my friend.

Jo laughed. Harshly, bitterly. I'd expected agreement. More tears. Not that, though. The sarcastic bite of her laugh cut me deeply because Jo was always such a happy person. If anyone was in need, she was the first to lend a hand. She didn't deserve whatever had happened to her.

"Hard for that to happen," she grated out, "when you can't even shift."

I blinked. "What?" I had to work my jaw several times to get that single word out. She couldn't *shift?* Now that was unheard of.

"Yeah," Jo said. "I didn't shift, Dan. I know my wolf is there. She's inside me. I can feel her a bit like you did leading up to your Soulshift. She's definitely there, just weak, somehow. Nothing happened last night. I waited, standing there naked, while everyone else shifted and took off. And I waited. And waited. And nothing."

"Oh, god, Jo," I said, reaching out to hug her again. "I'm so sorry. I should have been there for you. I can't imagine."

My guilty conscience reared its ugly head again, slamming me down, painting me as unworthy of this friendship. I'd *promised* Jo that I would be there for her, but as soon as the moon showed its face, I'd taken off without a care in the world, leaving my friend behind to suffer horribly.

"It's okay," Jo said, the epitome of grace and class. "I don't blame you."

"But everyone shifts on the first Wild Moon after their twenty-first birthday," I said. "That's... that's just the way it is."

There was precedence about Soulbonds not forming right away. It happened with many of the men since they often ended up mated to younger shifters, so some of them waited years. I was the first woman anyone knew of where the bond had waited, but there was at least precedence in a way. This though...

"I know," Jo said bitterly. "Which must mean

I'm not yet twenty-one."

"How the hell would that be possible?" I said, speaking before my brain kicked in.

There was a reason my mother had been a second mom to Jo. A reason why she'd practically lived at my house for the first ten years of our friendship.

"Jo, I'm so sorry, I wasn't thinking," I said, trying hard to pull out the giant clown shoe I'd just inserted into my mouth.

"It's fine," she said tiredly. "You didn't have to live with the drug-addict mother or alcoholic father. It's not the first thought that enters your mind. And I wouldn't want it that way. I don't wish that on anyone."

"Still," I said, "I'm your best friend. I should have known."

"You should have known my parents somehow forgot my actual birthday and started celebrating it another time entirely? Seriously? Come on, Dan. No. You didn't do anything wrong. Stop it, please. I'm already dealing with enough shit." She sniffed, flinging her blonde hair out of her face. Half of it just fell forward again.

I remained silent while we drank some of the tea, and Jo pulled herself together a bit. She regained her composure eventually, and I braced myself. Now that we'd talked about her night, she would inevitably ask me about mine.

"Have you found anything?"

"Huh? Oh, no," I said. That wasn't the question I'd been expecting. "I've been trying. All my money goes to tracking them down. I've been in touch with every other pack I know about and even some I've only learned of since living in the city. Nobody has heard a damn thing. It's like they just vanished. I don't get it."

"Me neither," Jo said. "They didn't leave anything behind?"

I shook my head. As I moved it, my eyes drifted to the hallway that led to my father's study. I paused, staring at it, remembering back to that night. My father had come home unexpectedly from one of his expeditions, ostensibly to surprise me on my Soulshift night.

He'd told me he had a gift for me. A Shift Gift, it was commonly called. He'd told me it couldn't be mine until after. Through his hints, however–my dad had been terrible at keeping secrets–I'd gleaned it was a book. Something he'd found or dug up during his expeditions. Straight from the past of our species. Yet when I'd tried to take a peek at it, he'd been unusually secretive.

After they'd gone missing, I'd gone into his study, and seen the wrapped package on his desk addressed to me. But I'd left it there. He'd said he wanted to give it to me in person. It had felt wrong to take it then. But now…

I got up from the couch without a word, nearly

pushing Jo over and almost spilling her tea in the process.

"What? What is it?" she asked, but I didn't respond. My mind was locked in the past on the night of my Soulshift.

The book was still there, sitting on his desk in the white paper just as he'd left it. My name was on it. I unwrapped it, forcing my fingers to tear apart the paper before I had the chance to consider what I was doing. If I paused to stop, I might not start again.

A note was stuck to the front of a leather-bound book, which was in unusually good condition for something that should be hundreds of years old. Too good of condition. This was something else. As I looked at the spine, I spotted a name embossed on it.

Thomas Wetter.

My father. I trembled. This was his journal. It had to be.

But why had he left it for me?

I opened the note with shaky fingers.

Dearest Little D,

Tonight is your Soulshift. Although you've been a woman in my eyes for a long time, tonight, you will take your next step. You will become independent of us and bonded with your wolf. You will find your mate, and together, you will start a family. I couldn't be a prouder father. My latest trip was quite the time, and I think you'll appreciate all that I've found. I wrote about it for you.

I love you,

Dad

I swiped at my eyes with my shirt, trying to find a dry spot to absorb the tears I was now shedding.

"Oh, Dad," I said, gripping the journal tightly.

It didn't explain what had happened to them that night, but reading the note made it feel like he was there beside me. I had read the entire thing in his voice.

I turned to tell Jo what it was. I'd heard her get up and follow me, and she had to be dying of curiosity by now.

"Anything good?" she asked, leaning against the doorframe.

I shook my head. "N–"

The front door exploded inward under tremendous force, ripping one of the hinges free as someone forced their way into my house.

CHAPTER NINE

Lars Aldridge entered the house like a storm surge crashing over a ship lost at sea. The overwhelming Alpha power washed over Jo and me, pinning our wolves down with ease and driving Jo to one knee.

Anger at the intrusion into my parents' house gave me a burst of defiant strength which I used to keep myself upright, though I was forced to prop myself up on the desk to do so. Resisting Johnathan's order had been a challenge but doable. Anything more than what I was doing now would be impossible with Lars' power beating me down.

"You," he said, addressing Jo, though he didn't even bother to look at her. "Get out, and don't think about coming back."

Jo cast an apologetic glance up at me, but I shook her off. This wasn't her fight. She didn't need to get in the middle of anything. Most of all, I didn't want her to get hurt.

"It's fine," I said quietly, urging Jo to leave.

She got to her feet, head bowed, and started to walk toward the front door.

Meanwhile, Lars stood in the middle of my family's living room like he owned the place. His eyes glared at me, golden fire blazing in their amber depths. Lars was bald by choice, and that, combined with the fierce white goatee that he rocked, made him look like some sort of outlaw biker.

I was fairly positive he'd chosen the look for that very purpose, intimidation, and right now, it was working. I was fucking terrified. Yet I couldn't bring myself to cower before him, even if Lars was clearly expecting it.

"Stupid meth-head spawn," Lars spat as Jo went past.

He snapped at her, his teeth going for her neck in a display of arrogance I found despicable. Jo whimpered and bared her neck to him, submitting on the spot as he blasted her with another wave of Alpha command.

This is the man you want to be our Alpha? I shot the words at my wolf, adding some contempt to it, showing her how little I respected her opinion when she chose to try and ignore displays like this. This was a prime example of why we couldn't stay here.

To my surprise, my wolf shook off the Alpha-induced lethargy. She, too, was angered by Lars' intimidation game against Jo. That wasn't how an Alpha should act in her mind, and she growled, the sound echoing in the back of my throat.

Lars' attention snapped to me at the sound. I'd hoped it would. If one thing were to force him to focus on me instead of Jo, it would be defiance, even the tiniest bit. He didn't brook any of that in his pack and had even attacked pack members for little more than what I had just done.

"*Leave*," he snarled at Jo, who scampered out the front door so fast she didn't stop to grab her shoes.

Meanwhile, I strode out of my father's study and down the hallway, approaching the pack Alpha. I didn't want him in the room. It was my father's study, his private area, except when he invited me in, and I intended to do my best to keep it that way until he returned.

I didn't let myself consider the idea that he was dead instead of just missing.

Lars let me approach, watching me come closer with something akin to amusement replacing the anger in his eyes.

"A defiant one," he mused quietly, lifting one arm to take my chin as I stepped right up to him.

I tried to resist, but he cranked my head left and then right.

"Useless pup," he spat. "Good for nothing."

I bared my teeth.

"*Sit,*" he snarled.

I sat abruptly, squatting down on my haunches as I took the full brunt of his Alpha, the single barked word slapping my wolf and me down. It took everything in me to twist my head up to look at him.

Lars stepped closer, practically thrusting his crotch into my face, making me instantly wish I hadn't twisted my head. He stood there for several long seconds, forcing me to all but inhale his crotch-tang. I wanted to vomit. It was so gross and derogatory. I should tear his fucking nuts off. That's what I should do. Shift and just rip them from his body. See just how well he did as a nutless eunuch.

I didn't, though.

"Good bitch," he said, rocking forward on his toes just a bit, bringing his dick even closer to my face.

I'mma do it. I swear by Vir, I'm going to fucking do it if he doesn't stop.

He did it again.

We growled, my wolf pissed off at his dominance show. We wanted Lars to know that if he weren't using his Alpha power on us, we'd go right for his throat and leave him a bloodied mess.

Turns out that a pack Alpha doesn't appreciate being told that. Lars' wolf burst from his face, and he clamped his jaws around our neck, pinning us to the floor in a heartbeat. He shifted back almost as fast, a truly impressive display of control. I could never have attempted anything like that.

Maybe growling back wasn't such a good idea. Remember, we want to survive this!

"Behave," Lars growled as he collected himself, tugging the tight black t-shirt he wore back into place. "Otherwise, I'll rip your throat out and give this piece of shit hovel a new paint job. Understood?"

Jaw clenched so tight I thought I was going to shatter a tooth, I nodded. I'd never heard Lars speak so angrily. He was already on edge, and if I kept pushing him, he would follow through with his threat. Still, I stared daggers at him as I did, letting him know I wasn't doing so willingly.

"Good," he said. "I'm glad we got that sorted out. I do hate making a mess."

I slowly rose to my feet, facing Lars, waiting for him to get to the damned point. The shithole liked to hear himself talk.

"I understand you rejected my son," he said at last. It wasn't a question.

"He ran home to Daddy and told on me, did he?" I said.

Why can't I keep my thoughts to myself sometimes?

Lars glared at me.

"I said I'll submit," I told him. "I never said I'd be polite."

"Insolent little shit," the Alpha rumbled, but he didn't pin me again.

I let the words roll over me. They were just words, after all. Once he said his piece and left, I was gone. This town was getting put in the rear-view, and I was never coming back. Lars could come looking for me, but I'd keep on the move. Anything was better than staying.

Anything.

"You will accept the Soulbond," Lars ordered, putting some command into his voice.

I braced myself against it, fighting the order.

"You will mate with my son," he continued. "And you will formalize the bond. Am I making myself clear?"

"Crystal," I said. "But you can go lick your own asshole because nobody else is going to eat the shit you're trying to feed me right now."

A vise-like hand grabbed my throat and threw me against the wall. I rebounded, but before I could act, Lars was there again, crushing my windpipe and pushing me into the wall.

"You can do this all day," I croaked out.

Lars relaxed his grip slightly. It was a mistake all around because now my mouth had an excuse to run itself before my brain could use the additional oxygen to think through what I was saying.

"Your son is a tiny-dicked bastard that I've already suffered through once. I'm not about to do that for the rest of my life. I can only deal with one of those. Tiny dick or an asshole personality. Your son got hit with the terrible twosome, however, so that's going to be a no-go for me. Got it? So, either kill me or let me go."

Lars listened passively as I busted out my monolog. When I finished, instead of flying into a rage and snuffing out my life, he did something unexpected. He leered at me, a strange glint in his eye.

"There are worse punishments than death, you know," he warned. "You should be careful."

What the fuck was that supposed to mean? Of *course* there were worse punishments. Like being forced to mate with his son. But that's not what he meant, I didn't think. So, what had he been referring to?

"You have one cycle," Lars said, casually turning and launching me into the couch.

The furniture's frame cracked as I slammed into it. I grimaced, hating how easily he could toss me around. It was a real powerless feeling when someone did that to you and you didn't want them to.

"One cycle," he repeated. "The next Wild Moon, you will take my son, or I'll end the Soulbond the only way we can. I'll kill you."

"Yeah," I said. "I got that part. Thanks. But I'd rather do it myself."

Lars strode toward me, fury in his eyes.

Oops.

"You are just like your parents," he spat, shaking with anger. "Let's see if you can learn faster."

I opened my mouth to ask what he meant by that, but before I could, he slammed a fist into my face, and I only knew darkness.

CHAPTER TEN

I was awake.

Except I wasn't awake.

It was strange. One moment I wasn't there, then the next I was present. I was even standing. That's how I knew I wasn't awake. Nobody suddenly comes to while standing up. Except I *felt* like I was awake. There was no odd haze like in dreamland.

But where was I?

"Hello?" I called tentatively, looking around.

It was a dark place. Not black, just dark. The sky above me was black and cloudy, the slightly lighter clouds visible against the inky backdrop. They were moving fast, roiling hard into the distance, a constantly moving scene.

Yet, I felt no breeze.

In the distance, lightning flickered, then went dark. A second later, sheet lightning tore across the sky. I shivered at the display of power from the angry storm. Seconds later, the rumble of thunder arrived, bringing goosebumps to the skin along my spine and down my arms. It was cool here, but that's not why I felt so weird.

Everywhere I looked, the landscape was desolate. The land was rocky and broken, the ground so black it nearly blended in with the sky. No signs of life. Nothing moved. There was no noise except for the rumbles of thunder. This was a lifeless place. Broken rock and little more. No plant life, no insects. Nothing.

Except me.

"Hello?" I called again, a little louder this time. "Is anyone there?"

Where the hell had Lars taken me? There was nowhere like this near Seguin, that was for sure. How long had I been out? It couldn't have been that long. My shifter healing meant it was probably minutes at most. Unless he'd drugged me.

Was I hallucinating? Maybe that was it. I reached out and pinched my arm. I felt the pain. That was odd and definitely didn't happen in dreamland. So, I definitely was awake. Except I wasn't.

I took a step forward, determined to figure out what was going on. Beneath my foot—I was wearing shoes now. Interesting—rock crunched and ground into dust. Even the ground was so devoid of life it crumbled at the slightest touch.

Ahead of me was a hill covered in black, crumbling rock. I tried to scale it. From the top, I could get a good view of the world around me. Perhaps I could find where I was or learn where I should go.

The eerie silence gave me the heebie-jeebies as I climbed, crushing rock underfoot with every step. Some places, I sunk to my knee, the black material of my pants warding off minor cuts from the sharp bits poking me.

Nice pants, too, I observed, wondering where I had gotten them. Can I keep them when I wake up? They fit perfectly.

Definitely dreamland of some sort.

I finally reached the top of the hill—it was a lot taller than it looked—and took in the view of the other side.

"What *is* this place?" I whispered, staring at the stunning sight in the distance.

Far off—I didn't know how far. There was nothing to help judge distance—a towering stone wall rose into the sky. It had to be the height of a short skyscraper, hundreds of feet high. It stretched from horizon to horizon as far as I could see. But most imposing of all were the giant gates set into the wall straight ahead.

They were made of stone, too, and clearly designed to open. The stone was a slightly lighter color than the black of the rest of the wall, and I swore if I squinted, I could see an arc of tracks in the ground where the gates' edges would swing open.

"What the hell..." I breathed, awed into submission by the sheer scale of it all.

Nothing like this existed on Earth, I was sure of it. The Great Wall would come up to this thing's shins at absolute best.

So, why the hell was I dreaming of it? I'd never had any crazy dreams like this before. Only normal ones. You know, like swimming through an underground shipwreck that happened also to be my father's Wal-Mart, while sitting in first grade listening to my teacher drone on, before looking to my left to see the heartthrob of my teen years taking off his shirt to reveal the first set of abs I'd ever seen in person and then waking up.

Yeah, normal dreams.

I stiffened in alarm as the hairs on my neck rose. This was no eerie landscape goosebumps. This was my wolf trying to tell me something very important.

I was no longer alone.

Closing my eyes, I took in a deep breath. I had no idea who or what I would find here in not-dreamland dreamland, and I knew I had to be ready to fight. Somehow, this was real without being real, and I definitely did not want to find out what happened if I was hurt, or worse, if I died while here. It was possible the entity that had crept up behind me was friendly, but if so, why hadn't it announced its presence?

I knew it was there, though. I could feel its presence behind me like a weight, pressing down on my shoulders. Turning slowly, I readied myself for a confrontation. I looked up as I turned.

Way up.

Like, craning my neck up. Whoever it was, they stood not two feet away and towered over me.

Tall, imposing, and, shockingly, almost impossibly sexy, *he* stood there, staring down at me with eyes of the royalist blue drilling right through me. His hair was blacker than mine and fell in gloriously untidy waves to his shoulders. He had it pulled back from his head, giving me a perfect look at the precise symmetry of his face, including a pair of lips compressed into an unimpressed line.

"What are you doing here?"

I stared. His *voice* was hot. Like, throw myself to my knees and rip his pants off kind of hot. Like I would let him do *anything* to me he wanted, just as long as he kept talking kind of hot. I quivered in my boots. Yes, apparently, it's actually a thing because I did it. My fake dream pants should have been turning to ash from the heat my crotch was exuding.

"Who are you?" I asked, staring at his angular, stubble-covered jaw for a moment.

He regarded me curiously, his eyes burning with a fire I couldn't explain. Dressed in a long black shirt that clung tightly to an impressively shredded form, he too wore black pants and black boots. Just like me. It was apparently the outfit of choice for this place.

I'd hate to see their fashion shows.

"How did you get here?" he repeated, his voice flowing over me a second time, turning my need-to-fuck meter up to eleven. This guy was sex on wheels. Or black boots. Whatever.

"I've been asking myself the same damn question," I said back. "Sorry, don't have an answer for you. Your turn. Who are you, and where am I? What is this place?"

The giant being stared down at me, and I swear he was considering crushing me right then and there. I'd have died a happy woman to go out with his hands around me. Which just goes to show that I had to be dreaming because who the fuck thought that in reality?

"You shouldn't be here," he said.

"Tell me about it," I agreed. "Just point me in the direction of Seguin, and I'll be on my way. I promise. Or maybe you can help me wake up. See, being that I'm unconscious and all, when this dream ends, I can wake up."

He shook his head, black hair bouncing as he did, before settling down into a perfect frame of his sharp face. It was like it was alive. Maybe it was. What did I know about this place?

"Dream?" he repeated. "This is no dream."

"Right," I drawled. "Listen, I've had some pretty good sex dreams before, but nothing like *this*, okay? I certainly couldn't have dreamed up this place and you. Not in one night, at least. But I *am* dreaming because I can't be here. So, I know it's weird for you, too, but you're gonna have to accept it. You're in my head."

Mr. Mysterious stared at me without speaking.

Then he opened his mouth, and a surge of water came forth, splashing all over me.

CHAPTER ELEVEN

I gasped in shock as the icy water slapped me across the face, bringing me back to reality.

Lars was towering over me, a bucket in his hand. He saw I was awake and grinned, tossing the bucket to the side. Angrily, I lunged for him before logic could kick in, but I made no headway. Metal clanked on metal, and I stayed firmly in place.

"What the fuck?" I spat, straining against the bonds trapping me to the chair as cold water dripped from my face and upper body. My skin puckered from the chill, my nips standing at attention like the fucking president was coming or something.

I looked down, wondering why they were so sensitive, which is when I noticed I wasn't wearing a bra. Or underwear. Just a black t-shirt and baggy blue shorts.

"What the fuck did you do to me?" I snarled, immediately assuming the worst.

"Nothing," Lars growled. "Unlike some, we have honor."

I nearly choked on my laughter at that, but unless I'd been unconscious for days, I couldn't feel anything that would indicate foul play. So maybe he was telling the truth.

"You still stripped me naked, you fucking pervs," I snarled, straining at my bonds. "How the hell do I know you didn't take a bunch of pictures or anything? Psycho bastard. Let me go!"

Lars continued to stare at me like I was on display or something. It was giving me major creepy vibes.

"Quite the dream you were having," he remarked at last.

I froze. He knew about that? How could he know about that messed-up place? How did I even dream something like that in the first place? It had been so *real* feeling.

"We never touched you, but your body was, shall we say, active, there." He chuckled nastily.

Ew. Gross. I didn't want to think about this asshole watching me while I had a sex dream. Vomit.

"Pervert," I said, my voice as cold as the water still dripping from me. "Is this how you get your rocks off these days?"

Alpha power reached out and slapped me, and for once, I was actually grateful for it. That stupid dream sequence was still filtering through my body, giving me the odd chill and flashback. Once the Alpha's command hit me, my brain cleared rapidly.

I would have time to overanalyze the dream and come to wildly inaccurate conclusions later. For now, I had to focus on getting out of my current predicament. Somehow. Given I had metal shackles around my wrists and ankles, securing me to a solid chair, I didn't exactly see a way out. Yet.

"I *was* going to give you time to come to the proper conclusion on your own," Lars said once I settled into the chair and fixed him with a sullen glare.

Bastard was just waiting for me to submit before he explained what the fuck he's doing.

"However, you've proven yourself to be too unwieldy, too unreliable. You're probably too stubborn of a bitch to realize that this is the only proper way forward for someone like you."

"Someone like me?" I growled. "You mean not a teet-sucking sycophant? Great. Fantastic. What's your grand plan now? Leave me tied to a chair for a month? As if that would get me to change my opinion of your son."

Lars smiled, his lips curving upward even as his eyes remained a blank, dull blue. It was very disconcerting, and I fell silent as fear slithered into my belly, working its cool tendrils through me. What was he going to do? Just how much shit was I in?

"You *will* change your opinion, you disobedient pup," he informed me. "You're going to spend the month here. As our guest."

I snorted. "That's a hoot. A guest. Guests are usually free to leave. You mean prisoner."

"Whatever term works best for you," Lars said, waving a hand dismissively. "Trust me. Being in such proximity to the Soulbond, it will be impossible for you to resist. Your wolf will want it. It will cry out for it, driving you desperately into his arms. You will *change* because of it, little wolfling. You won't be able to resist."

I couldn't speak. I stared at him in horror. He spoke with such certainty, such knowledge. It made sense that the Soulbond would change people. Make them more compatible to help with a lifetime of being together.

But knowing that it would affect me while I resisted it? Trying to force me into Johnathan's arms? That was a nightmare come true. I didn't want to give up who I was for anybody, let alone that prick!

"Yes," Lars hissed. "You begin to see. You realize your future. Fight it or accept it. One way or another, you *will* want it eventually. There is nothing you can do about that."

"Why are you so intent on this?" I whispered. "Why *me*? I'm not anyone special."

"Of course you aren't," Lars said as if that should have been obvious. "You are a no-one. But the line must be continued. The Wild Moon has chosen you to be my son's mate. My heir must be ready to rule the pack when I have…moved on."

Lars didn't seem particularly weak or even remotely close to stepping down from being the head of the pack. I didn't foresee Johnathan taking over for decades yet. What was the rush? There was only one possible reason.

"So, I'm nothing but a baby factory to you, is that it?"

"My bloodline is strong," Lars said. "It must be continued. Aldridges have ruled the Seguin pack for generations. We will continue to do so. You will do your part. Eventually. If it drives you insane from trying to deny it first…small loss."

The insidious smile on Lars' face had me feeling all sorts of unwelcome. He definitely did not care if I lived or died, so long as I bore Johnathan some heirs first. What a lovely father, looking out for his only son's well-being. Definitely not a psychotic tyrant of an Alpha. Not at all.

"There are plenty of women in this town who I'm sure would have your son's babies. Women from other packs, too. Trust me. I had to hear all about it when I dated John. You know, before I realized how much like you he was."

Lars' hand flashed down. I rocked back in the chair, my cheek ringing with pain. I cried out but quickly bit down. The last thing I wanted to do was give Lars the satisfaction of hearing me in pain.

"You will show him the respect he deserves," Lars hissed. "His name is Johnathan."

Well, that explained where *John* got his fanatical desire not to use the short form of his name. I thought it was his own thing, but nope. Turned out it was dear old dad all along.

Just how much independence *did* John have? Had he been allowed to date me without asking Dada for permission? Or was that all orchestrated and planned as well? I had to wonder now. After all, where was Johnny boy at the moment? He certainly wasn't in the tiny little room with Lars and me.

"Thirty days, little wolf," Lars said when I sat there silently, not bothering to speak anymore. "We'll see how well you fare. If you continue to deny it...you *will* go Wild. And then I will enact the law and do as I must."

"Oh, so tough of you to kill little old me," I muttered.

Lars fixed me with a glare. "Just like your family. I tire of your rebellious ways. Thirty days."

He was gone before I could open my mouth to ask what the hell *that* had meant? Rebellious ways?

My father was one of your biggest supporters, you oversized thundercunt. What rebellious ways could you possibly mean? Hell, even I never rebelled, other than recently when I rejected John. And that was well earned if I do say so myself.

So, what was I missing?

CHAPTER TWELVE

The small, windowless room in which I was being held made it impossible to tell time, but I figured several hours must have passed while I sat in the chair, unmoving.

No sounds reached my ears. Only the single dull yellow bulb overhead provided any light. The metal of the chair was cool to the touch. My wet clothing initially left me chilled, but as time went on, my body heat warmed it until I was just damp. Which was almost worse, in a way, since I couldn't scratch any of the million itches that broke out across my body.

"This sucks," I said to myself.

All the while, in the background of my mind, my Soulbond pulsed away, a link to a man I wanted nothing to do with. Or did I? Would it be so bad to submit to it? I would be happy with Johnathan. The Soulbond would see to that.

Fuck right off, I snarled at the thought, recovering my sanity. I shut those treacherous ideas down. There was no way in hell I was going to give up and become a broodmare for this twisted family. No way, not happening.

I struggled some more in my bonds, trying to twist my arms and use my shifter strength to break through them, but they held firm, leaving me feeling weak and useless. I tried to turn to see just how I was secured, but the tightness of my arms bound behind me meant I couldn't twist far enough to get a good look.

Lars had known what he was doing. Just how many other people had he held prisoner here? I could look down and see that the chair was bolted to the floor. Clearly, this hadn't been set up for me. It had already existed. Why?

Before I could contemplate that further, my Soulbond pulsed even stronger, and a moment later, the door behind me opened.

"Bravo!" I called, instantly knowing who it was. I tried to whistle but failed to make a sound. I've never been able to do that properly. I was really hoping for a one-time wonder, but alas, I failed at that, too, like so many things lately.

"Danielle," Johnathan said as he came around to my front.

"Vir's Oath," I cursed, more in annoyance than anything. "What is it with you and having to use people's full names? It's such a mouthful."

My ex shrugged, looking quite uncomfortable as he stood before me dressed in an expensive dark blue silk shirt, black pants, and chocolate-brown shoes. I noted he carefully avoided the water still puddled around me—there was nowhere for it to drain.

"Why is it you insist on those dusty old curses?" he countered. "Nobody swears by the old gods anymore, Danielle. Just you."

And my father, I thought sullenly. But what was the point? Johnathan had been indoctrinated by his asshole father. I wasn't about to break through that wall anytime soon, and I frankly didn't care to spend the energy trying. He wasn't worth it.

"So, did Daddy send you in here?" I shot back. "After all, he has to do everything for you. Like you're a child. Did you run in here and start crying to him when I told you to piss off? Running home to tell on me. Pathetic."

"I didn't tell on you," Johnathan snapped, clenching his hands into fists, his shoulders flexing until the veins in his neck stood out. "It was rather obvious what happened. You know, since you did it *in front of the entire pack.*"

"You deserved it," I said, shrugging as best I could given my situation. "It's not my fault you were a colossal asshole to me."

"You're exaggerating."

"And you're victim-blaming," I fired back hotly. "You don't even believe you were the slightest bit rude to me. Otherwise, you wouldn't have expected me just to accept you as my mate."

He clenched his jaws together. "It wasn't exactly my choice," he said through his teeth, showing his frustration at our situation. "I didn't mean to be."

I sat back in the chair, staring at him. He'd had no choice but to be a dick to me? But who—no, bad question, I know who. *Why* would his father put him up to that?

"By Vir, your entire family is messed up," I said, shaking my head. "I thought shit was bad for me when you told me I was adopted and you were right, but now that I'm seeing the real Aldridge family, I can confidently say yours is *way* more fucked up than mine. All of you are insane."

"Now that's not fair," Johnathan protested sharply.

I lifted my eyebrows before looking pointedly at my current shackled predicament and my clothes, which his father had put on me, by stripping off my other ones.

"Not to mention the mark I'm sure dear old dad left on my cheek when he hit me. Like the real man he is."

"It's fading," Johnathan said.

I sighed. "That's not the *point*, John." I used the

short form on purpose. "The point is that you guys are treating me like shit and then acting surprised when I won't immediately obey and become the good housewife who does whatever she's told. Look in a mirror! This isn't how you treat people."

John looked away, unable to meet my eyes as I gave him my best glare. I was surprised. Embarrassment was far humbler of a reaction than I'd ever expected from him or anyone in his family at this point. It suggested he knew what was going on was wrong.

"You don't know him," he said quietly after a moment, clenching and relaxing his right hand over and over again. "You don't know what it was like, growing up with him as your father."

I laughed. Hard. I laughed until tears streamed down my face and I was out of breath. Then I laughed some more.

Johnathan stared at me, unspeaking, the entire time. I eventually pulled myself together.

"Please," I gasped, still struggling for air. "Please tell me you don't *actually* expect me to fucking *pity* you, do you? After everything your stupid family has done to me and mine, you want me to think you're the *victim* in all this?"

He opened his mouth to reply, but I wasn't done. My outraged laughter quickly became white-hot fury.

"And even if it was real, don't *ever* expect me actually to give a shit, *John*. You're an adult, and you can make your own decisions. Do what's right if you think you're not like him. Set me free."

"I can't do that," Johnathan said quietly, shaking his head, staring at the floor. "Not unless you agree to be my mate."

Well and truly under Daddy's thumb, it seems. Can't even think for yourself.

"That's never gonna happen," I said coldly. How many times did I have to tell them that?

"Dammit!" Johnathan said, smacking a fist into his palm. "Can't you see I'm trying to help you out here? Come along willingly, Dani, and this will be easier."

He was trying hard to convince me, even resorting to using a short form of my name. I wondered how much that cost him. Not enough, that's for sure.

"No," I repeated.

"If you don't do this on your own, my father is going to leave you broken and bleeding for the next Wild Moon. You'll be so weak that you'll be lost to your wolf forever. Then he can come and hunt you down for sport. Don't let him win like that! Just accept our bond."

As he spoke, the Soulbond pulsed harder in my mind, filling me with warmth and happiness as I looked at Johnathan. Here was a man who would make me happy. Who I could feel fulfilled with, it said, working its insidious way into my mind, trying to twist my thoughts. The stupid thing didn't care that he'd ruined my family. That he was an asshole or had a tiny dick. None of that mattered.

My Soulbond wants me to be miserable. Perfect. 'Cause my life isn't already fucked up enough as is.

A part of me almost believed Johnathan's last plea. That he truly did not want to see me hunted down by his father, who would surely take pleasure in ripping my throat open for all the pack to see.

I couldn't trust that part of me, however, because it might be compromised by the Soulbond. I would have to rely solely on myself and pure logic. No emotions could be taken into account.

Which was fine with me because I wasn't going to let any of this influence my decision. I'd made it and was sticking with it. Besides, I was already working on my escape from this hellhole.

CHAPTER THIRTEEN

As it turned out, the Aldridges brought escape to me.

I guess my message about *never* mating with Johnathan didn't resonate with them. Perhaps they were mentally incapable of understanding just how much I hated him after the way he'd destroyed my family, dropping the little bomb about my parents adopting me in secret.

The worst part was, I knew they were right in a way. If I stayed with Johnathan, I would eventually forgive him. The Soulbond would see to that. Even now, I could feel it in the back of my skull, pulsing slowly, each gentle wave of golden happiness working to erase the burning fury I felt toward him. I could fight any physical torture these assholes tried, but this was something deeper, something more insidious.

I wonder if anyone else ever felt this way about

their Soulbond? It's supposed to be this wonderous thing, a time of magical happiness and alignment with another soul. But not for me. For me, it's the toughest fight of my life.

The renewed grating of snores on my eardrums yanked me out of my little daydream. I glared daggers at the nearby bed where Johnathan was passed out, doing his best to wake the entire house in his sleep. I did *not* miss that, but for once, his snoring was useful.

After an unknown amount of time in the dark, dim cell, more of Lars' minions had arrived. They'd trussed me up with rope and brought me to Johnathan's room. Once there, they retied me to the chair, but they'd left my arms bound in front of me, my biceps tied to the thick metal chair—and what did it say that this insane family had multiple chairs seemingly built for this purpose?—but I could still bend my arms, bringing my wrists toward my face.

By dropping my face, I could bring the rope within range of my mouth. As Johnathan slept peacefully, I started chewing my bonds, strand by strand. It was a painfully slow process, but I fueled my patience with anger. Fuck these people for thinking they could control me. My brain was my own, and I wasn't going to let them win.

A second presence made itself known as the room abruptly leaped into full clarity, my vision incredibly heightened beyond anything a human could see. The sounds of snoring became the rip-saw roars of a chainsaw as my brain filtered every sound through my suddenly acute hearing.

I grinned as my wolf lent me her strength. We chewed the bonds, biting deeper into the thick rope with every gnash of our teeth. Around us, the house slept, but we kept alert. Any noise could wake Johnathan, or worse, Lars. If we were going to do this, it had to be in utter silence. Together, we could escape.

Johnathan's snores filled the room as he rolled onto his back.

By Vir, I don't miss that shit, I thought, remembering the times I had slept over. "Slept" being a bit of a misnomer since I don't know how anyone could handle that much noise and still pass out.

At least it was covering any sounds we made as we worked on our escape. We looked up constantly, ears pricking at the slightest of sounds. Someone was still awake in the house, somewhere. I'd heard footsteps at one point, but they hadn't come near.

To the household, I was just a young, weak she-wolf. An easily intimidated woman who they could scare into submission with a few wrist restraints and threats of force.

As if I don't love being tied up normally, I thought with a silent snort. They weren't going to get their way with me. Fuck that.

Another strand parted under our teeth, and a low growl of success slipped out of my mouth as the bonds started to loosen. Success was closing in, and my wolf was getting antsier.

We must be quiet, I urged her, reasserting control from my human side, reminding her who was in charge.

The she-bitch didn't like it, but she didn't fight me either, remaining silent while lending me her enhanced senses so that we could do this together.

It would have been much easier simply to destroy the chair. Metal it may be, but it would still break if enough strength were applied to it. With my wolf, we could do it and be gone in a second or two. However, it would wake the entire house, so I had to go about it the slow and steady way.

I had to think about the future this time. There was far more to what I was doing besides freeing myself. I had to think about *after*. Even as I made it through one braid of rope and wriggled my hands out of the rest, I was planning six steps ahead. After the rest of the rope was undone, I had to turn to the next stage of my escape.

Getting out of the house.

Rising to my feet, my wolf and I padded silently toward the door, moving as stealthily as we could. Now was not the time for sound either. After we got out of the house—and we *were* going to get out—my wolf and I had another challenge ahead of us. Perhaps the biggest one of all, and I needed as big a head start as possible to succeed in that.

Assured that nobody was waiting outside the door and that my "mate" was still soundly asleep, I opened the door and slipped out into the hallway. The added padding of the thick carpet running down the center of the hallway allowed me to move in near total silence. My eyes flicked around, remembering the layout of the giant mansion. With three levels and an abundance of rooms and corridors, it could easily become confusing to those who had never been there.

For once, my history with Johnathan was going to play into my hands, guiding me toward the nearest exit. I moved slower than I wanted, forcing myself to exercise restraint and caution well beyond what *seemed* necessary. All it would take was one mistake, and the entire house would be after me. I couldn't risk it. So, I moved with agonizing slowness, one step at a time, transferring my weight as cautiously as possible.

I passed by empty rooms on either side of the hallway, reminders of a time when Seguin was full of shifters instead of a town half-empty and boarded up. A time when we had been more than we were now. I wasn't sure *why* the pack had been shrinking, but the past day or so was beginning to give me an idea of why some might leave and never return.

I didn't slow at any of the rooms, but just shy of the top of the stairs, I paused outside one. The door was marked with an intricate, painted scene straight out of our history books. It had always caught my attention, and it didn't fail to now. The shifter god Vir, Champion of Amunlea, the Goddess of all shifters, kneeled on one knee, giving his word to the Goddess that he would fight to the very end in her name.

The scene was called "The Elevation," and it represented the day Amunlea created Vir to be her Champion and general, the strongest god after herself. It was also supposedly the beginning of the fall of our species if one believed the old legends.

It's why we curse the oath that Vir swore to her.

All the artifacts my father had retrieved for Lars sat behind that door. I'd seen many of them myself, and as such, I shouldn't need to bother myself with more daydreams. I knew what was in there, from the many golden crowns to the jeweled pendant of Amunlea herself, supposedly, a glorious piece of jewelry. But it was knowing what was in there that made me pause.

It was a reminder of my father.

Footsteps coming up the stairs snapped me out of my history lesson. I whipped my head around, horror pumping ice through my veins. I froze, unsure of what to do. There was no way I could go unseen. The hallway was a straight shot and getting to the nearest hiding place would involve running flat out. That alone would alert whoever was awake that I was free.

Flattening myself against the door of the relic room, I took a slow, silent breath and whispered a quick prayer that whoever was coming up the huge, curved stairwell would head toward one of the other wings of the house. Then I could sneak down past them, open a window, and run into the night.

Please. Please don't come this way. Go another way. Any other way. Just not down here.

The door's alcove would keep me out of immediate sight, but I couldn't be missed by anyone walking down the hallway unless they were half-blind. Since Grandma Aldridge had passed away a year ago, there were no elderly members of the household I was aware of who might walk past me.

The footsteps continued. I leaned into my wolf, using her instinctual knowledge to figure out what I could about the owner.

Light. Not heavy. Female most likely, or perhaps a youngling.

The last would be the preferable choice. Now that I was one with my wolf, I could overpower a shifter who hadn't had their Soulshift yet. If it was a woman, however, then I could be in for a fight.

Whoever it was, they reached the top of the stairs and, as my luck would have it, chose to head down my corridor. Considering it led to the sleeping chambers of the primary Aldridge family, that was no surprise.

My heart sped up as they drew close, hammering so hard I swore whoever was coming had to be completely alerted to my presence. There was simply no way they were going to walk by unawares. Yet on they came, approaching step by step. My hand trembled as the time to strike came near.

I would have one chance at this. One shot to do this as quietly and quickly as possible, buying myself time to run.

Time slowed as the leading foot of my unknown victim appeared past the edge of the alcove. I waited till it was almost on the floor. Then I moved, lunging forward, timing my attack so I hit them when they were off-balance with one leg in the air.

My fist flashed out, connecting solidly with their jaw, their head snapping around. Success!

I watched in horror as Mariana Aldridge, Lady Aldridge and Lars' mate, toppled to the floor. I should have caught her, should have lowered her gently to the floor to minimize sound, but the shock of who I had attacked, followed swiftly by the fear of what Lars would do in retribution, left me rooted to the spot for several seconds.

Thankfully, she landed on the carpet, managing to miss the walls on her way down. I stared at her for what had to be an eternity, though it was likely no more than a second or two.

Run!

My wolf didn't care who we had attacked. She wanted out and was snapping at me to get a move on. It was time I listened to the beast within. She knew how to run. To run as fast as the wind.

We found the nearest window that would open and slipped out, not trusting the doors to be unwatched. Our feet crunched mulch and flowers underneath as we landed in a garden, but I ignored it, stripping the shirt and shorts off, trying not to focus on what was going to happen next.

This was the first time I had ever shifted outside of the Wild Moon. My wolf was ecstatic about being able to run free two nights in a row, and I did nothing to restrain her.

With my teeth clenched against the pain, I initiated the transformation. The hair on my arms thickened and grew longer, turning silver-white, as did the hair on my head and elsewhere, covering me in a thick coat of fur.

Bones cracked and reknit in a painful sensation that, thankfully, was fleeting, taking mere fractions of a second. Though that also meant all the agony was condensed into several waves of blinding pain.

Then, almost before I realized it had started, we had done it. We had shifted.

I pawed at the ground, feeling the power in my limbs once more. This time, however, it was fully under my control. I was in charge with only my wolf's instincts at the forefront.

Time to go, I thought, and we shot off through the darkness at a blinding speed.

I'd escaped the bonds and Johnathan's room. Now my wolf and I had made it out of the house, though the alarm would go up soon thanks to our unfortunate encounter with Lady Aldridge.

Which left only one part of the plan to go.

Time to get the hell out of Seguin.

Forever.

CHAPTER FOURTEEN

I adjusted the bag's strap on my shoulder once more as it slipped free, its weight pulling it down.

"Stupid thing," I growled as I slipped my left arm through the strap as well, so it rested on both shoulders, digging into my skin.

I'd been planning to travel light, but once I'd reached my parents' place, I had a hard time choosing what to take and what to leave. At this point, I knew full well not to expect the house to survive Lars' wrath. I'd escaped his prison, and on top of that, I'd assaulted his wife.

He was going to burn the place to the ground, I was sure. So, I took what I felt was important and what I could haul, then left as fast as I could. After all, it was the first place they would look for me.

This was the second, though, so I had to be

quick.

Bending over, I picked up a few bits of gravel from the driveway, shaking them in my hand as I walked to the side of the farmhouse. I switched all but one of the pebbles to my left hand. That one was launched in the air, clattering noisily against the window.

I cringed at the sound, but I couldn't risk going inside. If any of the pack enforcers arrived, I needed to see them coming so that I could run before they located me. But I couldn't leave just yet. Not without saying goodbye to the one person I had left. The one person who had never doubted me for a moment.

I chucked the second pebble, glancing around as it bounced off the glass. I didn't hear, nor smell, signs of anyone else, but that could change instantly. I launched the third pebble, my eyes already looking around the property.

"*Ow*," a voice hissed from the window. "What the hell was that for?"

I swung my gaze back around to see Jo sticking her head out the window and rubbing her forehead.

"Shit, sorry. Jo," I said, keeping my voice low. I strode up to the side of the house, so we could be as close as possible, thus keeping our voices down.

"What are you doing here?" she asked. "Why

are you…You're leaving, aren't you?"

I quickly nodded. "I had to come and see you. I had to say goodbye."

"Goodbye?" Jo repeated, frowning at me as she shook herself awake.

"I'm not coming back this time, Jo," I said quietly.

I looked around as I talked, watching for anyone approaching the house. Thankfully, like most shifters in Seguin, the Alustria family lived on an old farm. They had no neighbors nearby, and I could see all around me. Anyone who was sneaking up on me would be forced to reveal themselves long before they got close enough to catch me.

"What about the Wild Moon?" Jo asked nervously, looking up at the sky, where the moon was now waning. "What will you do?"

"Survive," I said. "If I stay here, if they force me to mate with Johnathan, I will be as good as dead. On the inside, at least. I'll find some way to be safe while I'm out there. To not harm any humans during the Wild Moon."

"I don't understand," Jo said. "Why? What happened? What did Lars want with you?"

I sighed. "You had some bum luck, not shifting," I said. "It'll happen, and I can at least assure you that when you do, you won't end up with the bad luck of being mated to Lars' son."

Jo rolled her eyes. "That would be nice. At least one worry off my plate. Why can you guarantee that to—Oh."

I nodded.

"Oh, no," she said. "You're serious? John is your Soulbound mate?"

I nodded again, gritting my teeth. "Yeah. And then I kinda sorta rejected him in front of the entire pack. Including Daddy."

Jo gasped. I quickly filled her in on the rest of the night's activities, watching her horror grow as she listened to the way the pack Alpha had treated me.

"What are you going to do?" Jo asked eventually.

"I don't know," I admitted, feeling my fears rise. I had no real plan, no idea of what to do. I would run.

And then what? Keep running for the rest of my life? With the Soulbond, Johnathan could find me anywhere if he wanted to. I would never be safe from him. Or his father.

"But you're Soulbound," Jo said. "You can't just escape that."

"I have to try," I said fiercely.

Jo disappeared from the window and seconds later came flying out the front door, wrapping me up in one of her customary hugs. Her head only came to my shoulders, but I accepted it anyway, giving her a hard squeeze.

"I'm going to miss you," she said quietly.

"I'll miss you, too, Jo." I meant it.

"Call me when you can, okay?"

I shook my head. "Can't. They'll probably monitor it and trace the call. I'll try to send word I'm okay from time to time. Letters, probably. Frannie will help me. Maybe email if I can learn how to do so without being tracked."

Jo smiled. We both knew my old boss at the Seguin Post Office wasn't a big fan of Lars. She would ensure my messages got to Jo.

"I'm sorry," I added, knowing I was pushing my luck, but this might be the last time I had a chance to talk with her. I had to get everything out. "I wish I could stay here, be here for you when you Soulshift. But I have to leave. I need to get away from John, and I need to find my parents."

I could see it in Jo's eyes. She didn't think they were alive. I couldn't blame her. It seemed impossible that after eight months they would still be alive wherever they were. But I had to try.

"Go get the world," Jo whispered in my ear, giving me one last squeeze. "You're gonna do great."

Blinking back tears, I patted Jo on the shoulder and headed to my father's old pickup, which was still parked in the driveway. That was why I'd come here. I opened the door and tossed the bag into the seat. This was it. I was leaving Seguin and never coming back. A new chapter of my life.

"Dan!"

I reacted instantly at Jo's cry. Pushing away from the truck, I let myself fall into a backward roll, tucking tight and coming up into a crouch.

A wolf landed where I had been standing. If I hadn't rolled away, they would have pounced on my back, claws ripping me to shreds as they bore me down into the seat of the truck.

I didn't recognize the gray and black mottled beast, but they sure as hell knew me. Most likely, it was one of the clans' enforcers sent out through Seguin to try and track me down.

"Get inside. Jo. This isn't your fight," I snapped. "Go!"

My last barked command snapped Jo into action, and she retreated inside, closing the thick door behind her. Once she was safe, I rose from my crouch, keeping my legs bent, arms out slightly to the sides.

I didn't want to give away much, but I was no longer the naïve country shifter who had left Seguin eight months ago. Nobody seemed to realize that my time in the city had changed me, and I was banking on that surprise to help me out of this jam.

I'd learned a lot in the city. Much of which I'd never even told Jo about. All of which was to say that I was much more confident in my chances against this wolf than I would have been when I first shifted.

The beast pawed at the ground, snarling at me. It wanted me to submit, to do as it wished.

"Not happening," I growled. "Like, at all. So let's get this over with. *Come and get me!*"

The taunting was something I had learned. It made people act without thinking before they were ready, and it was no different with this asshole. He launched himself at me in a head-on charge, intending to bowl me over and get his jaws around my neck.

Which is exactly what I'd expected. But as he came at me, his jaw met my knee in a flying kick. His teeth snapped together, and I swore one of them snapped, but I didn't have time to check. Though my attack had hurt my opponent, I still had to contend with another problem.

The wolf still massed more than me, and its nearly limp form slammed into me a second later, dropping us both to the gravel driveway. I grunted as thousands of tiny pebbles abraded the skin on my arms and legs, sending tiny shoots of pain across my body.

I rolled to my feet just as the wolf shook off my hit and started to rise. I dropped an elbow into its midsection, putting my entire bodyweight behind it. Ribs gave way, and the wolf yelped. Loudly.

“Shut up,” I hissed, poking it in the eye.

It howled in agony. Claws ripped at my clothing, and I grunted as one of them tore the flesh on my shoulder blade open.

I ignored it, grabbing one of its front paws and, with a sharp cry, yanking it as hard as I could. Bone broke, and the noise that came out of the wolf’s mouth sent shivers down my spine.

“I’m sorry,” I said, getting to my feet and putting some distance between us. “I don’t know you. I didn’t want to hurt you. But I’m not going back there. I can’t.”

In the distance, the howl of other wolves foretold the coming of reinforcements. I had mere seconds to get out of there.

“I’m sorry,” I repeated, meeting the enforcer's eyes for a moment before turning and racing to my father’s truck. I fired up the engine, spun it around, and headed down the driveway, spewing gravel behind me. I left the wounded wolf, Jo, and everything I’d ever known in my rearview mirror.

I didn’t look back.

CHAPTER FIFTEEN

I slammed back into the cage wall, momentarily seeing stars.

The crowd went wild around me, cheering and hollering for more, while in the background, bettors cried out for bookies working the tables, wanting to place new wages or modify existing ones. One person gasped audibly as I ducked a second punch and spun away, sweat dripping down the back of my neck, turning my tightly braided hair into a wet, sloppy mess.

Ahhh, I thought as I danced around the cage, eyeing my opponent. *It's good to be home.*

The stench of cigar smoke wafted through the converted industrial building—so much work had been done that I wasn't even sure what it had originally housed, but it had the high windows and brick exterior of an old factory or something similar.

All I knew was what it was *now*. An underground fight club. I know, I know, the first rule and all that. Well, this was my gig now. And truthfully, I was starting to enjoy it. Not only that, but I was improving.

Of course, thanks to my shifter healing, I was getting a *lot* of experience.

"Make 'em work!" a wavery voice called from my corner.

I sighed, swiping at my eye to keep sweat from dripping into it and blinding me again like it had before I took the last blow. That one had been unplanned, and those always hurt. I preferred knowing when the blow was going to connect.

My opponent—I didn't know who he was, and I didn't care—came at me again, shaking his head at me. They always did that, stunned that I, a woman, would look for *more* punishment. Well, they didn't have to understand me. Nor did they have to care. I beckoned him forward before glancing at the man in my corner for guidance.

Carl mimed punching, the movement making his cream-colored suit pull tight against his rotund figure. He immediately tried to sit up straight and adjust it, as if that would hide his increasing belly. I marveled at the way his stomach grew while his hairline shrank. It was like the two were perfectly diametrically opposed. Unfortunately, Carl was only aware of his stomach. He thought his hair was fine.

Men.

I casually ducked under a snap-jab, only to flinch as a crosscut slammed into my face and spun me to the ground. The jab had been a feint, and in my distraction, I'd fallen for it.

Impressive, I thought, spitting blood. I immediately ratcheted up my opinion of the man across from me.

"*Stay down,*" he growled at me, though it was muffled by his mouthguard. Clearly, he didn't enjoy beating up on a woman and wanted the fight to be done.

I looked over at Carl again, and he motioned for me to get up. To continue the fight.

Sorry, bud, I need the money from this fight, I thought, mentally apologizing to my foe. Not that I needed to bother. He was still going to win the fight. Just not yet.

I got to my feet. What would my parents think if they were to find me like this? Boxing in an unsanctioned club, fighting against men, all for money?

Probably would be happier that I wasn't a prostitute somewhere, I guess. I'd keep that in mind in case they ever turned up alive.

My opponent closed on me the second I rose. I backed up quickly, then threw a few quick punches his way, forcing him back for a moment. I needed to drag the fight out, but that didn't mean I wanted to keep getting knocked to the ground for it. I hadn't bled in two, or was it three, weeks now? I was frustrated.

Can't let it get to me. Need to stay calm. Have to lose the fight. Don't go off on your own again. You won't get paid.

I gritted my teeth, glancing yet again at Carl, trying to tell him he needed to signal the end of the fight already. But this time, Carl was staring out at the crowd, rubbing his greedy sausage-like hands together as more bets were called and taken. He didn't pay me any attention.

Angered, I lashed out with a kick as my foe closed. I hit his calf perfectly, and he howled in unexpected pain. Tonight, it was a boxing match. I'd just broken the rules. The ref, who was just one of the bouncers, shouted a warning at me. I nodded.

By Vir's Oath, you fool! Now you'll have to exploit that attack. Otherwise, people will think there's something strange going on with this fight. Good job.

So, I did just that, ignoring Carl's apoplectic reaction as I went on the offensive.

Sorry, Carl, you're gonna have to trust me on this one. I'm not about to do something stupid. We're still gonna get the money.

I attacked in a flurry of punches, but I let them be unguarded. I drove my opponent—what was his name again? I couldn't remember—back against the cage. I drove a fist into his side, but I pulled the blow. A true hit from me would have broken his ribs, even with the large, padded gloves I wore. I couldn't do that. It would raise too many questions.

I didn't want questions.

His defense was good, and at one point, he got a foot behind him on the cage and pushed off, his superior size driving me back. I struck back, dodging one of his blows and connecting against his cheek, snapping his head to the side. It was the most damage I'd done all evening, and I could hear the crowd starting to turn in my favor. Thinking I'd win this one after all. More bets were made.

There you go, Carl, I thought, going on the offensive again. This time, though, I purposefully overextended myself, giving my foe a wide-open chance as I struck too hard with my off hand, turning my body too far to the side.

He saw it. He took it. I went down.

The crowd went insane.

There you go, Carl. Be happy with that, I thought, not getting back up, acting the shit out of the fall as if I was knocked silly. I put my hands on the ground and tried to push up, but let them go limp and flopped back down, feeling nothing more than a fish out of water. It was ridiculous.

And I was going to get paid for it.

Eventually, I heard the ref call the fight with my opponent, Dino "The Monster" Mulvalia, as the winner. So, that was his name. I shrugged mentally. It wasn't like it mattered. He was nothing to me. Just a payday.

Around the makeshift cage, the crowd was beginning to subside, the excitement fading. Some were happy with the outcome, others not. It was like that every night. Footsteps approached.

"Okay, come on," Carl said, grabbing my arm and trying to pull me to my feet. "Let's go."

I got to my feet, still acting unsteady. I leaned on Carl. Sweat got all over his suit. Oops.

He grunted, and we made our way out of the ring, me moving unsteadily until we went through a set of doors that led to the changerooms. If a janitor's closet could be called such.

As soon as the doors closed behind us, he shoved me off him and started fussing over his suit. I didn't care. The man was a scumbag.

"Good job out there," Carl said, his voice watery, weak. "You really got the crowd going. Tonight is gonna be a fat take."

I shrugged. "Just make sure I get my cut, Carl," I said in a hard tone.

"Yeah, yeah. You know I'm good for it," he said, brushing me aside. "Probably five hundred for you tonight. That's a good one."

“Not enough,” I growled, standing up. “I need more, Carl.”

“Hey, we had a deal,” the fat greasebag said, licking his lips.

Due to my height and his average stature, I could look him in the eyes when standing, and I knew he hated that. Carl liked to look down at the world. He was a greedy, arrogant type.

“Seven-fifty,” I said, knowing not to push too hard.

Not because I was afraid of violence, but I knew if I tried to do more, Carl would drop me. He didn’t want confrontation. In fact, he ran from it. That’s why I was the fighter.

“Fine, fine,” he said unhappily. “If it’s there, then it’s yours.”

I knew it would be.

“Good. When’s the next fight?” I asked.

Carl frowned at me. “You got a death wish, kid? You’re already in the ring twice a week.”

“Make it three times, then,” I told him, lifting a wrist to my mouth and undoing the strap with my teeth so that I could pull it free.

“You’re gonna get yourself killed,” Carl protested.

I didn’t kid myself. Carl didn’t give a shit about my well-being. In this place, nobody cared about the fighters. They only cared about one thing. The money. Carl didn’t want to lose his prized cash cow, that was all.

"I need another fight, Carl," I said. "Either that or pay me more."

He licked his lips nervously, looking around, but there was still nobody in the hallway. "Fine," he said. "I'll get you another fight. But it won't be as big a take."

"Time for an upset then," I suggested. "Get me in with a bigger name. I'll beat them."

Carl's beady eyes went wide. He didn't know my secret, didn't know what I was, so of course, to him, it sounded insane.

"They'll never take it," he said.

"Make them. I need the fight."

Carl threw up his hands. "Okay, whatever! I'll see what I can do."

He turned and strode back down the dimly lit hallway, leaving me alone. I turned and headed into the changeroom. I needed a shower.

And a drink.

CHAPTER SIXTEEN

I half-flopped into the barstool and signaled at Jakoby, the bartender.

"The usual," I said when the giant Irishman looked my way and smiled through his bushy beard.

"Sure thing, Dani," he said, starting to mix up my drink.

I had no idea what it was called, but it had a bunch of colored booze and was tastily addictive. That was all that mattered to me.

"And a water, if you don't mind," I added.

The fight hadn't taken much out of me, but the adrenaline was fading, and I knew I had to hydrate. I wasn't wounded, but dancing around for fifteen minutes like that still had me working up a sweat.

"No problem, Dee," Jakoby said, swiftly filling a

glass with water and sliding it down the bar top toward me.

I nabbed it with casual ease and downed half of it in one go, barely stifling a sigh of relief at the cool, refreshing wave that worked its way to my stomach. Sometimes, water just hit the spot.

"For someone who's been here a short while, you sure are making friends quickly," a voice said from my left.

I slowly turned my head. At some point after I'd sat down, someone had come and occupied that seat.

He was dressed in an immaculate black suit, the material fitting him like it was made for him. As I took in more, I decided it probably had been. The shoes were shiny and expensive-looking, and the watch on his wrist screamed wealth. I didn't know who he was, but it was obvious he thought he was a big deal.

That impression died when I took in his face.

Pale skin contrasted fiercely with the black of his suit, but that wasn't what caught my attention. His eyes burned with a blue fire, practically glowing from the inside out, they were so bright. I inhaled sharply as they locked on to me with a stunning directness I simply wasn't used to.

He had smooth lines and sharp, angular corners to his face, sweeping cheekbones that framed a jaw straight out of a fashion magazine.

This man was walking sex, and I could practically feel it oozing out of him and catching me in its web. Like I was nothing but prey.

His predatory gaze did little to ruin that illusion. Whoever he was, he was used to having whoever he wanted. Most women would have trouble saying no to him, and I knew it wouldn't be easy for me either.

He smiled at me as I stared at him, running a hand through his blond hair, letting it fall messily back into place. It still looked good. I very carefully sat up straighter as he looked at me how a lion did a wounded antelope. Like he was the hunter, and I was his prey.

Not happening tonight, I thought, for once thankful that I was on my cycle. Usually, I hated how my body decided it despised me once a month for not putting a baby in it, but this one time, it actually came in handy, helping to dampen the arousal I could feel flickering to life within me.

This man was *dangerous*. I had to remember that. Besides, his come-hither looks and what appeared to be a rock-solid body likely meant he had no idea how to pleasure a woman. He was used to not having to try, I'm sure, and I didn't feel like adding my name to what must be a long list of disappointed lovers.

Yet, for some reason, my wolf disagreed with me. She spoke up, vocally so. This man was *at-*

tractive to her.

Are we into bad boys and stuff now? I asked her. When the hell had that happened? I was surprised that she was so active all of a sudden. Since we'd left Seguin behind for good, she'd been quiet. Until now.

Something about this man was attractive to my predator side, and that made me even more uneasy about the entire thing. I leaned into my wolf, using her abilities to test the air, but I couldn't pick up anything that smelled off about him. He wasn't a shifter, that was for sure.

"Is that a problem?" I asked, replying at last to his initial comment.

"Not for me," Mr. Unknown said with a smile, leaning back against the bar and staring out at the rest of the open space.

I waited, but he didn't say anything else. He simply continued to slowly sip at the bottle of beer in his right hand. Ignoring me.

What was the point in initiating conversation, then? I slowly turned away from Mr. Unknown. No way would I give this overdressed fop the satisfaction of having me talk to him more.

I leaned forward, resting my elbows on the bar as Jakoby brought my drink over. I took a long sip of it, listening to the sounds behind me.

The bar itself was a public establishment, registered and all that fun stuff, but it was invite-only on weekends and occasionally during the week. That way, only trusted patrons were allowed in, meaning they could host their underground fight network without fear of reprisal from the law.

Tables that would normally be laid out in the center of the room were stacked beside the bar to create more room, and I looked idly in the mirror behind Jakoby, watching the cage. It was empty now. My fight had been the last one scheduled for the evening.

I wondered more about Mr. Unknown. *Did he show up for the fight? Or just after? Why was he here, and why give me that line if he didn't intend on saying more?*

Beside me, he continued to people-watch. I chuckled internally. I was a shifter. A predator by nature, used to stalking my prey, taking the time necessary to get what I wanted. This man, he exuded the same attitude, but he wasn't *truly* a predator. He was human. If he thought I was going to grow impatient first, he was in for a rude awakening.

Or so I told myself. The truth was probably a little grayer than that.

I couldn't deny that I was intrigued by him.

In that instant, I knew I was going to lose the battle. I'd gone and admitted to myself that I wanted to know more about him. It grated to know he'd beaten me. I didn't like losing—even when I was paid for it—but I could be gracious about it.

"Do you have many friends here?" I asked, turning to face him.

The smug look of victory flashed through his eyes, but like a true professional, he didn't linger on it. I tilted my head in acknowledgment, letting him know I was fully aware of the little game we'd played. I wanted him to know that I'd *chosen* to break the silence, that my speaking wasn't done out of ignorance.

It made me like him more. This man was a professional. Used to getting his way, perhaps, but not an asshole about it. He just enjoyed the game.

"A few," he admitted with a tiny smile.

I swallowed against the sudden weightlessness in my stomach when he did that. I was so unprepared for my body to have that sort of reaction that I panicked and, desperate to do *something* to stall for time, I downed the rest of my drink.

Oops.

"Just a few?" I said as the liquid burned pleasantly into my stomach.

What am I doing?

"It's hard to make true friends in my business," he said quietly, his eyes sweeping the rest of the bar. "So, yes, just a few. Real friends."

"Yeah," I agreed. "People like that are too few

and far between."

"So," Mr. Unknown said. "Will I be seeing you around here more often?"

It was my turn to smile. "I suppose you'll have to come back and find out for yourself," I said, deciding to play it a bit mysterious.

Mr. Unknown chuckled, the smooth, velvety sound an instant point of attraction. Was there anything about this man that *didn't* ooze sex? I swear he could crook a finger at me and I'd explode simply from imagining what he could do with it. Okay, maybe not literally, but everything about him was designed to be as beautiful as possible.

From the messy, light blond hair to the pale skin, sharp jaw and suit that he wore like a second skin. This man was dangerous. Human or not, he was an alpha predator of his kind, and I knew it. Worse, *he* knew it. I suspected he was holding back in giving me the full treatment, though I couldn't figure out why.

"It's not often someone spars with me," he said, still smiling.

Is that what I was doing? Because it felt like I was trying my best simply to stay afloat. *Maybe that's more than he's used to? Maybe he's used to women simply submitting instantly, doing as he pleases.*

My mind wandered, curious as to whether he

had a place nearby, because a part of me wouldn't mind submitting to him. I'd never *been* with a real man, and all my senses were screaming at me that this man was one. That he could do what my ex never could.

Besides, where was the harm? I could take him if he truly tried something wrong. I wasn't going to be in any danger, and in my sex-deprived brain, that was the perfect time to submit. When it was all for fun. And pleasure. Yes, lots of pleasure, that much I knew he would give me.

Maybe life in the city doesn't have to be as bad as I thought it would, I thought, already mentally preparing to leave with him, even though he'd not invited me.

I leaned in just a hair, eager to draw in more of his scent, that rich, oaky aroma that I'd picked up a time or two already, completely at odds with the smell of booze and stale cigars filling the rest of the room. As I did, I stiffened, my nostrils filling with another scent. One I had hoped never to smell again.

There was an Aldridge in the crowd.

CHAPTER SEVENTEEN

"Is everything okay?" Mr. Unknown asked, leaning slightly closer.

I basked in his presence, savoring that sweet yet tantalizingly faint hint of cologne that he wore. This was a real man.

Looking into his almost unnaturally blue eyes —how were they so bright, even in a dingy place like this?—I forced myself to try and smile. For him.

"Yes," I said quietly. "Everything is fine."

Mr. Unknown stared at me without speaking for a dozen or so seconds. Judging me with his eyes. I could feel him taking my measure, and for once, I wasn't sure how someone was going to react. I hated not being in control. I hated being the one to react instead of leading. I was no Alpha, but I didn't like being forced to dance to someone else's tune. I liked *choice.*

"Bullshit," he said, somehow making the curse sexy.

It shouldn't be legal, but there he was, doing it anyway.

"Pardon?" I said, trying to compose myself as his sultry, come-hither business worked its hooks into my body, pulling me closer. I didn't want to go. I didn't want to ruin this by dealing with Johnathan. I just wanted him to reach out and touch me. To take me with him.

Wait. Johnathan?

I tested the air again, relying heavily on my wolf since my human side was all sorts of useless with Mr. Unknown this close. We sniffed at the air, filtering out dozens of different scents, instantly cataloging them in a way no human ever could.

Our eyes narrowed as we picked out the scent we wanted and analyzed it. Yes, it was him. We knew his scent and would recognize it anywhere. I tried to hide a sigh of relief. At least it wasn't his father. If the Alpha were here, I'd be in trouble.

I blinked at a noise in my ears. It was Mr. Unknown. He was speaking.

"Pardon?" I repeated. "Sorry."

Mr. Unknown cocked his head at me. "I said, it's bullshit. You're not okay."

I liked that. Jo would call me out on my shit, too, when I was blatantly lying. She would force me to talk about it. She'd said that it was good for me to share. To not bottle it up. I'm sure she hadn't had Mr. Unknown in mind when she'd said that, of course. Oh, well.

"Someone is here that I don't particularly wish to see," I said with a sigh, deciding for some reason to trust this man. A man whose name I didn't even know.

Mr. Unknown's response caught me completely by surprise. I'd expected him to grimace, to nod in understanding. The moment of blinding fury, however, caught me completely by surprise. It was gone almost as quickly as it appeared, but I *knew* I'd seen what I'd seen. He couldn't hide that, not with eyes like his, that practically glowed blue even in the dim bar light.

"Do you wish for me to see to it?" he asked in a quiet voice.

I shivered. For the first time, he spoke in a way that didn't ooze sex. Instead, it threatened violence. Death even. I wasn't prepared for that either.

Who *was* this man? A moment of clarity spiked through my sex-deprived brain, telling me I needed to find out more before I did something wild, like spread my legs for him. He was clearly powerful. That much was obvious. Nobody spoke like that without being able to follow through with it.

Still, he wasn't dealing with a human. Johnathan was a full-blooded wolf shifter. He would tear this man apart without even trying.

No, this one is up to me to handle.

"No, thanks, Mr. Hotshot," I said, forcing a laugh to try and ease the tension. "I can handle it just fine myself. It's the interruption that I don't like."

Especially when it's interrupting something so intriguing. *I don't know who you are, Mr. Unknown, but I'll be back.*

Now that I was leaning more into my wolf, I could more easily ignore his charms. Despite our nightly talks, my wolf was still obsessed with the Soulbond and returning to Johnathan. Now that she'd scented him in the bar, she wanted nothing more than to run over to him and submit. To mate.

If she had her way, I'd be putting on a second show for the bar patrons tonight. I might enjoy watching some good porn from time to time like any woman with a libido strong enough to warrant a battery subscription from Amazon, but hell if I was interested in *making* some.

Even I had my lines.

So, we weren't going to do that, I told my wolf, using no uncertain terms to get my point across. I reminded her we hated him. That we were not going to set female rights back a century or three by letting ourselves be bound to the man who had hurt us so badly. We deserved *better* than that. I reminded her that Johnathan had also ruined our moment with Mr. Unknown.

Ruining things was all he seemed to be good for. My evening. Our relationship, back when naïve little me had thought dating him would be a good idea. And most recently, my entire *life*, when in a fit of anger as a vindictive ex, he'd decided to expose the fact that my parents weren't my real parents.

Yeah, this man was not worthy of my love. Not at all. Fuck the Soulbond. I wasn't having any of it.

"I'll be back," I told Mr. Unknown, rising from my seat. "But I understand if you have to go."

Mr. Unknown reclined deeper into the bar, resting his elbows on it as he regarded me. His eyes trailed down my tall, willowy body, pausing at my feet before making their way back up. I shivered. I'd never been the subject of such intense, blatant scrutiny before, and I suddenly felt completely, and totally, unworthy of it.

He was a walking billboard for sexual pleasure and satisfaction. Everything about him was perfect to the point of overwhelming. And here I was, a tall skinny chick with tiny tits, tiny ass, and no sexual experience. He wasn't in my universe, let alone my league. This man would look at supermodels and have his pick.

Why on earth would I ever be of interest to

him? All I had going for me was that I was a wolf shifter. I was far stronger and faster than I looked. But none of that mattered when he had no idea what I was.

"This should be interesting," Mr. Unknown said as his eyes reached mine again. "Another for me, will you, Jakoby?"

The bartender nodded and immediately went to fetch him a second drink.

Apparently, Mr. Unknown didn't plan on leaving. What's more, I was getting the vibe that he *knew* what I was about to do. As if he was aware of everything going on and wanted to stay to see it through.

Which was impossible because even *I* didn't know what I was going to do besides get rid of Johnathan. Somehow. It was a lot harder than it sounded. Not that anything could stop me from trying.

Casting one last look at Mr. Unknown, who was smiling broadly in anticipation of whatever he thought was about to happen, I set out into the crowd, trying to track my quarry down. The place was still rather full after the fights, but it had emptied enough that I was able to spot Johnathan without much effort.

He was on the far side of the bar, heading the opposite way as me, weaving his way through tables and the crowd as his head scanned the occupants. Searching for me. His height let him do it as he towered over most humans. It wouldn't be long before he found me.

"Dani," a voice said from my side, distracting me.

I turned to see Carl approaching, a giant, slimy grin on his face.

"What is it?" I said, keeping an eye on Johnathan.

"Here," he said, pulling out a wad of cash. "Your take from tonight. Eight hundred. It was a better night than we thought!"

I eyed the money. If Carl had voluntarily upped my amount after I'd basically threatened him to pay me more already, than he must have taken in *substantially* more. It didn't matter. The money in his hand gave me an idea.

I knew how to get rid of Johnathan.

"I want you to take all the money and put it on me for the next fight," I said. "Use your front or whoever, but put it *all* on me. Got it?"

Carl frowned. "What are you talking about, Dani? What fight? There are no more fights scheduled."

"There's about to be one," I said, my plan coalescing in my mind.

"Tonight?" Carl sounded surprised. "But you already fought."

"Start spreading the word, Carl," I growled, practically wolfing out right there as I tapped into my other half, preparing her for what was to come. "Do it, or I'm done working for you."

I knew that threat would work. I made Carl a *lot* of money. A lot, both in my frequency of fighting, but also because I would win or lose against anyone that he told me to. I don't know how others hadn't caught on to the fact that I was throwing the fights, but it didn't' matter. Carl didn't want to lose out on his cash cow.

"Okay," he said, shaking his head. "Okay, fine. Who's your opponent?"

I pointed through the crowd to where Johnathan had paused, staring straight at me. He stood out quite easily, not just with his height, but the blood-red shirt he wore was enough to catch the eye as well. Even I had to admit he looked good in it.

Stop it, I snarled at myself, feeling the insidious touch of the Soulbond trying to work its magic on me. Make me want to go over to him. Take his hand and leave this place. Together.

Enough.

"Him?" Carl croaked in shock. "Dani, come on. I've set you up with other women or very low-tier men. But this guy, this guy is huge. He's going to *hurt* you, Dani. I can't do that."

Still staring at Johnathan, I reached out and snagged Carl by the collar, yanking him in close.

"Make the damn fight, Carl," I snarled in his

face, my wolf right on the surface.

I'd never treated Carl like this. Never spoke up against him or threatened him. My actions stunned him, and he stood shaking, almost trembling in my grip. He was useless like that.

"Bet on me," I told him. "And you'll win a lot of money."

That did the trick. The talk of money brought him around. All I had to do was appeal to his greed. "How can you be so sure?" Carl asked, still flustered at being so easily yanked around.

"Because this guy has it coming," I growled, staring at Johnathan, hatred burning in my gut.

I could add one more thing to my list of things Johnathan had destroyed. My new life here in the city. By showing up here tonight, he'd proven he could find me anywhere. I knew he could, but this showed he was willing to. That he would never stop following me. Never giving me any peace.

Oh, yes, I was going to win tonight. He just didn't know it yet.

"Okay, if you say so," Carl said, still not believing me. I didn't care. He was probably going to bet against me. His loss.

"Eight hundred on me," I snarled. "Remember that, Carl."

"Uh, yeah," he said, licking his lips nervously before heading over to the sound system and speaking to the DJ lounging nearby. The DJ looked at me and then at Johnathan. I could see Carl waving his hands, growing insistent.

Finally, the DJ threw up his hands and caved.

I grinned at Johnathan, who hadn't moved, still staring at me across the bar. He was waiting for me to make the first move.

Okay, I said and headed for the cage. I casually pulled open the door and stepped inside. I was wearing street clothes, a pair of black pants, a white t-shirt, and a normal bra. My hair was unbraided now, falling down my back in wet, wavy curls, courtesy of the lack of hair dryer.

People in the crowd were staring at me now, likely wondering what was going on, when the background music cut out and the DJ began to speak. I didn't hear his words. I just watched Johnathan's face, waiting for him to realize what was going on.

The crowd cheered at the prospect of another fight. They cheered harder when I indicated I would be one of the fighters. Johnathan was frowning at this point. I wondered if he had any inkling of what was about to happen.

"Her opponent tonight," the DJ said. "A newcomer to our crowd. Give it up for the Bloodman!"

Apparently, Carl had come up with a nickname for Johnathan. A spotlight clicked on, and the DJ pointed directly at my ex. I grinned as he blinked in momentary confusion, then waved his hands in a negative.

The crowd booed, egging him on with chants of "Fight!" It wasn't working, though. Johnathan wanted nothing to do with it. The crowd continued to get worked up. People were on their phones, texting and making phone calls. Probably calling people back for another fight.

"No!" Johnathan said, his voice carrying over the crowd. "I will not fight her."

I grinned from inside the ring and gave him the finger. "What's the matter?" I shot back, breaking out my big gun, the one I knew would force him into the ring. "Are you afraid? Are you a coward?"

Gauntlet. Thrown.

The crowd went nuts, and I waited. Both Johnathan and I knew he couldn't refuse now. Not without accepting that label.

We were going to fight.

CHAPTER EIGHTEEN

Just as I expected, Johnathan walked to the center of the bar. The crowd was taunting him like mad. They had no idea who or what he was. To them, he was just a human acting too scared to take on a girl.

Not that I would have expected this crowd of degenerates to ever think that maybe a man his size shouldn't fight a girl like me. If we were both human, this would be suicide.

But we weren't human. The crowd didn't know that. They just didn't care. They wanted a fight and blood.

As he came around, he stripped off his shirt, revealing an impressively muscular torso. I found myself looking at it for a moment. It had never been his looks that I'd had an issue with. Johnathan was as attractive as they came.

Well over six feet tall, he had the thick, powerful build of a bodybuilder, compared to Mr. Unknown's more lithe, athletic build. Both strong, but in different ways.

Now, why did I go and bring him into this?

"This is a dumb idea," Johnathan said as he climbed into the cage with me, an enthusiastic fan slapping the gate closed behind him.

"You coming here was a dumb idea," I shot back. "I told you I never wanted to see you again."

"We're Soulbound." He said it like that explained everything.

To him, it probably did. To me, it was nothing. Worthless.

"I don't care," I told him. "I want nothing to do with you."

"It can't be severed," he said harshly. "Stop denying it. You're only going to drive yourself insane if you try."

"I'd rather that than willingly go with you," I said, my voice cold. "I'd rather *die*."

"If you keep defying my father, you just might get your wish," Johnathan said. "I was barely able to keep him from coming here tonight."

"Am I supposed to thank you for that?" I said with a laugh, reaching back to braid my hair to keep it out of my face as best I could. I didn't have an elastic to tie it closed, but I made do. It was better than nothing.

"I suppose not," Johnathan said. "Why are you

doing this?"

"Because maybe it'll teach you to leave me alone," I said.

He shook his head. "If I win?"

"You won't," I said. "Remember, I already beat you once."

He flushed angrily at the reminder. "If I win?" he repeated hotly.

"If you win," I said, "then I'll go back with you. Willingly."

I had no intention of doing that.

"Fine," he said. "And if you win?"

"If I win, you leave me alone. Forever."

"Won't happen," he said bluntly. "I can't. The bond calls to me."

I gritted my teeth. "Fine. For a week, then."

That would put me precariously close to the next Wild Moon. Maybe by then, I'd have found a way to hide from him. To stay safe. Because, come the Wild Moon, both Johnathan *and* his father would be after me.

"Fine," Johnathan said.

I still doubted he meant it, but I should at least get the rest of the night to myself. That would be a small victory. I could find some way to run. To get away.

"Well, come on then," I said, lifting my hands like I was going to box.

Somewhere, someone rang a bell. There was no ref this time. No judge. It was just a straight-up fight until one or the other submitted. That simple.

Johnathan lifted his hands, and he came into the center cautiously. I circled the outside, forcing him to turn with me. He easily kept pace. I kept circling. And waited.

It took two laps of the ring for Johnathan to grow impatient. He launched his attack at me, a roaring hammer blow that would have leveled me. *If* he connected. I easily ducked under it and past him, driving my fist deep into his stomach as I did.

Johnathan let out an "*oof*" as I drove the air from his lungs, his body folding over the blow. I only pulled my punch enough so that I didn't send him flying backward, which would have drawn far too much attention from the crowd. But he dropped to his knees from the blow anyway. I tried to follow it up, but he rolled away from me, getting to his feet, slowly sucking in air.

"How *dare* you come here," I spat, advancing on him, not planning on letting him recover. "How *dare* you come to ruin my life again. How dare you think you own me!"

I feinted with my right and then darted to the side and connected hard onto his ribs. I let myself fall through the blow, avoiding his backhand and coming to my feet with some distance between us.

Johnathan growled and charged at me, moving faster than I expected. Faster than a human should. The crowd roared, obviously not realizing what he'd just done. I wasn't prepared for it, and he hit me like a linebacker, delivering a brutal bodycheck that hurled me back against the far side of the cage.

I hit hard and fell. The crowd gasped.

There was no time for me to waste. I forced my screaming muscles to respond, pushing myself away and to the side. Johnathan's knee came flying toward me, narrowly missing my skull. The cage shook as he made contact, and his bellow of frustration cut through the crowd's noise like a knife.

I got to my feet again, the entire right side of my body one giant ache. Nothing was broken that I could tell, but that impact had *hurt*. Johnathan came at me relentlessly now. Dull blue eyes were filled with frustration as he advanced. He might be winning the fight, but he'd been forced to dance to *my* tune, and he didn't like it.

Well, too bad, Johnny Boy.

"Just end this now," he growled at me. "You don't have to get hurt."

I grinned and snapped my leg out as he advanced. I caught him as he was transferring his weight with his step, and the force of my kick—

which I hadn't pulled—whipped his leg out from under him, and he fell. I scrambled to get on his back like some sort of spider monkey, holding on tight.

My arm slipped under his chin. This wasn't the type of fight Johnathan was used to, and it showed. He wasn't prepared at all for that move, and he didn't stop me from locking it in.

The crowd knew, however, and they shot to their feet, erupting with shouts and chants. I squeezed, holding on for dear life, doing my best to avoid Johnathan's wild attempts to pry me off while taking backward punches and elbows that sent flashes of agony through my body when they connected.

But I didn't let go. I had this fucker where I wanted.

"You should never have come after me," I said as his blows started to weaken. "Now you're going to lose to me twice, you little bitch."

I don't know if he heard that last taunt or not because he'd run out of blood to his brain and was slipping into unconsciousness. I braced myself, holding on tight as we fell to the ground. Thankfully, he didn't fall backward. That was probably the only move he could have made that would have dislodged me. Instead, we fell to the side. I grunted at the impact but kept holding tight until he was completely limp. Then I held on for a few more seconds before finally releasing.

Scrambling free, I got to my feet before Johnathan woke up with a roar, the blood returning to his head.

I slammed a fist into his face, keeping him down.

"You lost," I shouted over the bar patrons as they went ballistic. "Get the hell out and leave me alone."

He got to his feet, bleeding from his nose from that last punch. I braced myself for him to continue the fight. If he did, I wasn't stopping next time.

I don't know if he read that in my eyes or if the crowd's taunts were getting to him, but he didn't come at me again.

"Smart choice," I said. "Now get out of here."

Glaring daggers at me, he left the cage, grabbing his shirt and heading for the exit to a chorus of jeers and taunts.

I took a deep breath, letting some of the tension leave me. It was done. I would have the rest of the night to myself, at least.

Looking over at the bar, I spied Mr. Unknown still sitting there. He had a very, *very* smug smile on his face. I could tell he approved of what he'd seen.

Maybe my night hadn't been ruined after all.

I started to smile, only to have it fade as Mr.

Unknown got up and left without looking at me once before.

I stood in the middle of the ring, surrounded by chanting fans. Carl was pushing his way through the crowd, a smile from ear to ear. He must have bet on me after all. Which meant I had just won a large sum as well.

Yet, none of that seemed to matter as I watched Mr. Unknown walk away.

I was still alone after all.

CHAPTER NINETEEN

I eventually made my way from the cage to the back room, leaving the cheering adulations of the crowd behind.

It was the second time I'd been back there that night, but this time I had no clean clothes, nothing to change into. I sat on the bench, sweat still dripping down my forehead, ripped clothing stained with blood. Apparently, my hit against the cage had torn open my shoulder. It wasn't bad, but blood and a white shirt didn't play nicely together.

The door was on my left, while in the back right corner, the open shower waited if I chose to use it. Lockers were on my right against the same wall I was now leaning against, cursing my idiocy.

"How could I have been so *stupid*?" I hissed to myself.

Did you really think you could come here and make a new life for yourself? That he wouldn't find you?

The city of Kellar wasn't exactly far away or anything. A few hours' drive from Seguin, no more. I should have gone farther. Another country. Hell, maybe another continent. Perhaps that would have weakened our Soulbond to the point that Johnathan couldn't have found me.

Instead, I'd just run back to the only other piece of comfort I knew and hoped would be enough. Like an idiot.

"So naïve," I whispered, disappointed in myself for falling for it all.

Outside, footsteps came down the corridor toward me. I looked up as the door opened, wondering what Carl wanted.

"You," I said, shooting to my feet as Mr. Unknown entered the change room. "I thought you'd left."

"I did," he said bluntly. "Then I came in through the back."

"Oh," I said, tugging on my shirt, wishing desperately that I'd used the time I'd had to clean up. Even just rinsing my face, washing off some of the blood. Anything that would have made me more presentable to Mr. Unknown.

Why couldn't I be all done up? Dressed to the max, a bit of female warpaint on my face, the whole bit? That would have been nice. He would certainly be a little more attracted to me then.

I could see it happening. Him walking through the door and taking in my appearance. He'd say nothing, but he wouldn't have to. His hands would grab me and throw me up against the dirty shower, hiking the back of the fancy dress —because, of course, I'd be wearing a fancy dress to impress someone like him even though I hated dresses—so that he could feel the soft, smooth skin of my rear.

His touch would make me moan and thrust myself back toward him. Right then and there, he could take me if he wanted. I wouldn't care. My screams would echo down the hallway as he showed me what a *real* man was like. Made me his for that moment in time.

My body was responding just to the thought of it. That's how badly I needed some casual, rough sex. To just be *taken* and all but used. I could imagine his hands on my hips, pulling me back against him, and it was intoxicating. Growing heated at the idea, I almost went for it. I almost touched him.

What are you doing?

I caught myself just in time. The wolf inside me voiced her disappointment, along with the heat between my legs, which I wasn't expecting. Since when did she want someone other than Johnathan?

Alpha.

Although my wolf wasn't truly speaking to me, I could pick up on the concept she was saying. This man was strong enough, Alpha enough, for her to find him not just attractive but hot enough to want to go to bed with.

Can I use that? Use him as some sort of shield from Johnathan? Something to keep my wolf and I distracted from the Soulbond?

Maybe. The only problem was, I didn't even know the guy. Yet I wanted to give him something only Johnathan had ever had? While I didn't intend to die a born-again virgin, perhaps I should get a grip on myself. I hadn't made a good choice with the first person I'd slept with because I hadn't known who he truly was.

I'm not going to make that mistake again. Besides, you're on your period, get a grip. He might not care, but we do. Standards, girl, let's try and find some.

"About finished?" Mr. Unknown said, interrupting my little inner conversation.

"What?"

"That fight," he said as if I hadn't spoken. "It looked personal."

I grunted. So ladylike. How could he possibly resist me now?

"That's not good," he told me.

I shrugged. What was I supposed to say to

that?

"Not all of life's problems can be solved with violence," Mr. Unknown continued. "Sometimes they can. But often, you need another approach. You need to find that with him. To solve your problem."

I shrugged again. Right now, despite all his hotness and ultra-sexy personality, I really didn't want Mr. Unknown or anyone's help. I wanted to either be fucked so hard I had bruises, which I was still trying to figure out *why*, or be left entirely alone. There was no middle ground.

"You need to find out what's eating at you."

"I *know* perfectly well what's eating at me," I snarled abruptly, not appreciating his tone.

It was Johnathan and our stupid Soulbond. It was his ability to find me wherever I was. It was his ability to ruin anything and everything in my life. It was the fact that if I didn't give in to the Soulbond soon, it was going to destroy me.

I could feel it at all times. Pulsing away with positive thoughts about Johnathan. Trying to change my wolf's and my feelings toward him. To suppress memories and thoughts that were negative and push a positive narrative. It was always there in the back of my mind. I had to fight it constantly.

I was *tired* of fighting it already, and it had only been a few weeks. What would happen in months? Years? Would I eventually cave? Would I lose who I truly was to this insidious, *evil* thing inside me? Who would I become? *That* scared me.

Mr. Unknown was giving me a long, appraising look.

"Do you *truly* know what's eating you?" he said at last, his tone gentler than before. "Or do you just think you do and you're using it to avoid something else?"

My parents.

I frowned. I swore he was reading my mind, looking past the outer layer and deeper into me, into my thoughts and fears. I still had no idea what had happened to them, not even a clue. All the money I won went into looking for them. It's why I insisted on fighting so often.

But so far, I hadn't found a damn thing. Not a single shred of evidence or clue as to where they had gone. It was like they'd just disappeared. Completely. Turned into dust. It made no *sense* and that too gnawed away at me because of how things had ended between us.

"You should do something about whatever it is," Mr. Unknown said.

"I can't," I said in a quiet tone. "I don't know …" I trailed off.

It wasn't Johnathan, after all. It was them. I missed them. I missed my family. I had no way of knowing. No way of finding out what had happened to them. I'd looked for clues.

In my mind, a picture of my father's journal appeared. The one from his study that he'd intended to give to me as a shift gift. I'd swiped it when I'd broken out of Aldridge Manor and returned to my old home for clothing and supplies. Something had driven me to grab it, but until then, it had stayed tucked away in the bottom of my bug-out bag.

Unread.

"See," Mr. Unknown whispered with a ghostly smile. "I knew there was more. Now *do something* about it," he urged.

Before I could speak, he nodded sharply and then left, leaving me alone in the room, aroused, confused, and more than a little scared.

Can you read my mind?

I cast the thought out there, wondering if I would get a response from him. Either he could read minds, in addition to being addictively hot, or I was just easier to read than I liked to believe.

When I got no response, I knew what the answer was.

"Damn," I hissed.

What was worse was that he was right. Although I'd been paying other people to look for evidence about my family, I'd been avoiding doing anything about it myself. It was going to be painful, but Mr. Unknown was right. I had to do *something*.

Now was the perfect time for it, as well. I'd just sent Johnathan packing for a week, hopefully more. Which meant I could get out of town, and *that* was good because I was coming up on four weeks since I'd left Seguin.

Lars' countdown was running out.

I didn't know what was going to happen, but one thing I *was* certain of was that I didn't want to be anywhere near a population center when the next Wild Moon arrived.

That meant it was time for me to leave Kellar.

CHAPTER TWENTY

Thomas Wetter.

That was the name embossed on the spine of the book. It was the only lettering on the exterior at all, which was standard for his journals. I'd only ever seen their spines before, facing out from their place on the shelf he kept them on. I suppose it *could* be something else, but I trusted my gut on this one.

Closing my eyes, I reached down and placed my palm on the brown leather cover, imagining my father writing in it, hunched over in a tent somewhere out in the wild. He loved that. Exploring the unknown. It was what drove him and made him happy. I sighed.

"I'm sorry, Dad. I'm trying," I whispered to nobody in particular. "I don't even know where to start. It's just so hard."

My voice broke on the last word, and I slumped back against the futon that doubled as both my couch and bed. I rented a room in an apartment building in a less than reputable part of Kellar. All my money had gone to the search for my parents. A futon had seemed like the most sensible of purchases, somewhere I could sit or lie down as needed. No point in buying two pieces of furniture with my meager income.

I preferred to eat.

The half-eaten bucket of ramen sat on the cheap plastic stool that served as my coffee table, dinner table, and nightstand all in one. I eyed it, but I wasn't hungry. Not anymore. The thought of opening the journal and reading my father's notes filled my stomach with a lump all its own.

My father.

Adopted, perhaps, but still the man who had raised me. I ran my fingertips across the journal's cover. I'd spent many a day trying to figure out how I felt and what the truth of it must be.

Doubts larger than the Atlantic still existed inside me, and unless I could find my parents, they would always be there. Without the truth, a part of me would always wonder. But with the complete and utter lack of clue as to where my parents had gone, I had to decide for my sanity.

Did I believe the people who raised me had truly loved me?

That was the question I needed to answer for myself. I could not go through the days constantly flopping back and forth. Had they loved me and raised me as their own, simply not feeling the need to tell me because they saw themselves as my parents?

Or was there another reason, a more sinister reason, behind the lies and deception? Had they not wanted to tell me because of some other reason? It wasn't just them keeping the truth from me either. Clearly, Johnathan had gotten the information from someone, which meant others knew I was adopted.

They'd known all along, and not one of them said a damn thing. I've got a lot of questions. Questions that need answering.

There was only one person who would give me those answers, and he was currently in locations unknown. I refused to believe they were dead. Not until somebody could show me their bodies. No, my parents were out there somewhere, hiding, for reasons I had yet to decipher.

When I caught up with them, though, they would explain everything, from my adoption to their disappearance.

Gonna need more money to do that. Tracking them isn't cheap.

"Stop avoiding this," I said, forcing myself to acknowledge out loud that my focus was wandering away from the task at hand.

My father loved me. I chose to believe that. I chose to believe they hadn't faked it all. I had too many happy memories, too many things that felt too natural to be anything but real.

It was easier to believe that than to continue thinking I was all part of one big sham, a charade. There was nothing about me that would warrant such action. I was just a regular old she-wolf.

Okay, maybe not quite normal. Not many of the pack reject their Soulbond after searching for it for most of a year. But, otherwise, totally normal.

Nothing worth such a cover-up. Which was why I was confident my parents had cared.

"Damn," I said, tracing circles on the cover of the journal. "Why is this so hard?"

I swallowed heavily, putting a finger under the cover, ready to flick it open.

"I miss you guys," I whispered to the empty room. "I should have stayed and listened. Should have let you explain."

Blinking back tears, I took another long breath. The night of my Soulshift, the same night I'd found out I was adopted, I had confronted them about it. I'd laughed and asked them if I was their real daughter. It was funny to me at the time. Because why wouldn't I be?

To my horror, they had hesitated. That's when it all came crashing down, and I couldn't handle it. Between my wolf doing her best to drive me insane and the pressure of my Soulshift, finding out my life wasn't what I thought it had been was too much.

So I'd run out of the house.

That was the last time I'd seen my parents. The last time we'd spoken. It gnawed at me that I'd left it like that. Without any closure.

This is how you start, I told myself, focusing on the journal. *Fine.*

My index finger nosed open the cover. The first page was blank, devoid of any writing, but that didn't mean there was nothing there. A single white business card lay pressed firmly against the spine, trapped there until the cover was opened.

Aaron Greiss.

That was all, that and a phone number. I flicked it over, but the back was empty as well.

"Weird," I muttered, setting the card back down.

I'd never heard that name before, but that didn't mean much. My father must have had all sorts of contacts outside of the pack to help him with his journeys. This must be one of them.

Turning the pages, I got to the first entry. It was dated about six months before his disappearance. This was his most recent journal. I thumbed through the entries, not reading any of them yet. I had another thought on my mind.

"Interesting."

The writing stopped a little past the halfway point of the journal. It wasn't finished.

"Now, why on earth would you gift me a journal that you hadn't filled?" I mused, tapping my chin in thought. "What were you trying to tell me?"

The more I considered it, the more I was certain something had happened on his last trip. Something he couldn't tell me about. Or didn't want to. No, that couldn't be it. If he were trying to protect me, he wouldn't have gifted me the journal. After all, he'd never let me read one before. Now he was *giving* me an unfinished one?

That has to mean something, I thought. I just didn't know what.

My eyes lingered on the last page, his final entry.

Today was productive. I'm certain that this valley is where I will find it. At this point, it's only a matter of time before I find Shuldar. I must be thorough, however. The ancients were keen to hide from the outside world, that much I have gleaned from the bits and pieces I have found. Why, I do not know, but they did not seem to want to be found.

Still, I am confident that at some point, I will find it. All the clues point to here. To this valley. Even the most recent artifact we have recovered confirms this. I must take it back to Lars for verification, but I am positive he will agree. I'm so close! This is it. The big discovery.

The journal entry ended. I frowned at the dried ink on the cream-colored page. What artifact had he recovered? I remembered when he came home unexpectedly for my Soulshift. He'd said he had to update our Alpha on what he'd found. What had he told Lars? Why hadn't he put more information in the journal?!

Sighing, I flipped through the pages, back toward the beginning. Eventually, I would go through it, entry by entry, but for now, I was looking for anything that stood out, anything that caught my attention. Anything that—

"What the fuck?" I gasped, sitting upright, staring at the page in shock.

There was no journal entry this time. No words on the page. Instead, there was a sketched image.

It was the being from my dreams. Sure, he had a pair of horns jutting from his head and was holding a long spear of some sort, but there was no mistaking the angular jaw, the long black hair, and the eyes. They were filled with black ink in the journal, but in my mind's eye, I saw the blue fires burning in them.

"That's impossible," I whispered, stunned. "What the hell does this mean? Where did you get this image?"

There was no name attached to it. I flicked back a page, but the only information I could find was that my father had copied the image from a drawing he'd found on a cave wall.

I stared at the image for a long time, willing it to come alive. This was important. It had to be. That man had appeared in my dreams. Except he'd claimed they weren't dreams. Visions, then? Who knows. It proved I wasn't insane, for starters, but also, I knew now I had to find out more about who it was in the picture.

Answers. I needed answers.

Slowly, I thumbed through the rest of the entries, but there was nothing else. No more drawings. The last page flicked free of my thumb and rested flat. The business card slid free, and I pushed it back against the spine with my index finger.

I frowned at the card, deep in thought.

CHAPTER TWENTY-ONE

The business card spun between my fingers, twirling round and round as I stared at it as if eventually something would be revealed about the card's owner.

Of course, it wasn't a magical business card, so it just kept spinning, over and over. I was stalling. Which was ironic, considering I'd slept the night without making any rash decisions, letting myself wait until morning before I took one course of action or the other.

Shocking, I know, but who said an old dog couldn't learn new tricks?

"Either you call it, or you don't," I told myself.

The card spun on.

Light streamed through the single window in my room, a welcome contrast to when I'd come home the night before and sat staring at the journal with nothing but the single overhead light to read by. It was sunny today. Clear skies, and it looked like it was going to be rather nice out.

Finally, I snapped the card down on the table and took out my pay-as-you-go cellphone. It wasn't a smartphone. I didn't spend money on that. It was simply for making or receiving phone calls. Cheap and easy, and if I didn't use it much, hopefully untraceable.

Maybe I'm giving Lars too much credit. He's never been a huge technology buff. Likes to do things the old-fashioned way, or so he says. Besides, he has Johnathan to track me, anytime, anywhere.

I shivered, hating that reminder.

Okay, fine. Time to put up or shut up, Dani. You want to find your parents? Stop being a wimp and dial the damn number.

I flicked open my phone—yes, it's a flip phone, so what?—and punched in the number, stabbing a finger at the send button before I could rethink my decision. It was just a phone number. Nothing bad was going to happen from calling it.

"Hello there," a sultry Australian voice greeted me. *"The customer you have dialed is unavailable. Please leave a voicemail after the tone."*

Whoever it was hadn't programmed their voicemail. That was irritating because it gave me no clue as to who Aaron Greiss might be.

The tone beeped, and my message was live. I momentarily panicked, unable to say anything.

Whoever listened to the message would hear nothing but heavy breathing at first, and boy, wouldn't that be open to misinterpretation.

"I knew Thomas," I said at last, unsure of why I opted to leave out that I was his daughter. "We need to meet. Walkers Bar. Four o'clock. Today. I'll have the red hat on."

Hanging up, I spent several long moments working to collect myself. There. I'd done it. I'd set the meeting with whoever was on the other end. This Aaron Greiss, an unknown contact of my father's. There had to be a reason the business card was there. My father must have intended for me to call him.

Maybe he had information on my dad. I pushed that thought down. Hope wasn't what I needed right now. Practicality, and information, those had to be my pillars.

I snatched up my phone and headed for the door. I had somewhere to be.

The trip across downtown took me about half an hour. It would have gone faster if I'd taken the bus, but I wasn't about to spend money I didn't have just to avoid walking. Not to mention, public transit in Kellar was always crowded, and there was always one person who decided to do something disgusting on the bus that went against all etiquette on how to be a human being.

Last time, it had been a lady shoving her face with sunflower seeds and leaving the drool-covered pile of shells on the seat next to her. Yuck.

As I walked, the buildings got cleaner and taller, and the architecture went from brick and concrete to glass. I was heading from the slums to uptown, where the money lived in the city. I didn't like it. Everything was too modern. Too angular and lacking in character and diversity.

Give me my old farmhouse over a fortieth-floor condo any day. I'd take its creaks and charms and haphazard layout in a heartbeat before living in a place like this. To some people, though, this was their home or office. Or both. And if I wanted to get an update, it was where I had to go.

I paused outside an average tower. Some thirty floors, maybe more. Lots of glass. Gray exterior. No sign out front proclaiming any singular company's dominance. The first time I'd visited, I'd sworn I was in the wrong place. Now I knew better, and I proceeded through the lobby with confidence, no longer shocked by the size of the arched ceilings like I had been seven months ago after being given the name by someone.

The elevators closed around another occupant and me, and I tried not to tap my foot in impatience as we paused at the fourth floor to let her out. It's not like I was in any sort of hurry. I wasn't late. Nor was I early. It's impossible to be either of those when you didn't have an appointment.

The elevator chimed as we hit the sixth floor, and I exited, my shoes echoing on the cold marble tile that had been installed in the exterior corridor. I passed by several office doors, each with a sharp placard labeling the business in gold lettering. Most were lawyers, though one was a publishing house that thought a little too highly of itself, in my opinion.

Then, I reached the one I wanted. The sign simply read, *Finders.* Nothing else. I'd thought it a bit presumptuous, but the more I'd learned about the reputation of the man inside, the more I figured it was an apt description.

I didn't bother knocking, instead letting myself in. As usual, a woman with thick, beautiful curves sat behind the desk, her skin dark enough that it practically blended in with the expensive mahogany of the desk. She looked up, smiling to reveal perfectly white teeth.

"Miss Wetter," she said.

It probably wasn't a good sign that the smile faded as she said my name. Oh, well.

"We weren't expecting you."

"I know, Elaine," I said, feigning a yawn. "That's because if you do, he always makes it a point to be out of the office. Hence, I show up like this, and he has no choice but to meet with me."

Elaine was, as far as I could tell, the only other

employee who worked at the firm. She was there whenever I showed up. I had begun to harbor suspicions that one of the offices had been converted into a bedroom for her so that she was never far from work.

"Well, he's—"

"I know," I said, waving her off as I headed for the door behind her. "He's not taking visitors. The usual. Don't worry. I'll tell him you tried to stop me."

Elaine sighed, and I saw her reach surreptitiously for a buzzer on her desk that would alert him I was coming.

I grinned, tossing Elaine a wink. We played this out on a weekly schedule now, and she no longer bothered to try and stop me.

The door had one of those nearly opaque glass windows set into the upper half, the kind that muddies the view of what's behind it, but if something dark moved against a bright background, you still saw it. As I approached, I saw a generic blob that had to be the man himself get up and rush for the door.

"Hello, Max!" I boomed, strolling into his office, intercepting him just shy of the lock and deadbolt. "So nice of you to come and hold the door for me."

Maxwell Simmons, best private investigator in all Kellar, so it was said, stared back at me with resigned anger in his dark brown gaze.

"Miss Wetter," he said through gritted teeth, going along with my little charade. "So good to see you. Please, come in."

He grabbed the door and held it open for me to walk in, though I knew full well he'd rather slam it shut in my face. *Sometimes you have to play nice when the visitor is paying, Max. That's just how life goes.*

I almost went around the desk and plopped into Max's seat, just to see his reaction, but I stopped short of that. Don't let anyone say I'm not reasonable.

"Why do you always refuse my calls, Max?" I said, speaking before he had a chance to return to his chair. "It's like you don't want to talk to me."

"In my business, Miss Wetter, it's easier for me to call when I have an update or a question," he said with feigned patience. "Otherwise, I'd spend as much time calling clients to tell them I have no updates as I would actually trying to find the people they want me to."

"So, what update do you have for me, Max?" I asked, all but ignoring his spiel. I knew why he did it. I didn't care. My money, I wanted updates.

"Nothing, Miss Wetter," he said with a sigh. "Just like I've had nothing for you all these months. I keep telling you they are gone. There isn't a single shred of anything to indicate that your parents have gone anywhere or done anything. Not one iota, which grates me to say because I pride myself in finding anyone."

"I know, Max. You come highly recommended, don't worry. I'm not going to let this stop me from sending someone who might need help to you."

Max nodded thankfully as he sat back in his chair. He was middle-aged, probably late forties, if I had to make a guess. He shaved his head, though he wasn't quite bald. I think he thought it added to his image when he needed to play tough guy. While he was in the office, he wore a standard black business suit with a white shirt and, oddly enough, a red tie. It was unusual, but Max wore it well.

"Thanks," he grunted. "But that doesn't help me with the fact I haven't found anything on your parents."

"You're still trying, though, right?"

He shrugged. "You keep paying."

That was his way of saying yes. Max was a reputable sort. Mostly.

"Okay," I said, taking out part of my winnings from the night before—for once, I wasn't giving over everything I had. The extra fight with Johnathan had earned me a bit of a respite since Carl had done exactly as I'd asked and bet everything on myself. "Well, here's this week's installment. You're going to keep looking, right?"

"You keep paying," he repeated. "Though, I can't promise anything will change."

So, in other words, he'd keep doing his job, but he didn't think it likely he'd find anything. But if I were desperate enough, he'd take my money. Like I said. Reputable. Mostly.

"Put more resources on it, then," I said, making a snap decision and putting half my remaining money on the desk as well.

Max sighed. For a second, I thought he would refuse it. But in the end, he nodded and scooped up the cash. He tucked it away in a drawer and then looked back at me across the desk, arching his eyebrows ever so slightly.

I got the hint.

"Call me with an update next time, Max," I said as I stood. "I hate coming down to this end of town."

"Will do, Miss Wetter," he said.

We both knew he wouldn't and that I'd be back next week. With more money.

Max was the best in the business. I wasn't sure what else I could do to track down my parents. If he couldn't find them, then how could I? I didn't know the first thing about finding someone who didn't want to be found. No, I had to rely on Max.

Well, him and perhaps the man I was going to meet with later today. Maybe he could give me some clues.

Assuming he showed.

CHAPTER TWENTY-TWO

Walkers Bar wasn't anything special.

That was precisely why I'd chosen it. Set inside an old Victorian-era house in the historic part of downtown Kellar, it occupied both floors. The upper floor was dedicated to tables and a more private, secluded drinking experience. The main floor, meanwhile, had been renovated to be mostly open concept, with a large floor along the right side that could house tables or dancing, depending on the night. I'd been there once or twice over the winter, but I was by no means a regular.

As I walked in, my eyes rapidly adjusted to the dim interior. Although it wasn't an upscale bar, it was far from a dive. Everything was clean and well-kept. It was simply designed to mimic the look of a house that was two centuries old. A few regulars looked up as I entered, but I let my wolf take over my body language as I strode toward the bar, and the looks faded.

No prey here. I was a predator, and I wanted everyone around me to know it. I had no idea who I was meeting, but I wanted no trouble from anyone else until they showed, so I put on my best resting-bitch-face look and slumped back onto a barstool to watch the door.

"Can I get you anything?" a waitress asked as she passed by on her way behind the bar.

"Water for now," I said, shaking off my demeanor just long enough to be polite. "I'm waiting on someone."

"Sure, can do," she said, moving on, barely having slowed to take my order.

I surveilled the place, but none of the people inside looked like the type who would associate with my father.

And how are you supposed to know what that type might be? Have you ever met any of them before? Stop judging books by the cover. Stay aware.

There was always the chance that the person coming tonight *wasn't* a friendly. That they were someone my dad was chasing. He could have left the card as a warning. To stay away from the person. Like the dragons on old maps of the unknown areas. *Here be dragons.*

Not that dragons actually existed, but it was meant to signal danger. I needed to keep my guard up in case my dad had been doing the same. For all I knew, this man could be the one behind my parents' disappearance.

Or he could be my father's mechanic. I just didn't know. This was step one in my search for answers. Follow up any and all clues my dad left behind. I'd avoided reading his journal for long enough, but thanks to Mr. Unknown the night before, I was spurred into action.

I briefly wondered about him. Who was he? Why had he been there in the first place? Again, lots of questions, no answers.

Story of my life.

The door opened. I tried not to stiffen as a man in a yellow and green polo and beige slacks entered, walking his golf-shoed pompous posterior straight to the bar to order some British-sounding drink so fast and with such an accent I quite literally did not know what he said.

The waitress did. I heard her respond with an affirmative. I wondered if Mr. PGA knew how much the waitress disliked him. Probably not at all. His type didn't pay recognition to those they thought beneath them.

He grabbed his drink with what I swear was a snobbish sniff and disappeared upstairs. Not my man, then. He'd have come over to me if he was the one I was waiting for. I blinked, reached into my purse, and pulled out the red baseball hat. I'd said in the message I'd be wearing it, so I had better stick to my word.

As I was fumbling to get my hair properly braided and tied off through the opening in the back of the hat, the door opened. I kept fumbling with my hat as I looked up, desperate not to let a single person enter with scanning them.

I needn't have bothered rushing. The man was walking straight toward me. Not the bar. Me. Which made complete and total sense as I lifted my eyes a bit higher, locking gazes with a pair of crystal blue orbs that burned with a fire that sought a matching flame within me.

And found it.

I sat up straight, hissing as I broke out in goosebumps, hat forgotten.

"You," I said as Mr. Unknown strolled up to my chair. This time, he wore a deep maroon suit that looked like pure chocolate against his vitamin-D deprived skin. It fit him like a glove, and I had to try my hardest not to let my gaze wander south.

"Hello, Danielle," he said, my name rolling off his lips like an orgasm for my ears. I shivered, glad I was wearing a shirt thick enough that my now rock-hard nips wouldn't poke through. Not that he needed any help knowing I was instantly aroused by his sheer presence. This man was a hunter, and he knew prey when he found it.

"How do you know my name?" I asked, speaking the first question that came to my mind that wasn't "my place or yours?"

"The announcer last night might have said it a time or ten," he replied smoothly, his velvety tenor going straight between my thighs.

Okay. Enough. You're here for a reason, Dani. Keep your head in the game and not in La La Land. Time to be mature.

"I see," I said. Great response. Real smooth.

"Yes." He adjusted the collar of his suit, undoing the top button of his black dress shirt.

It revealed the tiniest bit of skin. I licked my lips as if I was about to lick that newly exposed skin, tasting his skin, the slight hint of sweat that I was sure was present.

God, what was wrong with me?

Frustrated at my inability to focus, I sought out my Soulbond.

Golden energy washed over me like a cold shower, dampening my enthusiasm for the walking sex mannequin. I wanted *Johnathan.* Not this wannabe. I needed a real Alpha.

Annddd, that's enough of that, I thought, wrenching control away from the Soulbond before it got too strong. My wolf whimpered her dislike of my actions, but I swatted the beast aside. I had a mission here. It was time to focus.

"May I sit?" Mr. Unknown asked, gesturing at the chair next to me.

"Actually, I'm waiting for someone," I said.

He smiled at me.

"But if you give me your number, I can call you back. Maybe we could get together for a stronger drink," I suggested, pointing out the water I had yet to sip.

What are you doing?

The instant I suppressed my Soulbond, Mr. Sexbot was working his mumbo jumbo on me again.

"That would be nice," he said, flashing two rows of perfectly white teeth at me. "I think I might take you up on that." He reached into his suit pocket and handed me something.

After a moment, I reached up to take it. Several moments later, I registered it in my hand and looked down. It was a white business card with gold lettering embossed on it.

Aaron Greiss.

CHAPTER TWENTY-THREE

"You," I said, shocked back into my chair.

"Me," he agreed.

To stall for time, I turned and picked up the water that had been sitting patiently on the counter, waiting to be drained. I made up for lost time by putting half of it back in one go. I then promptly coughed as some of it made it into my lungs.

Off to a really good start. Really badass of you. Coughing on water. Some tough shifter chick you are.

"Who the hell are you?" I asked as he sat down anyway, correctly deciding I wasn't going to invite him. Not anytime soon, at least.

"Aaron Greiss," he said as if that answered everything, instead of leaving me with more questions.

"How did you know Thomas?" I asked, switching gears.

Aaron smiled, giving me another full glimpse of those teeth that I'd swear were implants if everything else about him wasn't also stupidly perfect. He was just a genetically gifted individual.

"You mean your father?" he said.

I stared, too astonished to realize I might be in a world of danger in addition to being hopelessly outclassed in the knowledge department. Not that it made Greiss a supergenius or anything. I was just that bad at the moment.

"How did you know that?" I asked, then clamped my mouth shut. "It's probably too late to deny that we're related, isn't it?"

Aaron nodded. "A little. But it wouldn't have done you any good anyway."

"Why?" I was getting tired of asking all the questions, but I was so hilariously unprepared right now it didn't matter. I was still getting answers. Maybe some of them would actually be helpful.

"Your father talked about you all the time," Aaron said. "I think he liked to brag."

"Oh," I said, stomach twisting itself into uncomfortable knots.

This was the same Dad who I'd run away from

without giving him the chance to explain the truth after twenty-one years of raising me and doing things like this.

"You knew him well, then?" I asked, struggling to compose myself.

"He was an explorer," Aaron said. "Like myself. We have worked together in the past on different projects. Most recently, we were looking for something together."

I nodded. This much I knew. My father hadn't been shy about telling me what he was after.

"Shuldar," I said quietly. The ancient, lost shifter city. From a time when we had been a species united in one pack. Ruling the PNW from our homeland. A time of godly worship and obedience.

Supposedly.

"Yes, Shuldar," Aaron said. "Your father was insistent that an ancient civilization had formed a true city out here."

I bit my lip, trying to keep my face neutral. That effectively confirmed my father hadn't told Aaron about shifters. Not that I'd expected him to, but there were humans who were invited into our world every so often. It was rare but not unheard of.

What would you have told him if you found the city, I wonder?

"It's nonsense, of course," Aaron continued.

"No evidence of any city out there has ever been found. The Mayans, Incas, and Aztec are all south, very south, or *extremely* south of here. No Indigenous tribes ever formed actual cities, as we would think of them."

"Yeah," I said quietly, my mind elsewhere. "Tell me, Aaron. Why were you at the fights last night?"

He shrugged. "Heard you were in town. Wanted to see why."

I considered my response. Aaron *seemed* genuine. I was having a hard time finding any sort of lie or maliciousness to his responses. It felt like he meant everything he said. Of course, he could just be an excellent liar. It's not like I had an excessive amount of experience at successfully figuring out when I was being lied to.

So, I would have to go out on a limb and either trust him or thank him for coming and move on. Which would provide me with precisely zero answers. Beyond that, he and my dad had apparently worked together.

Not enough.

"My father is missing," I said, deciding to lay my cards on the table.

"I'm sorry," Aaron said tightly, a troubled look creasing his beautiful face.

I decided I didn't like it when he wasn't happy. A face that beautiful deserved to smile. My brain started to wander, thinking up different ways I could make him grin. Fun ways. Intimate ways.

I chugged more water, surprised to see that it had been refilled. This waitress was a star.

My mind momentarily distracted from creating a porno with Aaron, I focused back on the *real* issue at hand. Which most definitely was not my lack of a sex life. Though that seemed like it *was* becoming more of an issue the closer we got to the next Wild Moon. I couldn't recall having ever been this perma-horny before.

It would get me in trouble if I didn't do something about it, but I simply didn't have the time to care. I had to worry about Johnathan and his psycho father tracking me down, not to mention find my father. Oh, and I needed to keep paying the bills while I was at it. Sex just wasn't on the priority list.

"What do you want from me?" Aaron asked.

"I want you to help me find Shuldar," I said without a clue in the world as to *why*. But as I said it, it felt right. I needed to go there. Don't ask me why. I hadn't gotten that far, but as soon as Aaron had brought it up, I'd felt a pull to the northeast. To the mountains where Shuldar was supposedly hidden, lost to the centuries.

"It's pointless," Aaron said, rolling his shoulders to settle the shirt back into place. "We've searched for it for years and came up with nothing. That's not likely to change now. It's a wild goose chase, Dani."

My name sounded like chocolate on a rainy day coming from his mouth, but I couldn't let my body get distracted by his sinfully delicious everything. Not right now, at least.

"I need to find it," I said, leveling my gaze at him.

"I don't work for free," Aaron said. "Your father had a benefactor that paid me."

"Shit," I muttered. Lars must have been the one putting up the funds. There was no one else. Unless my father had more shady connections that I didn't know about, which seemed a lot more feasible now than it had twenty-four hours ago.

"Money upfront," Aaron added quietly. "I've been stiffed too many times."

"How much?" I heard myself ask.

He named a figure.

I choked again, this time on air. "You're nuts! That would take me weeks to amass. At least!"

Aaron shrugged, tugging the suit tight against his shoulders as he did. I tried not to stare.

"Will the same benefactor–he never would mention who it was–bankroll you?" Aaron suggested. "Or maybe your father or mother left you some money?"

I shook my head. "They disappeared without a trace. Both of them, and I've been throwing my money at trying to find them."

Aaron was silent for a moment. "Don't beat yourself up over that," he said quietly, reaching sideways to rest a hand on my forearm.

I nearly threw myself at him. His touch was cold but enticing at the same time. I wanted more, but something told me I shouldn't. He was dangerous. Tempting, but a man to be wary around.

"There's nothing wrong with what you've been doing," Aaron told me, slowly withdrawing his arm, not without a bit of sadness on my part. "From what I know of your father, it's not like him to up and disappear."

"It's not like either of them," I said. "Something happened, and I don't know what."

So, why did I feel pulled to find Shuldar? Why was that suddenly so important to me? Did I think my parents would be found there? Had my parents decided to run away to the lost city? Without telling anyone?

Each question I posed to myself felt wrong. What was at Shuldar was for *me*? I felt it, not in my mind where my wolf lay or my Soulbond, but somewhere else. Somewhere…deeper.

I had to get there. No matter what.

"I need to find Shuldar," I repeated.

Aaron nodded. "You have my price. I prefer precious metals, gold, or gemstones."

"That doesn't sound shady at all." I gave him a

flat look.

"Coming from the woman rigging an underground fight club," Aaron said calmly.

I frowned. He had a point. I wasn't precisely on the up and up either, so it would be a bit hypocritical of me to judge his method of payment now, wouldn't it? Fine.

"What guarantee do I have that you can lead me there?" I asked.

"You don't," Aaron replied, downing a drink I hadn't even noticed him order. "Just like your father didn't."

"Perfect," I muttered.

"You have my number," Aaron said, rising from his chair and heading for the door. "Call me when you have the money."

"Yeah," I said, watching as he left.

Once he was gone, I sighed. "Now, where the hell am I going to get that kind of money?"

CHAPTER TWENTY-FOUR

Danielle Aria Wetter. You have the absolute worst ideas sometimes.

"And this one takes the cake," I said, staring up at my objective. The place where I could get the money to pay Aaron to help me find Shuldar. It was the only place I knew housed such a sum of money that I could get my hands on. Unfortunately, it also happened to be the *last* place on earth I ever wanted to visit.

Time to get at it. Clock is ticking, and the Wild Moon is nearing.

I didn't have to remind myself of that. I could feel it inside me. Both my wolf and my Soulbond were growing more active. Stronger. Trying to take control of me. The longer I denied the Soulbond, the more it pulsed within my mind, whispering good things about Johnathan, urging me to take him as my mate. To accept the truth, that he was good for me. That's why I was here–

Enough, I snarled mentally, silencing everything. *I did not come back for him. I came back for money.*

I shivered as my brain went silent and stared up at the line of trees running parallel to the road, blocking the view of what lay beyond. A double row of lamp posts ran up the gravel driveway, flanking the single-lane vehicle entrance. I couldn't see beyond the trees, but I knew what lay on the other side.

Aldridge Manor.

The sprawling, three-story mansion belonging to Lars Aldridge, Alpha of the Seguin pack, and quite possibly the person I hated most on the planet. Followed closely by his son, who also happened to reside there. And here I was, contemplating not only going up there and revealing that I was back but going *inside.*

Shuddering at the idea, I forced myself to look past it. I was doing this for the greater good.

I laughed to myself. Not that it mattered, it was highly unlikely that they would buy my lies anyway. There was just as great a chance that they would believe me as they would toss me back into that windowless cell in the basement.

There's nowhere else to go, though. Nowhere else I could get that much cash or gold in such a short period. This is my only option.

I wasn't happy about it, but the Wild Moon was mere days away. The sense of urgency inside me grew by the day. I *had* to find Shuldar. It was imperative.

I just didn't know why yet.

You're stalling, I told myself, knowing full well that's precisely what I was doing. Can you blame me? If I went up the driveway, I was going to have to pretend like I'd come around. That I was considering accepting Johnathan as my mate. I might have to *kiss* him.

In my mind, I retched at the idea. Gross. I'd hoped I was done kissing guys who used far too much tongue. Ugh. Unfortunately, time was running out, and I had no other options for money. Which meant it was time to get on with it.

My long legs easily carried me up the driveway. I was past the trees and had entered the house's shadow when a giant, black object shot out from the side of the house. It snarled in fury, the Alpha command washing over me.

On instinct, I started to fight it. Sheer principle said I had to shrug it off and resist because submitting to Lars was just about the most unappetizing thing I could think of.

Fake it! You have to fake it!

Lars was almost on me, his wolf covering ground at terrifying speed, and I forced myself down to the ground. I showed my neck, hoping he wouldn't tear my throat out anyway, just to spite me. I wouldn't put it past him.

"You," a human voice came as Lars shifted back. It was full of derision and hatred.

Which I guess made sense. He didn't have any reason to like me.

He shuffled closer. "Look at me."

I grimaced. He was doing his macho masculine dominance shit again. Bracing myself for what I knew I was going to see, I turned my head, trying to open my eyes after they were past his groin.

I failed.

What the fuck, dude? Why you gotta shove your junk in everyone's faces? Hasn't a girl ever told you that a penis is really not attractive or impressive when it's just limp and flopping around like a deflated string balloon?

"Why are you back?" Lars growled down at me.

I focused on his face, ignoring the pint-sized anteater inches from my face. *Apparently, some things run in the family.*

"The Wild Moon is almost here," I said quietly, trying to play the part of the meek and subservient woman. Anyone with a shred of intelligence would know I was faking it, but Lars was so caught up in himself that I'm sure he *expected* this out of me to the point that he would never consider I could be faking it. He didn't believe anyone could be strong enough to defy him.

Or stupid. Most definitely stupid. Don't go inflating your own ego here, either. This is a plan born of sheer stubbornness and idiocy. Nothing more.

"So it is," Lars smirked as he looked down at me. "And?"

He wanted more. He wanted me to say it.

Fine. Whatever it'll take to convince you.

"And," I said, trying to make myself whimper as I spoke, "I can't run forever."

Lars nodded.

Holy shit, is he buying this?

I cast my eyes down, not wanting him to read the hope I could feel blossoming inside me. This might work, after all. Maybe I'm not a terrible actress!

"Good," Lars said, nodding once sharply as if making up his mind. "I'm glad you came to your senses."

"I did," I told him, steeling myself. This next part was the trickiest of all. "But I'm not here willingly. I still don't want this, so if you expect it to work, I have some terms."

His teeth clamped down on my neck. I whimpered and yelped for real, caught off-guard by the sudden attack as I was pinned to the gravel driveway, the sharp stones scraping roughly against my face.

Even when he released me, I stayed like that. There was no point antagonizing him further.

"You *dare* to dictate to me? The Alpha of your pack?"

I took a deep breath and nodded. "If you want this to work out, then yes, I do dare."

Bracing myself as I finished speaking, I prepared for his next attack. I doubted he was going to just kill me at this point. I knew at a minimum a part of him would be interested to hear what I was going to propose.

"Interesting," Lars growled, standing up and taking a half step away from my curled-up form. "Good. I like it. An alpha's mate should be strong. Unyielding. What do you propose?"

I got to my feet, proving not just to Lars, but also to myself, that I was as strong as I was pretending to be. Hopefully.

"I'll give you what you want," I said quietly, staring into his amber eyes. "I'll stand by your son's side. I'll bear his children."

"And?" Lars barked. "That's what's expected of you, woman."

"And in return," I growled, showing a bit of the defiance I was feeling on the inside. "Your son doesn't touch me unless I say so. In public, I will play the good mate. In private, he leaves me the fuck alone. We live separately. I don't have anything to do with him or you."

Lars gave me a long stare as he considered my terms.

"Deal."

He didn't stick out a hand to shake on it. I was beneath him for that. We had gone from me bargaining to Lars agreeing to the terms as if they were *his* orders. It was almost impressive how easily he took command of the conversation like that.

"Okay," I said as we stared at one another, him naked, me dressed in jeans and a sky-blue, loose-fitting long sleeve.

It was weird. Really weird.

"Follow me," Lars growled, heading to the front door.

Now, I know as a wolf shifter I should be uncaring about nudity. And I am, really I am. Mostly. But walking behind Lars, while his ass cheeks clapped in the sunlight as he strode toward the front door, was just too much. He looked *ridiculous*. I'm not sure if this was supposed to be some sort of power move on his part, but damn if it didn't ruin the scary aura that he usually had around him.

Lars reached the door and pushed it open, heading inside without checking to see if I was there. I had to jog forward to grab the eight-foot-high door and haul it open again. Otherwise, it would have closed in my face.

Ass, I thought, but my glare faltered as I saw a figure move at the top of the curved stairs ahead of us.

"What is she doing here?" Johnathan asked, staring down at his father and me, his back to the hallway where I'd attacked his mother during my last escape. The same hallway that housed the relics my father had retrieved on his missions. I tried not to smile as my plan came one step closer to fruition. Now all I had to do was survive long enough to escape with Aaron's payment.

No big deal. Right?

CHAPTER TWENTY-FIVE

"Your soulmate is here," Lars said, gesturing behind him. "She has come to her senses."

"Has she now?" Johnathan said archly, crossing his arms. He still didn't descend the stairs.

"I have," I spoke up before Lars could say anything more. I didn't want Johnathan getting any false impressions. I had to make it *very* clear to both Alpha assholes what the rules were while I was here.

"Of her own free will at that," Lars said. "She's a strong one, Johnathan. A good Alpha's mate."

"Seriously?" Johnathan said, gaping at his father. "After what happened the last time she was here? After how she treated Mother?"

Lars chuckled. "Mary should have been more aware of where she was going. She'll get over it."

And that sealed it. If I'd had any remaining thoughts of actually somehow making things work with Johnathan and his family, they died there with the dismissal of his mate. Women weren't valued in the Aldridge household, and I don't know why I ever thought differently.

My Soulbond pulsed in my head, and I lifted my eyes to meet Johnathan's. *Damn. This isn't going to be easy.* The closer I was to him, the more my body and soul ached to go to him. Even now, I was filled with the desire to go to bed with him. It was foreign, at odds with the disgust my mind and brain felt, but I couldn't deny it didn't exist.

No wonder Lars had been confident and agreeable. He knew the Soulbond would turn me. No matter what my terms were now, it would eventually push it all aside, turning me into the perfect mate for Johnathan if I gave it the time to do so.

Which I wasn't going to. I had mere days before the Wild Moon, and I knew if another one came over me while Johnathan was around that I wouldn't be able to fight it. I had to get what I'd come for and get as far away from him as possible before it happened. Or live in servitude like Lars' mate for the rest of my life.

That's a hell no from me. I will not *end up like that!*

"I don't like it either," I said to Johnathan, glaring up at him. "But when you showed up in Kellar, it showed me the truth. I can't run from this. I don't like you, and I don't like admitting that. But I'm not going to run forever. So we're going to compromise, and that's that."

I strolled past Lars and up the stairs, aiming to bypass Johnathan and head down the hallway to the guest quarters. Courtesy of my time dating Johnathan, I knew the layout of the house rather well.

"A compromise," he rumbled as I approached. "How is that?"

"Ask your father," I said. "I'll be in my guest quarters."

"Guest quarters?" Johnathan asked, looking past me at his father, then back at me.

I smiled broadly at him, teeth and all. "All good things take time. Surely you have the patience to wait for your mate, don't you?"

Johnathan's jaw clenched, the veins in his temples standing out. He didn't like this one bit and was quite obviously having a hard time with his temper.

Oh, well. Maybe you shouldn't have been such an asshole, and we could be mated happily ever after. Sorry, not sorry. Dick.

I let my eyes convey my thoughts as I walked past, fighting hard on the inside not to sashay my hips a little as my Soulbond pulsed stronger than ever. That was expected, however, and I'd braced for it, preparing my mind not to be distracted as I walked down the hallway.

I very carefully did *not* look at the relic room as I passed. No sense in giving anyone the slightest clue what I was planning. Better to catch them unawares if that was possible.

Not long after I'd shut the door to my chosen guest quarters–I'd chosen the farthest one possible from Johnathan's room–he entered. No knock. He just waltzed in as if he owned the place.

His dull blue eyes locked on me. I forced myself to look at the bridge of his nose instead. This close, the pull toward him was strong. I had to resist in any way I could.

"Well?" I said as airily as I could. "Did you chat with dear old dad?"

"Yes." The single-word reply came out clipped and short.

"So, do we have a deal?" I crossed my arms and tried to stare him down.

Johnathan sighed. "You really do hate me, don't you?"

I gaped at him, stunned by the confusion in his voice. "Of *course* I hate you. I fucking loathe you. You ruined my damned life, all because you couldn't handle being dumped. So, yeah, I hate you. Just a little bit. I wouldn't expect any loving or tenderness for the first, oh, ten or twenty years."

Hopefully, comments like that, pretending that I was thinking about the long-term, would help keep at bay any doubts Johnathan or Lars had. Maybe.

Johnathan bit his lip. He wasn't happy about the arrangement, but I didn't give a shit. He'd made his own bed. Now it was time he slept in it. Alone.

"How long are you going to be staying in the guest quarters?" he asked gruffly.

"Until I've got carpal tunnel in my wrists and nothing but dead batteries," I said, scoffing at the idea that we'd share a bed anytime soon.

"What about children?" he asked, lifting a hand, palm up, in question.

"I just got here," I said. "We'll discuss conjugal visits later."

He eyed me, and I saw suspicion creeping into his gaze.

"Of course I'm not happy," I snarled before he could say anything. "I hate this. We're Soulbound. But I can recognize reality just as well as you can. So, just leave me alone, and I'll see you at dinner, okay?"

Johnathan shook his head. "I'm not buying any of this. Three days ago, you fought me in the ring."

"Three nights ago, I kicked your ass in the

ring," I corrected.

He bared his teeth at me. I gave him the finger. It was the truth, whether he liked it or not.

"There's no way you're submitting to me now, not so soon after that."

I sighed. Time for a bit of honesty. "It's not about that," I said, voicing my actual feelings about what that night had taught me. "It's about what your presence did."

His forehead wrinkled between his eyebrows, but he stayed quiet, letting me continue.

"You showing up there reminded me that I'll never live a life without you. Or your father. You would always both be after me. Always showing up to ruin whatever life I tried to make for myself."

Johnathan nodded. "I'm drawn to you like you're drawn to me."

That wasn't at all how I'd meant it, but whatever, if it got him to agree with me, I'd go with it.

"So, I thought about it. At least if I come here, I can live *my* life in a place I'm familiar with and at least be happy to the extent I'm not looking over my shoulder all the time. If I need to pretend that I like you when we're in public, then so be it."

He opened his mouth to speak, but I slashed a hand between us.

"But that is in *public*. Not private. Are you understanding that yet? Is it getting through your brain?"

I swore I could hear his teeth grinding from across the room.

"Yes," he said tightly. "But I'll find a way to make things up between us."

"Bring my parents back," I said, naming the only thing that might make me hate him less.

He stared at me. "How the hell am I supposed to do that?"

"Exactly," I said. "But you may as well get started now. So get out, and I'll see you for dinner."

I pointed at the door, and he took it.

CHAPTER TWENTY-SIX

An hour passed before I was interrupted again, a gentle knocking at the door interrupting my solitary brooding.

I glanced at the clock on the intricate carved wooden nightstand and shrugged. I honestly hadn't expected the Aldridges to go that long without bothering me. Rolling off the bed, I strode toward the door, wondering if it was Johnathan this time or his father.

Yanking on the door, I paused, caught completely off guard. It was neither.

"Lady Aldridge," I stammered, mentally preparing myself for a fight. But she stayed at the door.

"Miss Wetter," she said primly.

"Please, let me apologize for what happened the last time I was here," I said, feeling myself start to sweat profusely. Why was she at my door? Why didn't she seem angry? "I didn't know it was you, and–"

"It's fine, child," Marianna said, though her face didn't match her words.

"Right. Okay. Well, I'm still sorry. Um. What can I do for you?"

She lifted her hands. That was when I noticed the blue box in her hand. It wasn't very thick, but it was as long as my forearm.

"This should fit you," she said, looking me up and down. "It's a bit big on me, but those gazelle legs of yours will make up for that, I think."

I stared. "What will fit me?" I asked a bit more suspiciously, eyeing the box. What was going on here?

"Take it." This was a command, and I found myself reaching for the box before I'd even thought it over.

"Um. Okay?" I took the box, holding it in my arms. "Now what?"

"Perhaps, darling, you should *open it*," Lady Aldridge said, speaking to me as she would to a dim-witted child. The "darling" was very much not a term of endearment. In fact, it was quite the opposite. This woman hated me like I hated the rest of her family, except she was doing a much better job of expressing it while managing to hide it at the same time.

I could learn some lessons, I'm sure.

"Right," I said, feeling silly. I held the box balanced on my left arm and pulled off the top.

As I'd begun to suspect, there was clothing inside.

"It's a dress."

I looked up as Lars sauntered down the hallway, looking entirely too proud of himself. Immediately, my stomach lurched, winding itself into a ball of stress. Something was going on. Something not good.

"I'm not wearing this," I said, glancing down at the burgundy outfit lying amid the white tissue.

"Actually, you are," Lars growled, coming over. "For tonight."

"Tonight?" I could feel the jaws of his trap closing around me. "What's tonight?"

"Oh, hadn't you heard?" Lars chuckled, coming up to stand next to his mate.

I noticed Lady Aldridge tense as he wrapped a hand around her shoulder, but Lars didn't seem to notice. I briefly wondered about the dynamic there, but the Alpha's next words left me too stunned to do much more than gape at him.

"Why, the party we're having," he said. "Here, of course. With many guests."

I snarled angrily. "We had an agreement–"

"And that agreement," Lars rumbled, standing tall, looking all Alpha and imposing as he cowed me. "Was that in public, you would be the loving mate. We must introduce you to the pack. I don't care if you like it or not. They must know that my son's mate has returned. Do we understand one another?"

I sensed he was ready to blast me with his Alpha power if I tried to resist. This was a battle he wasn't willing to back down on. One way or another, I knew I'd be at that ball.

"Fine," I said through gritted teeth. I hadn't planned on staying that late, but it was looking like I wasn't going to have any choice in the matter.

Of course, if everyone is going to be downstairs in the ballroom ...

"Fine," I repeated. "I'll do it. But don't make a habit of it."

Lars smiled. "I'll see you tonight, then."

I closed the door in their faces. Lars' angry growl was easily audible, and I smiled, taking solace in my small act of rebellion.

Taking the box with the dress in it to the bed, I pulled it out, the burgundy, spandexy material soft to the touch. I laid it down over the comforter and looked at the midi-length bandage dress. The bust plunged deep between the breasts. I was going to have a *lot* of skin on display tonight, it seemed.

The pencil-cut skirt might have stopped just above the knees on Lady Aldridge, but on me, it was going to be more of a mid-thigh hem. Just what an egotistical, horny male would want a woman to show up dressed in. It was pathetic.

There was another knock at the door. I went and got it. George, one of the Alpha's enforcers, was standing at the door with two bags and another box.

"Can I help you?" I asked. I'd never really interacted with George before, but in a town as small as Seguin, everyone knew everyone.

"For you," he said, dropping the items into my arms and then marching off without waiting.

"Right," I said, juggling the bags and box so I could shut the door before bringing them back to the bed.

Shoes, makeup bag. Sticky bra–three sizes worth, thankfully, so hopefully one would fit–and last but not least, a pair of black undies.

"I really hope these are new," I muttered to myself. They looked new. So did the shoes. Peeking at the strappy black three-inch heels, I noted a tag on them. They were also the right size.

Had Johnathan remembered my shoe size? That's kind of cute. I didn't realize he'd paid so much attention to me. I–

"Stop it," I snarled, catching myself. The Soulbond was devious like that. It permeated every thought, twisting it into something positive. It was trying to make me fall for him.

I surveyed the haul of goods in front of me. The Aldridges were expecting me to go the whole nine yards for their party, it seemed.

Well, fine. If I'm going to do this, I may as well do it right. Give them what they want. If I went along begrudgingly but still giving them what they expected, perhaps none of them would make a scene when I retired early from the party.

"Okay, time to whore it up, I suppose," I grumbled, only half upset about it.

The dress *was* really cute. But I would much rather be wearing it while at the side of someone who deserved it.

Like, say, Aaron…

CHAPTER TWENTY-SEVEN

A stranger looked back at me from the mirror.

The days of a stable life and having fancy clothes and makeup seemed so long ago now, even if it had been less than a year. It was amazing how quickly people could adapt to changes when they had no other choice.

All in all, though, I was forced to admire myself in the mirror. I actually thought I looked pretty darn good. I'd put on minimal makeup, just a hint of highlighter, some eyeliner, and mascara. My hair was straight and pulled to one side, falling in front of my right shoulder. The length helped conceal *some* of the open plunging bust, but after tonight, everyone was going to know I didn't have a whole lot going on up top.

I tugged on the hem of the dress, pulling it lower, trying to stretch it to keep it closer to my knees than my crotch. I'm not sure I was successful. Sitting would be a tedious activity tonight. Probably best if I didn't do much of it, lest someone get a full viewing of my underwear.

Staring at the person in the mirror as they looked back, I wondered what my parents would think of me, of my decisions. Here I was, dressed up like a good little slut, trying to rob the Alpha of our clan, all to go on a wild hunt for a city nobody had been able to find for centuries for a reason I couldn't explain even to myself.

I should be looking for them instead, trying to figure out where they had gone, and most importantly, *why* they were gone. It was all so vague and mysterious. Would they forgive me? Or would they hold it against me that I hadn't done everything in my power to find them?

I hoped it was the former.

My Soulbond pulsed with golden joy, and a moment later, someone was knocking on my door. I cringed, knowing perfectly well who was at the door. It had only been a few hours, and I was already starting to lose the fight with my Soulbond. Every thought of him had me smiling at the corners of my mouth, and now, knowing he was here, I was filled with a warm glow.

"We hate him," I said out loud, reminding all the various parts of me that Johnathan was persona non grata.

"Dani, it's me," came the call through the door.

"No shit," I muttered crudely, not caring who heard me.

I left the mirror behind, going to the door and pulling it open.

"Wow," Johnathan said in hushed tones as he took me in. "You look…incredible."

So did he. I'd forgotten how well he cleaned up. He stood outside my door, one hand in the pocket of his tux's pants, wearing the shit out of it. It didn't fit him like a wet blanket the way Aaron's had, but that didn't matter. It hung off him differently, emphasizing his strengths, and in that sense, it was the same as the way Aaron wore his suits.

Black with silver pinstripes, he had a crisp white shirt underneath, and it was paired with matching pants and pointed black shoes shiny enough to see yourself in. All in all, he looked *good*. My Soulbond drummed away in the back of my mind, amplifying my reaction, but a part of me knew it wasn't all because of the damn connection.

He looked good.

He was also an asshole, and I used that thought to ground myself. Even now, his eyes were fixed on my extremely modest bit of cleavage, and I wondered if I should grab a tissue to mop up the drool.

"Put your eyes back in your head, buster," I

said. "None of this is for you. You've had your look, now behave. We're in public tonight, and I won't have you staring down my dress looking for a hint of nipple like some high schooler, okay? You're going to treat me like a damn lady in front of everyone. Am I clear?"

My words lost some of their bite as the gentle pulsing of the Soulbond stripped some of the ice from my tone against my will, but I saw enough to know he'd gotten the point.

"Clear," he said, clearing his throat. "Shall we?"

I nodded and stepped out of the room. He tried to take my arm, but I snatched it back. "Not until necessary," I told him in no uncertain terms.

I had to. If I let myself slip, it would be nothing at all to give in to the increasing drum in the back of my mind that wanted us to be together.

Even before we reached the stairs, I heard the low buzz of dozens of conversations ongoing at once. I must have smiled because Johnathan looked over at me and paused.

"What's so funny?" he asked.

"Just trying not to cry," I fired back, steeling myself as we approached the top of the stairs. It was that time. Time for me to fulfill my end of the bargain.

Stay strong, I told myself, slipping my arm through his.

Immediately, the Soulbond burned stronger.

We started down the stairs. “Don’t even think of kissing me just because we’re in public,” I said under my breath as we descended, several sets of eyes turning to watch us. “You will be a proper gentleman and only kiss me on the cheek. But softly. Don’t you dare mess up my makeup. Got it?”

“Um, yeah, got it,” Johnathan said.

I turned to look up at him as we reached the ground floor. He looked a bit flustered.

“Are you *nervous*?” I whispered under my breath.

He shrugged. “Have you met my father? He’s somewhat demanding. I want to make him proud.”

I blinked. That was almost adorable. It would have been extremely so if his father wasn’t a ginormous douchebag.

“How did you know I was adopted?” I asked, deciding to try and take advantage of this momentary bit of weakness. I pushed with my Soulbond, with everything, trying to make myself as appealing to him as possible, leaning on our connection, clearing my mind of all the hate I could.

I was desperate.

“Not now,” he said, escorting me through the doors and into the ballroom.

For once, I agreed with him. As we entered,

easily fifty pairs of eyes turned to look at us. Smiles broke out on dozens of faces as we passed. I was among the pack upper crust. The enforcers, the powerful families, the wealthy. Even in a dusty farming town of only four hundred, there was going to be those with and without.

I was now surrounded by those who had it, or who brown-nosed Lars enough to be granted audience into his social circles.

They all started coming forward, congratulating us, telling us how happy they were and that we would make good pack rulers once Lars moved on. I didn't think Lars had any intention of giving up his power any time soon. Based on the language he used every time I'd heard him, he was planning to stay Alpha until he died.

I wondered briefly if I could use the Soulbond to pressure Johnathan into *removing* his father.

He cast a look at me, a tiny frown creasing the skin between his eyes for just a moment. Had he been able to tell what I was thinking there? Or had he just interpreted the general mood coming from me?

"Come on," he said. "Time to do the rounds. This is part of it."

"As long as we get food after," I said, my stomach growling.

Johnathan nodded, and I let myself be dragged into the middle of the fawning crowd. We chatted and moved about, me hanging onto his arm while Johnathan showed me off like I was a prized show horse. Or heifer. I didn't really know which description was more apt, but I did know that I hated it. I was an object to these people, nothing more.

Good for babies and bread, or some shit, I'm sure.

The thought of bread set my stomach to growling so loud that it interrupted our current conversation with Lester Pirron, a farmer whose only claim to power was that he had more land than anyone else.

"If you'll excuse us," Johnathan said graciously, "I think we should find one of the food tables."

"About time," I muttered as he guided me away. "I'm fucking starving. Where's the buffet?"

Freed of my responsibility to stand still and keep my mouth shut, I started looking around, taking stock of the gathering. I wasn't looking at the guests, but rather the servants, who were really mostly lower-level enforcers enlisted into the role for the evening.

They would be the ones I'd have to avoid when I made my escape. I needed to know what I was up against.

CHAPTER TWENTY-EIGHT

"Is it just me, or is the music getting louder?" I asked, my stomach now pleasantly full of some sort of cheese-covered bread, bits of steak seared to perfection, and a glass of sparkling water.

I longed for the wine, but given what I was about to embark upon, keeping my wits about me was the larger priority. Any misstep later would likely lead to me having an appointment with a metal chair in a windowless room.

"It's time for dancing," Johnathan replied.

I looked at him aghast. That wasn't at all the answer I'd expected. "What?"

"It's a ball," he said with a shrug. "There's dinner, dancing, political discourse."

"Don't talk to me like I should know these things," I snapped. "Not everyone lives in your little snobbish society, *John*. Most of us live in the real world, where this stuff doesn't happen."

Johnathan's face tightened, but he nodded. "Fair point. To answer your question, however, dancing comes after the food."

"Right," I said, considering my options. What did I have to say that could get me out of this? There had to be some combination of words that would work.

"If you don't dance with me at least once, people are going to ask questions that will make my father mad," Johnathan said, reading my panicked look with ease.

I cursed silently. I had to do this, didn't I? Suspicion was the last thing I needed right now. Which meant...

"Fine," I said, reluctantly concluding I had no choice. I was going to have to dance with him. "One dance."

Johnathan smiled and reached for my hand. I threw up a brief prayer to any of the shifter gods who might be listening to help me out. Perhaps Mino, the shifter god of luck, would be with me. I certainly felt like I could use it. Even as we walked toward the open space at the front of the room, I could feel eyes turning, watching me.

Just stare at the dress. At the silly amounts of leg I'm showing. Please don't watch my clumsy ass try to dance like a real lady. 'Cause it ain't gonna happen, folks.

With a flick of his hand, Johnathan spun me through a slow circle. I didn't know the first thing about formal dancing, but I could follow clear movements like that. I twirled, part of me wishing I had more of a ballgown on so that it could swoosh out to the sides as I stepped around.

"Oh," I said, suddenly short of breath as Johnathan stepped in close and pulled me tight to his chest after I finished my circle.

"Hi," he rumbled, and I struggled to maintain my composure as he brought me forward and then to the side and around and back. All of it within his personal space.

This was what I'd been afraid of. The proximity. My body was practically on fire. My wolf was rising to the surface, powered by the strength of our Soulbond to Johnathan. It was an immovable force, and it had caught me unprepared.

Damn, he even smells good. How is that possible? Why am I infatuated with his scent? And his hands on my back. So big and strong. I wonder what they would feel like if I just stopped resisting? Would it be even better?

I could do that. I could let my barrier down and accept him in. The scary part wasn't that I knew I could, it was just how *easy* I knew it would be. As if my willpower were but a speck compared to the blazing golden bliss of the Soulbond as it drummed away inside me.

"Is everything okay?" Johnathan asked as the music died down, the segue to another song evident even to my addled brain.

Had I just lost myself to the entire song? Had we danced through the entire thing without me realizing it? I shivered. I had. Now *that* was scary. I'd come dangerously close to losing myself entirely. And all it had taken was one song in his arms. If I stayed for another...

"No," I said, shaking my head. "I don't feel good. It's, uh, my stomach, you see. I haven't been eating well while I've been gone. So much rich food. I need to go freshen up, then I'll be back. Then we'll have one more dance, and you'll escort me to my room, just so any curious peepers believe we're retiring together. Got it?"

Johnathan smiled. "I can do that."

"Good," I said, starting off.

I was brought back around when he didn't let go of my hand. His eyes were locked on me, and he smiled. A real smile, and I looked away. That was the look that had won me over when I younger. He had a killer smile, perfect teeth, just the right amount of dimple in his cheeks, and it always seemed to reach his eyes.

"Thank you for that dance," he said, meaning every word of it.

Then he lifted my hand to his mouth and brushed his lips over the back of my knuckles before letting me go.

I smiled and, against my own will, gave him a small curtsy.

What are you doing? Stop it! This isn't your real life. Get a grip.

Pulling my mind back together after the extra blast of power from the Soulbond and trying to ignore the tingling on the back of my hand, I headed for the doors.

Nobody stopped me. Not even Lars. Evidently, I'd put in a good enough showing to be allowed a bit of leeway for the time being. That was good, very good. I took the stairs at a slow, regal pace, despite my desire to break into a flat-out run. There were two reasons for that.

First, the front hallway always had people in it. Enforcers dressed up as servers, or couples passing between the other rooms on the main level. If they saw me running, that would blow my entire cover.

The second reason was that if I ran in this dress, my ass would be hanging fully out in about three steps. The ballroom had gotten enough of a view of my modest-sized tits over the course of the evening, and they didn't need to see more. Not for free, at least. Not unless they wanted to bankroll Aaron for a second week.

Reaching the top of the stairs, I started for my room. The original plan had been for me to get changed first into something a little less conspicuous. But as I passed the artifact room, I changed that. Adapting on the fly was key, and right now, *nobody* suspected me. Going to my room first would increase the time I was gone from the ballroom and the likelihood that someone would come looking for me.

I faked rolling an ankle as an excuse to stop and look around while I rested a hand on the wall next to the door. Nobody was in sight, and nobody came rushing forward to see if I needed help.

It's now or never. Do it.

Taking a deep breath, I pushed open the door and slipped into the artifact room. It was dark, and I dared not turn on the light, lest someone walking by see it was on and poke their head in. I was going to have to rely on my wolf for this.

Reaching out to her, I leaned on her powers. The room brightened considerably, but so did my pull to Johnathan.

Enough. We're not going back there. Ever. So get over it.

She pouted but subsided for the moment.

The room was a dazzling array of ancient shifter artifacts, items that had either been kept over the generations or found by my father and others like him as they sought out the ancient city of Shuldar.

There was enough evidence in the display cases or mounted to the walls to convince anyone that we'd once had our own civilization, away from humanity. Books and tapestries, statues, even some ancient weapons such as spears and a sword. I wondered briefly who we would have needed to fight off with those. Humans?

But those weren't what I was after. I moved to the center of the room. Where Lars had his most prized finds on display. He brought everyone to this room anytime he had visitors from another clan. It was his way of demonstrating he thought himself the superior.

Alpha politics are for children, I thought.

In the very center was the item I'd come for.

A foot-high statue made of pure gold. It was human from the neck down, sporting a pair of breasts and a carved loincloth. The head, however, was that of a wolf. The eyes were emeralds, and a crown of rubies and diamonds was set into the statue as well.

"The Idol of Amunlea," I whispered, staring at the figurine just sitting there. Lars didn't even have it behind a protective barrier. He feared nobody, it seemed.

Arrogance. It's a great deterrent until someone more stubborn comes along. Or, in my case, desperate.

"Sorry, bud," I chuckled, snatched up the golden idol of the empress of the gods, and walked as quietly as I could to the far wall. I opened the window, and after a quick peek to ensure all was clear, I punched out the screen.

Hating myself for what I was about to do next, I leaned out the window and, as carefully as I could, dropped the idol three stories down into a flower bed.

"Forgive me, Amunlea," I whispered.

Then, I set to tearing the dress. It was a shame to destroy something so nice, but it was too restrictive. I needed to be able to move. I couldn't shift and still carry the idol, so I needed the freedom to run.

That done, I climbed onto the edge of the window. Just before I jumped, I heard voices in the hallway behind me.

"She said the food had gotten to her, father. She's not used to eating such rich food."

That would be Johnathan.

"Of course she did. She's been living on scraps like some pathetic gutter rat. Too bad. I did not throw this ball for her to hide in her room."

And that would be Lars. Ever the caring host.

I grinned and then dropped from the window without a second thought. It wouldn't be long before they discovered I wasn't in my room, but it would take them some time to realize they'd been robbed.

Scooping up the idol, I took off into the night. This part of the plan had gone flawlessly. It was time to get back to Aaron and give him his hefty fee.

Then we could find whatever it was my father had been searching for. What it was he wanted me to find.

CHAPTER TWENTY-NINE

My throat dropped into my stomach as the elevator whisked me upward at a rapid pace.

"Urgh," I muttered, adjusting the straps of the backpack I had slung over my shoulders. The straps were digging deep through my shirt and into the skin, courtesy of the heavy weight the backpack contained. The sudden extra weight as the elevator shot higher had caused them to dig in even deeper.

"You had better be worth this, Aaron," I grumbled to nobody in particular–the elevator was empty aside from me–as I waited for it to come to a stop.

After escaping Aldridge Manor, I'd run to where I'd stashed my dad's truck, then driven the few hours back to Kellar. I'd crashed at the back of a truck stop, waiting for daylight before getting in touch with Aaron.

He'd directed me to meet him at his offices.

The elevator slowed, my stomach returning to normal, and the doors opened, spilling me out into an ultra-sleek-looking lobby, filled with rectangular light fixtures, rich dark hardwoods, and brilliantly white tiled floors.

There was no secretary at the front desk, so I strode past to the offices. There were six in total, but only one, at the very end of the hall, seemed occupied with its door ever so slightly ajar.

I walked right up to it and went in without knocking.

"I can see why you need to charge so damn much," I growled, unslinging my backpack and dropping it onto his desk.

Hopefully, it scratched it a bit. The huge U-shaped construct likely cost half the amount of gold I had been lugging around. It would serve him right.

Aaron grinned at me. "Your father often said the same thing. But he always paid as well. My services are well worth it, I assure you."

"Right," I said, shifting my weight from side to side.

Truthfully, I was uncomfortable in a place like this. I was wearing jeans, black knee-high boots, and a gray sweater.

Aaron was wearing the shit out of a black

three-piece suit. Even the shirt was black, though it was a bit glittery, reflecting the light in fun patterns. He rose as I watched, coming to sit on the corner of the desk next to me.

He didn't even look in the backpack, simply taking my word for it. Instead, he stared at me, those oddly bright blue eyes searching my face for...something. The intensity of his gaze left me unsettled and incredibly aroused.

Maybe it was because I didn't feel the need to fight it with him as I did with Johnathan, but every time he looked at me, I nearly threw myself at him. Which probably wasn't a good thing. Any man who could turn me into a puddle of desire with a simple gaze did *not* have my best interests in mind.

"Thank you for this," he said, sliding the backpack across the desk to his side of it.

I watched him slide it away from me, peeking inside.

"Impressive," he said.

"We good, then?" I asked a bit bitterly. I didn't like handing over my culture to him. I could feel it even now as he pulled the statuette away from me. I didn't want to let it go.

But I didn't have a choice. I needed his help, and I needed it fast. I could get the money from fights–eventually–but it would take too long, and the next Wild Moon was almost upon us. I didn't know what would happen then, so that's why we had to move now.

"Yes," he said, answering me, though his eyes were asking me a question. "We're good."

"Spit it out," I said. "What?"

He licked his lips, then spoke. "What do you expect to find out there, Dani? Your father never found anything."

I almost told him I thought he was wrong. That my father *did* find something. But that was just a hunch, a theory on my part. My instincts told me something was out there in the mountains northeast of Kellar. Something I had to find.

"I don't know," I said instead. "But he left me that journal for a reason, and I have to know what it was."

"Very well," Aaron said, accepting my words.

I guess when you're getting paid as much as he was, it didn't really matter if I did or didn't find anything. His fee was covered, and that was that.

"Great." I really wasn't sure what else to say here. Making a comment about business being over with, so now we could get to the pleasure didn't seem like it would go over well.

"I'll start the preparations for the expedition," Aaron said, standing up. "It will probably take around ten days for me to have everything ready."

"Ten days?" I cried. "Not good enough. We can't take that long."

Aaron frowned at me. "Are we in a rush? That wasn't specified."

Of *course* we were in a rush. But I couldn't tell him about that. He didn't know about us, about my people, and what happened on the full moon. I had to be gone. I needed to be out there when it came. I didn't know why, but I just knew I had to be in the mountains when the Wild Moon came over the horizon in a few days' time.

Everything was counting on it.

"Two days," I said firmly. "We're leaving in two days."

Aaron opened his mouth to argue. "I don't–"

"Two days, Aaron," I growled, putting my foot down. I shoved his super-sexy good looks and the effects he had on my body to the side and stared him down. This was a non-negotiable point, and I needed him to take me seriously.

He took a long time to respond, staring at my face–not just my eyes, but the whole thing, which was a bit unnerving–before he finally responded.

"Fine. We'll do it your way, two days."

"Thank you," I said, giving him a firm nod, preparing to head out.

"But if we're going to leave that fast, then you're going to have to help me."

I paused. "Help you with what? I thought I was

paying you. Isn't that enough?"

"Not to leave that quickly," he said with a chuckle. "You're going to have to help me get my team together."

"Team?" I said, dumbfounded. "This is the first time you've mentioned a team!"

Aaron just stared at me, waiting for an answer. He wasn't about to explain himself. That much was clear.

"Fine," I said grumpily. "Where do we start?"

He grinned at me, and I nearly gave him the finger. Aaron was enjoying the victory, and if I got lippy, he would probably like it even more. So, I gave him sullen silence instead. I'm so mature.

"The docks," he said. "Tonight. Ten."

CHAPTER THIRTY

"I still don't understand why I'm here helping you," I complained as we exited his car and headed down toward the waterfront. "I'm paying you. You're supposed to do all the work."

Aaron shrugged. "I need someone to keep watch. Have my back. My normal guy isn't back yet, and if you want to move faster, this is the way it has to be."

"I'm not your thug," I growled.

"Really?" he shot back. "Because the other day in the ring, you beat that other guy rather handily. It was impressive."

"That was different," I said, declining to explain as to how or why. I had emotion on my side that day. Johnathan deserved that ass-kicking. "Besides, these guys could have guns."

"They won't," he said with a confidence that

surprised me.

"We're at the docks. How can you be positive nobody will have guns? This place is seedy as hell," I told him.

We walked along the sidewalk, headed toward a cluster of buildings. On our left, the commercial docks were fenced off by a ten-foot-tall chain-link fence topped with razor wire. Stacks of shipping containers as tall as small apartment buildings loomed over us, the sparse lighting creating a wild play of shadows and darkness.

Above them, the lifeless cargo cranes lay still, like ancient beasts in silent slumber, looking down over their territory. The gentle lapping of water against shore could be heard if I focused hard enough, along with the soft groaning of thick ropes as a giant container ship rocked against the dock.

In the daytime, this place was bustling, alive with energy and the calls of dockworkers. At night, however, it was eerily empty and deserted. I listened carefully to my instincts here, even with Aaron at my side. At one point, the hairs on the back of my neck rose, but looking around, I couldn't see anything that would cause alarm.

The faded lights of several dockside taverns and shops greeted us as we approached one of them, *The Winking Scow.*

"Such imagery a simple name can evoke," I muttered. "I just *know* this is the one you're going to take us into. Isn't it?"

"I can't surprise you with anything, can I?" Aaron said. "Remember, watch my back. Stay out here."

The way he said that, with the quiet belief that I could protect him, made me pause and consider. Did Aaron know what I was? Could he possibly be aware of the existence of shifters? Or did he just want to make me work for this trip as a way of protesting the short departure time?

Infuriating. The man is infuriating.

Yet, whenever I was around him, the drumming of the Soulbond–long since grown above the gentle pulsing it had started with–was diminished. Not erased or cut off, but dulled. Easier to resist. Like he was a constant source of cold water being poured over me. I appreciated that immensely, which was why I wasn't too upset about helping him.

I eyed the outside of the *Scow*, noting the half a dozen lookouts lounging around at tables or leaning against the wall. All of them were trying to act innocent or occupied, but it was clear they were there to keep unwelcome guests out.

"Nah, I don't think I'll be waiting out here like your butler," I growled, surprising Aaron with a burst of speed as I walked past the lookouts–several of whom rose to try and stop me–and pulled open the door to the bar, walking inside.

I paused.

My wolf's vision let me penetrate the deep gloom of the bar with ease. Most of me wished it didn't.

Very quickly, I noted I was by far the youngest and least well-traveled woman in the room. None of them turned to look at me, but many other heads did. Eyes dulled by alcohol and other substances stared at me, and I'm not sure I've ever felt dirtier in my entire life than in that single moment.

I tried to look past them. I wasn't afraid of any of these men. If I needed to, I could fight my way out of the bar, but it was unsettling to be the object of attention to so many men in the decrepit bar.

It had been nice once, I'm sure, long ago. The giant beams running crosswise were huge and reminiscent of a time when wood was the material of choice for building. A horseshoe-shaped bar stuck out from the back wall. A sunken pit on the left was crammed with tables and rough-looking types. Half the lights had gone out over it, and the few remaining were centered over a poker table.

To my right, more tables and some booths ran along the exterior and crowded the interior. A couple of doors on the right-hand wall might have been bathrooms, but I doubted I wanted to find out their current state. My mental sanity was already stretched thin.

Behind me, Aaron entered. Eyes turned to him as well. Dressed in his typical suit, he stood out almost as much as I did. At least I had the smarts to wear a black jacket and black pants.

Aaron had chosen his cream-colored suit again. In a place like this, it made him a prime target. I was going to have my work cut out for me.

Yet, as he walked by me, the crowd parted, letting him through like fish before a shark. And make no mistake, Aaron was a *dangerous* shark. I still didn't understand how, yet, but his arrogance wasn't born of money. It was born of competence. Everyone just knew not to mess with him because it wouldn't go well for them.

I went to follow, but the crowd was already closing in behind him.

"I'm with him," I said, pointing.

They didn't care.

This was a test. I'd told Aaron I could handle myself, and now he was letting me show him.

Fine. I can handle a test.

I started forward anyway. The closest drunk, a man probably in his thirties but looking twice that thanks to substance abuse, came at me, leering at me with a grin that was missing at least five teeth and breath that could stop a T-rex in its tracks.

"Hey, honey," he said as he came close, reaching for my chest. "How much for the night?"

I let him take a step closer. Then I grabbed the outstretched arm, pulling him in even as I turned and drove an elbow into his stomach before standing up sharply, my shoulder catching him in the jaw.

The drunk dropped like a sack of fish and heaved his stomach out onto the wooden floor, adding to the mix of other liquids and substances.

I was really glad I hadn't worn nice shoes. If I'd stepped in here in a pair of Louboutins, I'd have a much harder time restraining myself.

"Next one gets a broken bone," I said to the assembled crowd. "Dealer's choice on which. I'll break an additional bone for everyone after who tries to touch me."

The crowd parted for me, revealing Aaron's back as he headed toward the sunken pit.

That's what I thought, I said as I strode forward, head held high, my wolf howling in victory.

I stopped at Aaron's side, looking past him. He was watching the poker game with interest. Four characters were playing, not including the dealer.

The leftmost was a pockmarked, salty old man with skin that bespoke a lifetime on the sea. Probably a fisherman. He wore a black slicker jacket and had a ratty old Yankees hat.

To his right was a younger man with the look of a construction worker, down to the hi-res vest he wore. Probably a dockworker, I surmised, noting the safety boots and slightly higher quality of his black sweater, not to mention the fact he looked like he had all his teeth.

"That's our man," Aaron said, nodding to the third player. "Jaxton, my quartermaster."

Jaxton had black hair that was gelled into a spiky look, reminding me of a popular boyband hairstyle in the early years of the new millennium. He wore a black turtleneck and fingerless gloves. He was also holding a pair of nines and had another pair of sevens with one of the cards on the draw.

"Come back later," Jaxton said, without looking up. "I'm busy."

"We can't," Aaron told him. "We're leaving in two days now. Time to get to work."

Jaxton sighed. The final card was overturned, and it was another nine. He was going to win the hand, I thought.

"How many?" he asked as the bets went round. Jaxton raised by several large chips.

"Seven," Aaron replied.

I frowned, assuming they were talking about people given this was his quartermaster, Aaron had another *four* members of his team. How many employees did he have? And why did he need them?

"Seven, okay. Where?"

"Mountains. Same as previous," Aaron replied, the two of them having half a conversation.

"Okay, I'll get it done," Jaxton said, laying down his hand. "Now, leave me alone. I'm on a win streak here."

The player to his right laid down four aces. "Not quite."

"This is all your fault," Jaxton said, still without looking up at Aaron as the other player, a hardy man with the look of a ship captain, swept up the chips on the table. "You ruined it for me. I expect a bonus."

Aaron chuckled, then turned to me. "Okay, time to go."

I followed him outside. There was no trouble this time from any of the patrons. Nor did the lookouts bother us. I guess if we came out in one piece without causing a fight, they assumed we were okay.

Aaron kept walking. He was heading up the sidewalk, back toward his car.

"Wait a second," I said, grabbing his shoulder and spinning him around. "That's *it?* That was all you came here for?"

"Yes," Aaron said indifferently.

"We could have fucking *called him*," I spat.

"He doesn't have a phone."

"You don't need me for this," I said, my voice dropping to a growl as I got into his face. I didn't care how sexy he was, how dangerous he might be. I didn't like being used.

He didn't flinch. Now *that* was confidence, though of course, he didn't know I could tear him limb from limb if I wanted to.

"No," he said calmly, his blue eyes staring at me unblinking. "I didn't need you, you're right. I did, however, need to see just how committed to this you are. This won't be an easy journey."

I backed off slightly. "It's camping and exploring in the mountains. How difficult could it be?"

Aaron gave me a long look as if to tell me I should know better. *How much do you know about everything?* Not for the first time, I had to wonder just how well-informed Aaron was. And who had told him I was in town in the first place? Had he been keeping tabs on me?

"How can I trust you?" I asked. "How do I know you're not lying about my father?"

"Now that is a fair question," he said, reaching into his pocket, pulling out his phone. "Here. Look at these."

I waited while he unlocked the device and then handed it over to me. It was an image gallery. Of him and my father. Together. Smiling. Laughing. They were all taken out in nature.

"Your father was a good man," Aaron said. "I valued his friendship. You have nothing to fear from me. The choice is yours whether you will trust me or not, however. If you do, meet me tomorrow in the warehouse district just up the road from here. I'll text you the address. If not, then we'll consider this thing canceled."

He took the phone and walked into the night, leaving me alone.

"I notice you didn't say anything about a refund," I called after him.

It was a good point, though. Was I going to trust him, or wasn't I?

CHAPTER THIRTY-ONE

Three days to go until the Wild Moon, and I was out grocery shopping.

"Gathering supplies," as Aaron put it, which made it sound way more badass than pushing a cart around a store. Probably helped with his ego.

He pulled us up to a giant warehouse. Several other cars were parked outside. I got out of the car, the plush white leather of his Mercedes SomethingFancy-Class–I didn't know cars, nor did I pay attention when he'd told me–starting to rub me the wrong way. It was too comfortable for me.

"I figured when you said the warehouse district, you wanted to go to one of the markets there," I said, staring up at the drab, gray building covered in corrugated sheet metal without a sign on it. "Why didn't we do that or go to a grocery store?"

Aaron looked at me, blue eyes twinkling with laughter. "This is cheaper."

"You're such a stereotypical rich dick," I muttered, falling in step as we walked toward the doors. It was easy to keep up with him, my gazelle legs coming in handy for once.

"You don't get rich by spending your money," he replied so easily he must have been sitting on that line. "Besides, your payment won't cover grocery store prices."

I goggled at him. "It *what*? That's impossible. Though if you wanted it to, you'd probably have to take a lower cut yourself."

"Not happening."

"Shocking," I said. "But tell me, why are we *here*?"

"The people inside owe me a favor," he said.

"Right," I replied as if that made all the sense in the world.

"They don't want to pay it," he elaborated. "So, we're going to get the supplies I need anyway."

"I told you, I'm not your hired muscle," I snarled. "You work for me."

Aaron smiled at me, the look making my legs wobble slightly. "I know."

God damn him. So arrogant and sexy. I hate it. I hate him. But I wanted him. It was undeniable.

I wasn't going to be stupid enough to let myself jump into the sack with him. That would ruin a perfectly irritating client-employee relationship. A girl could daydream, though.

I needed to step up my game of being purposefully antagonizing, though. Aaron had me way outclassed on that level, and he deserved to suffer as much as I was.

"Well, shall we?" he asked, gesturing at the man-door set into the wall next to the large roll-up delivery doors. "Time is ticking."

He was right. I didn't *want* to be his muscle, but if we had to fight to get what we needed, then so be it.

My wolf, sensing violence, came nosing to the surface. I called on her senses, her strength, and her speed. Shifting was a no-go around humans, but it wasn't an all-or-nothing proposition. We were one, the beast and I, and with the Wild Moon drawing nearer, a good fight would hopefully leave her tired, making my life easier in the coming days.

"Fine," I growled. "Let's go."

Aaron nodded once, pulled open the door, and waltzed inside. I followed, trying to focus on the interior of the warehouse and not his fantastic ass. My wolf was ready for physical exertion of any kind, it seemed. Fighting or fucking, it didn't make a lick of a difference to her just now. For me, on the other hand, it made a *huge* difference.

This is not what I need right now. Focus. You could be in danger. Aaron could be in danger.

You wouldn't know it by the way he strode into the warehouse, acting like he owned the place. Did the man even know what fear was? Respect for your enemy? Whoever was here, they didn't respect him enough to pay their debts, assuming Aaron was telling the truth. That meant they were confident. I would have to be wary. If these people thought they could take Aaron, it meant they would be some tough customers.

"What's this?" I asked, staring around in shock at the inside of the warehouse.

"Have you never been inside a storage warehouse before?" Aaron asked dryly.

Grinding my teeth together so that I didn't clock him one, I looked. The place was…normal. Brightly lit with all sorts of warning signs, clean floors, men walking around with hard hats and caution vests. It looked like, well, a storage warehouse. Huge racks of metal shelving rose into the heights, stacked full of crates and skids of wrapped items.

"What were you expecting? A secret villain hideout with guns, tanks, and an arsenal big enough to take out the East Coast, all just sitting out in the open?" he teased.

I was blushing furiously, and I hated it. "Maybe," I growled. "You made them out to be bad people."

Aaron shrugged, stepping back as a forklift went by beeping loudly to warn anyone nearby. "They certainly aren't nice. Nice people repay favors."

"You just love messing with me, don't you?" I asked, relaxing.

"Maybe," he chuckled under his breath. "Now, let's get my stuff."

I followed him through the warehouse. He walked confidently, knowing where he wanted to go without issue.

"Paul Byron!" he called abruptly as we reached the loading docks, the area open of shelving but filled with skids and items ready to go onto trucks for delivery to their next destination. "I know you're here! Show yourself!"

Most of the workers nearby ignored Aaron, but he didn't seem to take that personally.

"What the hell do you want?" a voice spat from behind us.

I turned. The man approaching had to be Paul Byron. Only someone his size could comfortably threaten Aaron. The giant troll approaching was easily six and a half feet tall with a belly to match. His legs were thick as tree trunks. If we weren't on pure concrete, the ground itself would likely rumble with each step. A beard covered a weak chin, big, bushy, and unkept, the complete opposite of his head, which was bald, and beyond red. Ruddy, alcoholic cheeks completed the look.

"I want my stuff," Aaron said in a voice so cold I blinked in surprise.

This was the first time I'd heard him speak with anything approaching anger. Anyone who had a shred of intelligence in them should have known not to disrespect someone who could speak like that.

Paul Byron didn't care.

"Get lost. I told you last time, if you fucked me over, I was done with you," Byron growled, stopping in front of Aaron, looking down at him by four inches or more.

"I paid for these goods," Aaron said just as harshly. "I expect delivery."

"You paid me what you owed me last time, plus interest and late charges. Nothing more," Byron said. "You want them, it'll cost you."

"That wasn't our deal," Aaron said, voice going flat.

I flinched at that, and he was on *my* side. Byron should be blanching in fear. Instead, he just hiked up his denim overalls and laughed.

"Get out of my warehouse, *Greiss,*" he snarled, dismissing Aaron and turning to go.

"No," Aaron said, and before I could react, he punched Byron in the face. Bone crunched audibly.

The other man reeled backward under the blow, blood spurting from his nostrils, roaring loudly.

"What the *hell*?" I hissed, stunned at the sudden development. "I thought you–"

Half a dozen men came charging out from behind various skids, summoned by their boss' pained bellow. I glanced at Aaron, but he was too busy focusing on Byron. Which meant the rest of them were left to me.

"You and I are going to have some words after this, *Greiss*," I growled, mimicking Byron's contemptuous use of Aaron's last name.

Even as I spoke, I was positioning myself between the gang of thugs and my employee. I didn't miss the irony of it at all, either. It was painfully evident. I was paying Aaron to be his bodyguard.

I've got to get a better lawyer, I thought to myself, smiling as I positioned myself, blocking the path.

"Out of our way, lady," said the first thug, a tall, slim man with a thick brown goatee who reminded me strongly of the second-in-command from Star Trek.

Clearly, he lacked Riker's charm. Shame.

"Sorry, no can do," I said with a peppy smile. "But if you want, I can help you lose thirty pounds in thirty days? All you have to do is take some pills three times a day!"

"What?" The man blinked at me, then looked at his buddies.

Behind me, Byron shouted angrily. "Stop staring at her titties and get over here, you mongrels."

"Rude," I said, glancing over my shoulder. "I don't have any titties for them to stare at. Way to hurt a girl's self-confidence." I thought about it, tapping my chin. "Or maybe he's trying to help. What do you think?"

"What the *fuck* are you talking about?" the first thug said, stepping forward, arm extended, clearly meaning to brush me aside as they went to their boss' aid.

"It's my side *hustle,"* I growled the last word as his hand swept toward me, and I moved.

Ducking under his arm, I drove a knuckled fist into his kidney. The man doubled over, and I snapped my upper body down, balancing on one leg. My other leg came up and over my head in a display of flexibility I did not care to repeat, the sole of my foot catching him right in the face as he tried to stand up.

"Ow," I hissed, my groin shooting bright darts of pain through the rest of me. "That was dumb."

But I'd always wanted to try that move. Now I knew better. Leave it to the pros. The really, really flexible pros.

"Anyone else?" I asked.

Two more men came at me. "Ugh, fine," I said, dancing to the side easily, then simply shoving. I used a bit of extra strength, and both men went tumbling down.

They all came at me at once, and I ducked under a deluge of blows. I kicked and elbowed and punched, but six on one is tough, even for a shifter. I drove two of them back, but to do so, I opened myself up, and a knee caught me in the chin.

I saw stars. What I think was a fist–I couldn't see straight yet–caught me in the temple, and I staggered back.

"Go *down*, bitch," the leader snarled, back in the fight now. "You three, go help the boss."

I heard footsteps clatter as they tried to pass me. I reached out blindly and grabbed hold of one as he went by. I spun and heaved him, using my ears to guide me. I was rewarded by the sound of two bodies colliding and going down in a heap.

Shaking my head, I cleared my vision just in time to see Jaxton drop down out of nowhere and intercept the two thugs heading for Aaron's back.

"Not today," he growled.

With backup on my side, Jaxton and I drove in at the thugs, and in short order, we had three of them on the ground, groaning in pain. One of them had a broken arm. I was pretty sure Jaxton had caused serious issue to another one's knee, but I really didn't care enough to inspect.

"*Enough*," Byron said, spitting blood from where Aaron had him pinned up against a crate of equipment. "Fine. Take your shit, and go." He pointed at a trio of skids. "Don't ever come back."

Aaron stood back, straightening his suit, and nodded. "Thanks, Byron. Pleasure doing business with you."

Then, he turned and headed for the skids, passing Jaxton and me. "Truck here?" he asked.

"Yeah," Jaxton said. "It's outside Gate One."

I stared at the two of them, conversing as if nothing had ever happened.

Who *were* these people? Why had my father ever worked with them? They were insane. Which probably meant I was insane.

In the back of my head, the Soulbond drummed again. It was growing louder with each passing night. I could hear it at all times during the day now. Even Aaron's presence was slowly losing the battle, the beating of its desire for Johnathan slowly breaking through.

These men might be completely nuts, but they were on my side, and right now, they were the only hope I had to find whatever was out there that was calling to me before it was too late. Before I was changed by the Soulbond forever.

CHAPTER THIRTY-TWO

The next morning, I was tired and more than a little cranky. The night had been a long one, spent tossing and turning and waking up in a cold sweat more times than I could remember. The moon's pull was growing stronger, and so was my wolf.

Not even coffee could fix my mood. It was that bad. I stalked across the parking lot of our meeting place, which Aaron had told me to be at after our expedition to the warehouse. It was a long, squat, concrete affair, one of those commercial buildings that had gone up quickly in the late seventies, with a bunch of units next to one another.

Every five or so units, there was a break in the buildings to allow vehicles to access the rear. One tree was planted at the front of each unit, none of which looked to be in good shape. Unit Four was where I wanted to go. It had a pair of roll-up doors installed in the front, and faded lettering above them proclaimed that once upon a time, "Al's Auto Care" had called the place home.

Judging by the weeds growing everywhere, I doubted Al had been there anytime recently. It was the perfect spot for a secret clubhouse. Exactly what a man would choose.

I ducked under the roll-up door that was halfway down, noting that it felt as dour inside as it looked outside, the gray skies and generally blah weather of the day matching the well-worn interior. Two lifts still stood in place, but otherwise, the inside was devoid of anything related to its former life.

Instead, a handful of people stood around a wheeled chalkboard, drinking coffee and doing nothing. They all looked up as I entered.

"Am I late?" I asked, frowning. The dash in my dad's truck had said I was twenty minutes early.

"No," Aaron said, appearing from the little office off to the left.

He wasn't dressed in his traditional suit at all. It was still all black, one of his two preferred color schemes, but instead of the formal wear, he'd traded it in for something more practical. Black tactical boots, thick pants that wouldn't rip or tear as we trucked through the wilderness, and a heavy black shirt. Strapped around his waist was a utility belt that I felt was filled with practical items, not what necessarily came with it. He wore it with experience, clearly used to the weight.

"You've changed," I said dryly.

"You sound surprised."

I shrugged. "I figured you would be the type to wear camo-everything. I find it hard to believe they were so out of stock you had to resort to this."

Aaron stared at me, a mix of irritation and resignation. "I should have asked for more money."

I snorted. "Are you going to introduce me? I know Jaxton there, but what about the rest of your merry band of misfits?"

"Hey," one of the others said, a grin plastered on his face. "I resent that remark."

"That would be Dave," Aaron said. "He's our tech guy."

Dave was tall, though I didn't think he could quite look Aaron in the eyes. He had the look of someone who had once been extremely fit, but now the muscle was covered in a layer of fat. Bald, with thin eyebrows and a lopsided grin, I immediately pegged him as the funny one of the group. Easygoing and able to poke fun, I felt we would get along best. He nodded, and I smiled.

"You know Jaxton, our quartermaster."

"And not too shabby in a fight," I said.

Jaxton dipped his head in acknowledgment.

"Alexi is our tracker."

I focused on the next member of the team. Average height, blond hair–though not as brilliant as Aaron's–pale blue eyes, and a wide, blocky face that spoke of Nordic lineage, or perhaps northern Slavic, based on the name. I wasn't sure. He met my eyes, then looked away. That was all the greeting I was getting, apparently. A real charmer, that one.

"Pieter here is our chef," Aaron continued, moving on. "And an expert driver."

The smallest of the group, Pieter was a scrawny little thing even shorter than me with curly hair sticking out from under a green beret hat. I almost wrote him off as the least dangerous member of the group.

Until I saw his eyes. Tiny dots of brown, they focused on me with uncanny intensity. Something told me I shouldn't look away, not at first. This man wasn't entirely stable. I held the gaze. *Take a good look, buddy. Trust me when I tell you, you don't want to mess with me.*

Eventually, Pieter nodded, apparently satisfied with what he'd seen. I wasn't sure what that meant, but that was fine.

"And him?" I asked, nodding at the sixth and final member of the team. "Who's he?"

The unnamed member had his back turned to me. He was leaning against the upright support of the lift.

"That's Fred," Aaron said dismissively.

Fred didn't turn around.

"And what does Fred do?" I asked.

"Fred's a labor grunt," Aaron said as if that's all that was necessary.

I looked at Aaron, then at Fred. He was taller than Aaron, broader in the shoulders, too. His hair was short, black, and very thick. He turned around, revealing a taut face and brown eyes that revealed absolutely nothing about him. An extra bump in his nose spoke of it being broken a time or two in the past, but otherwise, there was nothing remarkable about him at all.

Yet, he gave me the creeps.

"A grunt. Right," I said, making it very clear I didn't believe him.

Was that a bulge I spotted under Fred's shoulder? It was tough to tell, the black of his clothes made it all blend even with my vision, but I was fairly positive. So, Fred was the gunman.

Why did we need a gunman?

"Why do we need this many people?" I asked. "Plenty of these jobs could be doubled up."

Aaron shrugged. Clearly, I wasn't winning that fight. *Okay, fine. You win this round, pretty boy.*

I waited for Aaron to explain what happened next, but he was looking at me. They were *all* looking at me.

"Well?" Aaron prompted when I raised an eyebrow at him, giving him a face full of *what the fuck is going on?* attitude.

"Well, *what*?" I asked. "Are we waiting?"

"Are you going to tell us what we're doing? What the mission is?"

I stared at him. Was he stupid? Did he get hit in the head too hard by Byron yesterday?

"I already told you what we're doing," I said, obviously missing something here. "We're going out to the mountains where you and my father went, northeast of Kellar. We're going to explore the last area you guys worked together. Then we're going to find the abandoned city hidden out there."

Everyone was looking at me now. Most of them with mixed amounts of disbelief. I looked over the group, then back at Aaron.

"You didn't tell them, did you?"

"I thought it would sound better coming from you," he said blandly.

"You mean less crazy."

He looked upward in thought, then nodded. "Yeah, less crazy."

"You guys signed up for this without being told what we're doing? Without even asking?"

The team shrugged in near unison. A sure sign

of a group that's worked together plenty of times.

"You all are fucking weird," I muttered. "And crazy."

"Don't forget you're part of the team now," Aaron said. "So, include yourself on that list."

"Oh, I'm at the top," I said, shaking my head. "At the very damn top."

I'm chasing a wild theory into the complete unknown, based on some vague hints and a gut instinct I got from reading my father's book. I stole one of my race's most important artifacts to do so. I'm trusting a man I've never met before, all while running from my Alpha and his son, the man I'm supposed to be mated to.

Yeah, definitely crazy.

"The thing is, I'm aware of my faults," I added when nobody else spoke.

Alexi spoke up, his words heavy with an Eastern European accent but intelligible enough to tell me he'd been here for some time. "What information do you have?"

I sighed. "Not much. My father has been looking for this city for decades."

"Yes. We have worked with him before. Never find city," Alexi said. "Where is your father?"

"Missing," I said. "I'm hoping that whatever is out there, whatever he wanted me to find, will help me locate him."

"So, we are going in blind?" Alexi asked.

I nodded, confirming it. "Yes. Do you want out?"

He shook his head.

"Anyone else?" I asked, looking around.

Nobody spoke up. They were all in. Like I said, a bunch of crazies.

"Did you ever take this many out with my father?" I asked Aaron suddenly, wondering if he was bringing such a large group because I was there and didn't really know what I was doing.

"Sometimes," he admitted.

"Why? I don't get it. How could you possibly need this many people out there?"

"These mountains are dangerous," Fred said, looking at me with brown eyes that tracked my every movement with computer-like precision.

He didn't elaborate, and after a minute of waiting for him to, I gave up.

"There's no way Fred is your real name, right?" I asked. "Is it supposed to make you seem less threatening? Because it doesn't work. Just so you know."

Fred stared at me.

"Whatever," I said, turning back to Aaron. "It's just camping and exploring out there. What's so dangerous? You keep saying this. I grew up in the country. It's fine."

"Growing up in a farm town is different than

where we're headed," he said. "No cell reception. No other humans for hundreds of miles. It's rough territory, and it's very easy to get lost and killed out there. We go as a team. As much for our own protection as yours."

"Okay," I said, not fighting it. If Aaron wanted to bring his frat brothers with him, I wasn't going to argue. "Then, let's do this."

Aaron nodded, and without a word, the others got up, filing out the back door. I followed. Waiting were two large, beefy-looking pickup trucks packed to the brim with supplies. The white one had a trailer attached to it, though it was empty.

Everyone but Aaron went to the white truck and climbed in. Aaron went to the slightly smaller black pickup, a new-looking Ford.

I hopped into the black pickup as well, taking the passenger seat.

"Are they that afraid of you?" I quipped as I got in and buckled up.

"I told them to let you ride alone with me," Aaron said quietly, firing up the engine with the push of a button on the dash. "I figured you would be more comfortable that way."

I frowned. That was uncharacteristically nice of him. Was he hoping for road head or something? It wasn't going to happen, and he had to know that. So I waited for the catch, but Aaron was done speaking. We pulled out, leaving the rundown building and my dad's little pickup behind.

Two days until the Wild Moon. Two days to find something my father hadn't found in years of searching.

I was so screwed.

CHAPTER THIRTY-THREE

"What's that?"

I looked up to find Aaron glancing over at me, his eyes flicking between the road and the book in my lap.

"My father's journal," I said, trying not to let myself get distracted by those damnable blue eyes of his.

They have no business being that intriguing.

Bright. They were bright, not intriguing. That's what they had no business being. They were like the sky but with an electric glow to them. Were they contacts, maybe? I couldn't rule that out, but I was positive I'd never seen someone with eyes quite the shade of his.

So much for not getting distracted. I fell for the trap again.

We were hours outside of Kellar now, human

civilization well behind us. The meadows had given way to forests, and we were slowly climbing higher into the foothills at the base of the mountains. Another hour, or maybe two, and I figured we'd be into the mountain range. It was hard to tell. The damn stone giants were incredibly deceiving in size.

"His journal?"

"Yeah. He gave it to me as a shi–a gift," I corrected, almost making a huge mistake. I was feeling too at ease around Aaron. I couldn't afford a slip. Not now. "He meant to, at least. He never got the chance before he disappeared."

"I'm sorry," Aaron said with uncharacteristic kindness. "I liked your father."

"Thanks," I said. "But I still think he's out there. Somewhere."

Aaron very clearly didn't state the obvious, that the odds were incredibly unlikely. I appreciated that from him. I wasn't dumb, I knew it was unlikely, but I wasn't ready to give up hope. Not yet.

"Your card was under the front cover," I said quietly. "I think he wanted me to come to you. That, combined with the last entries. It's like he was telling me I needed to come out here myself. To find something. You're positive he didn't find anything last time?"

"Nothing that he told us about," Aaron said.

"I see."

"What does his journal say?"

I stared down at the entry I was reading.

I talked to Lars today after returning home. I explained to him I knew I was on the right track, that we're closing in on it. It won't be long now before we find Shuldar. He was angrier than I've seen before. Spoke about time running out. That he needed to find it and soon. I've never heard him speak like that, not to me at least.

I flipped forward the pages by about a month.

I don't know what Lars wants me to find. He no longer confides in me.

How did I explain what these bits and pieces meant to me? That I was beginning to think that my father, once a staunch supporter of Lars, might have been coming to worry about him. That perhaps he was no longer as loyal as I once thought. Perhaps he'd *never* been.

There was something else at stake. Something that was driving Lars' search for Shuldar, and my father had sensed it, too. There wasn't enough to go on, though. Not enough to fill in the pages upon pages of blanks. I doubted anyone who didn't know my father would have been able to pick up on it because it was more what *wasn't* written than what was.

The lack of support and eagerness to continue.

Had he been stalling?

I sat up straight. Was that it? Had my father figured out the location of Shuldar, and he'd been stalling, trying to delay Lars? But why? What was Lars up to that he needed to find Shuldar so badly? It made no sense.

"I just wish I could talk to him one more time," I said quietly, closing the book. "I have so many questions. This gives me some clues, but it's not enough. It doesn't explain what's going on, what I'm missing."

Aaron nodded, drumming his fingers along the steering wheel. "Your father always told me you were smart. Smarter than he was. If he left you some clues, then you'll find them. I believe it."

"Thanks," I said quietly.

In the sky, the sun began to dip, and the drumming echoed faintly in the back of my head, pushing through the blanket Aaron seemed to drape over me. Even in such proximity, I wouldn't be able to ignore it for much longer.

What were you trying to tell me, Father?

CHAPTER THIRTY-FOUR

After nine hours of driving and two pit stops, Aaron pulled his truck off the road–more like an old logging trail by this point–and proceeded to lead us on another two-hour journey foot through the forest.

"Long way out," I grumbled as we climbed a rather steep incline.

I tried to keep my complaining to a minimum. It was hard, but I managed, especially since I was carrying little more than a heavy backpack, while the others were burdened down with large rucksacks stuffed to the brim with gear. Other than Fred, I honestly wondered how they all managed without falling behind.

"We'll get there tomorrow," Aaron said. "Near the end of the day."

"This is where you always came with my father?" I asked.

I didn't see any signs of a city around us.

"You'll see," Aaron said, following comfortably behind Alexi, who was leading the way, following some sort of trail only visible to him.

I glared at his back. Aaron was just as comfortable rucking through the mountains as he was navigating the streets of Kellar or blending in with the upper crust of society. He was a chameleon, and it irritated me. I wanted to know who he *really* was.

We continued to climb the ridge between two mountain peaks, and the closer we got to the top, the more I began to buzz with excitement. Whatever it was, it had to be on the other side, didn't it? I could *feel*...something out there. It called me.

Feeling renewed in purpose and spirit, I surged ahead with a burst of energy, passing Aaron and falling in just behind Alexi.

"How do you spot where we're going?" I asked. "I don't see any signs."

"Experience," Alexi said gruffly, not elaborating.

"Is it some sort of hidden markings that tell you where to go? Something my father laid down when he came this way?" I wanted to know, eager for more information. We were on the right track. I knew it.

"No."

Alexi was no help. He lengthened his stride and soon pulled ahead of me, even with my legs doing their best to keep up. I was too excited to be mad, so I just dropped back, walking silently next to Aaron, waiting for him to say something.

"Wow," I whispered as we crested the ridge. "That's beautiful."

Ahead of us, a valley spread out and away for miles. A vibrant swath of green covered the valley floor, except for where a river cut through from the northwest edge of the valley, down to the south, before flowing eastward out of sight.

Behind us, the sun was setting. Its rays fell perfectly between the peaks to our left and right, highlighting the third mountain in the north end of the valley, the ridges between the three forming the valley itself.

"Yes, it is," Aaron agreed, taking a moment to admire the golden light covering the landscape in front of us.

Then, he put a foot forward and began to descend the ridge. I stayed behind while the rest of the team came up. Each paused to admire the beauty of Mother Nature for a few seconds before heading down after Aaron.

Fred was the last one to reach the top. He'd been watching our rear, which is one reason why I'd been up near the front. He gave me the creeps for a reason I couldn't explain. Maybe it was just his silence or the menacing aura about him. Either way, I didn't like it.

"If somebody did build a city out here," Fred said gruffly, shocking me with his sudden eloquence. "They certainly picked a beautiful place to do it. Sunsets out here are grand."

I nodded. "Yeah. That far mountain will be picturesque in an hour or two."

"Even now," he said, and then he was gone before I could respond, following the rest of his team.

I watched him go. I hadn't expected that of Fred. Clearly, he wasn't just a dumb triggerman. There was a depth there I had missed the first time around. I knew I wouldn't underestimate him again.

"What would your friends say if they knew about your soft side, Fred?" I whispered as I left the top of the ridge behind and moved down into the valley.

It didn't take long for me to catch up with the others, and in another hour, we reached a flat, open meadow at the base of the ridge. We crossed it and found ourselves on the embankment of the river.

"We'll make camp here tonight," Aaron said. "Crossing the river is best done during daytime. It's deeper than it looks and fast flowing."

I didn't argue. I could hear it rushing past, the low rumble of so much moving water impossible to miss, even a few hundred yards from it. Water was probably my least favorite thing. A pool was great. But a deep, murky river where I couldn't see the bottom that was also moving fast?

I shivered. No, thank you.

Around me, the team was setting up their tents. I wandered over to Aaron, basking in the numbing sensation I felt in his presence. It was no longer complete, but it was better than nothing.

The lower the sun set, the more active my Soulbond became, and I was grateful for even the slightest relief. It was preparing me for the Wild Moon when it would be freest to act, and I would be at my weakest.

My wolf would be in command, and if she decided to follow the pull of the bond, I wasn't sure I'd be able to resist. Controlling my beast was hard enough on a regular Wild Moon.

Although, I won't be around the pack this time. Perhaps things will be calmer. Less intense.

I snorted.

"Something funny?" Aaron asked.

"No," I said, shaking my head, unslinging the pack he'd handed me from his truck and setting it on the ground. I wanted to get my tent set up so I could lie down and relax. The more we walked, the antsier I got. My body was practically tingling.

Rifling through the bag, I came up short with what I was looking for. Glancing around the camp, I saw the rest of his team disappearing into their tents. Fred had set up what looked like a tiny burrow of a tent I swore wouldn't even fit himself, but he somehow slid in with ease.

Dave and Jaxton shared a two-person tent, while Pieter and Alexi were finishing setting up an identical tent.

"Aaron," I said, watching as he pulled a tent from his bag.

"Yeah?"

"Where's my tent?" I asked.

Aaron waved a hand at the tent he was setting up.

"Oh," I said, feeling somewhat chagrined. Here I was preparing to get all cross with him when he was setting up my shelter for me. "That's kind of you. Thanks. You didn't have to do that, though. I'm not incompetent."

He shrugged. "You're paying."

"This is true," I agreed.

"Besides, it's my shelter as well."

I froze. "What did you just say?"

"You're paying?" he asked, looking up from where he was crouched as he slipped the poles through hoops on the tent's side.

"No, after that," I said tightly, trying not to feel

stupid.

"That it's my tent, too? What? Is there a problem with that?"

"We're sharing?" I asked, swallowing tightly as I looked at the size of the tent.

Aaron looked up at me, eyes glowing with that familiar irritating twinkle. "Yes. Why would we bring an extra tent just for one person?"

I glanced at Fred. "Fred did."

"Fred chose to haul it on top of everything else," Aaron said. "Fred does what Fred wants to do."

"Fred has a real name," I pointed out.

Aaron stared at me blankly.

"Whatever. Okay, we can share."

The smile that lit up Aaron's face had me wanting to make a mad dash for the tent, hauling him in after me. It promised all kinds of wicked fun, the sort of fun that would distract me from the beat of the drums in the back of my head urging me to shift and head back, to take Johnathan as my mate. To forgive him for the past so that we could have a future.

Maybe I should sleep outside.

I immediately nixed that idea, however. If I were on my own, I would probably shift and do just that, letting my wolf out, running off some of her exuberance this close to the Wild Moon. That wasn't an option with Aaron and the team around, so I had no choice.

I was going to share a tent with him.

"Something wrong?" Aaron asked.

"Look, I'm going to make this clear and say it only once," I said, trying to sound tougher than I felt. "We're sharing a roof over our head. Nothing more. No funny business, got it?"

Aaron looked me over and nodded once. "I'm a professional. Unless you ask for something, I'll be good."

I rolled my eyes. "In your dreams, buster."

He winked at me, and I nearly swooned. That's not fair. No man should have that kind of power with the mere movement of an eyelid. It should be outlawed, banned. Forbidden. Like he was.

My wolf disagreed. Vehemently. She howled and slammed against the mental shackles, straining to get free. She very much liked the idea of "funny business." Aaron was another predator, a *true* Alpha, unlike Johnathan, and whenever he demonstrated that, she went wild for it.

Now, if only we could just stop thinking about Johnathan all the time, not just when Aaron is sexing it up.

She also didn't have anything resembling morals or decency, which is something I tried to pretend I possessed.

Not happening, I told her in no uncertain terms. *Certainly not out here, in the middle of no-*

where, with five other men who will hear everything.

My wolf sniffed, and I got the distinct impression she was implying I was a prude.

Control yourself with the Soulbond bullshit, and we'll talk.

Silence was all that greeted me. That's what I thought.

I needed a distraction.

"What is the plan in the morning?" I asked.

"We'll ford the river," he said. "After that, it's up to you."

"You're so certain what we want is on the other side," I said, glancing at the river.

"Actually, I'm not at all certain you'll find a damn thing," Aaron said. "Your father worked the area to the west of here on his own several times. Said he found promising signs, but never said anything specific. We've worked everywhere else this side of the river together over the last year. If there's going to be anything, my guess is it's on the other side. But I don't know. There could be nothing there as well."

I nodded. What I'd read in his journal seemed to say the same thing without actually saying it. My father had gone into great detail about his finds on the south side of the river. The artifacts he'd found, all of which were now in Lars' possession.

Except for one golden idol of Amunlea, I thought

wryly.

However, again, by focusing on what he *hadn't* said, I noticed he didn't utter a single word about the other side of the river. Not even a speculation.

Curiouser and curiouser.

CHAPTER THIRTY-FIVE

Something was wrong.

I woke up with a start, looking around frantically, trying to still my thundering heart.

The tent was empty, but from outside, I could hear voices. Light was in the air. Morning had come. I listened for a moment longer, picking out the individual voices of the team members, including Aaron. Nothing seemed amiss. Everyone was calm and going about their morning routines.

Sliding out of the sleeping bag–Aaron *had* provided me my own one of those at least–I quickly dressed, pulling on black hiking pants and a dark blue top that was lightweight but thick enough to stop bugs. It was form-fitting, and I got a few glances from the team members when I emerged, but that was all. They were professionals.

“What is it?” Aaron asked from his crouch by the fire, the first to pick up on my changed mood.

“I’m not sure,” I said, taking deep breaths, trying to calm myself. I needed the thundering in my ears to stop so that I could focus.

Aaron rose to his feet in an easy, fluid movement and walked over to me. His presence was once again like an icy blanket, helping numb my Soulbond, dulling the incessant pull.

I looked at him as the thundering in my ears dulled ever so slightly. Could he know the effect he had on me?

“What is it?” he asked, looking out at the sea of trees surrounding our little campsite. “Did you hear something?”

“No,” I said. “I don’t think so. Just…woke up sharply. Something felt off.”

Aaron stayed nearby for a few moments longer, but when nothing happened, he gestured back at the fire, pulling me over. “Breakfast is ready,” he said, indicating a pot of coffee and some sausage and biscuits that Pieter had put together.

I let him pull me over, ignoring the thrill from his fingers around my arm. Whatever I had sensed when I woke, it was gone. For now.

Snapping up a plateful of food in seconds, I followed it with a cup of bitter black coffee. I hated it that way, but it was better than nothing. Grateful, I thanked Pieter with a nod. While I ate, I continued to look around, trying to figure out what had woken me.

Shortly after breakfast, we forded the river, having walked half an hour to find a suitable spot to cross. We only had to wade through water up to our waists while pulling on a rope that Alexi had secured behind us to keep us in place. It was tricky, the current was strong like Aaron had said, but we made it across without issue. Alexi left the rope behind, tying the loose end to a trunk to provide easy crossing on our return.

I waited for us to proceed, but we just stood around.

"What?" I asked, noticing that most of the team was either staring at me or flicking glances in my direction.

I looked down. My nips were popping out of my shirt thanks to the cold water, but that couldn't be helped, and I really didn't think these men were so immature that they couldn't handle that.

"Why are you all looking at me?"

"They're waiting for you to tell them which way to go," Aaron said. "There are no established places to go on this side of the river. It's all uncharted."

"Oh. Right."

I pondered that question. We were now on the north side of the river, all of which was unexplored territory. We could go any direction. All I had to do was point.

"Let's followed the river for a bit," I said, struck by sudden inspiration. "Keeping northward."

Many ancient cities and civilizations built near rivers. There was a good chance that if we walked the riverbanks, we might come across something.

Aaron nodded, and once more, Alexi lead the way. I fell in step behind him, Aaron at my side, while the others filtered out behind us, with Fred bringing up the rear. I glanced back at him, watching the way he looked behind as much as in front. Was he ex-military, perhaps? I doubted I'd ever get a straight answer from him.

We walked for hours. Twice we came across rocky outcroppings that forced us to move into the forest to get around them before we could continue. We didn't find anything. With each passing hour, I grew more frustrated, more anxious. Where was it? It had to be out here somewhere. My father wouldn't have led me out here otherwise.

"This is pointless, isn't it?" I asked, trying to keep my voice down so the others wouldn't hear. "There's nothing out here. I made a bad decision bringing us here."

Aaron shrugged and signaled for the team to

come to a halt. He looked at me. "What's going on?"

I shied away from the question. "We're not finding anything. This is a wild goose chase. We came out here for nothing."

With a flick of his wrist, Aaron sent the rest of the team on ahead, leaving us alone.

"What is it?" he asked more sharply. "What aren't you telling me?"

I grimaced, unable to stop my eyes from flicking behind us. How did he know, dammit? Aaron was far too perceptible for my liking. I'd been doing my best to ignore it, but as the day wore on, it had been getting harder. Even with Aaron so close by. I was getting distracted because I could feel Johnathan. He was close by and getting nearer by the hour.

"Do you want to take the lead?" I asked. "If you have any suggestions, now's a good time to let me know. Because I don't know if I have any."

"Treasure hunting can be a tedious and boring thing," Aaron explained. "This is one of the things I meant when I said these are dangerous lands. It's easy to get lost but also to get dejected. This valley is hundreds of square miles in size. You could hide dozens of old abandoned cities in here and still walk through without ever seeing signs of one. Don't be so hard on yourself."

"Thanks," I said, his little pep talk helping

to reinvigorate me. He was right. I'd thought it would be easy, simply waltz in, cross the river, and bam, Shuldar would be waiting. Of course, it wasn't going to be that easy. My father had spent years looking. I wasn't going to find it in one morning.

"This is why they pay me the big bucks," Aaron said with a grin. "For my way with words."

I rolled my eyes. "We should keep going."

"Which direction?" Aaron asked.

"Hmmm." I paused to think, but I couldn't come up with anything. My senses were being played with.

Behind me was Johnathan, and my Soulbond reached out to him. It called me, guiding me back the way we had come. Part of me wanted to go that way. But underneath that, far more subtle, was the call of the valley. Something had brought me here, had encouraged me to seek it out, against all logic and reason.

Why? What?

I reached into my mind, shoving my way past the golden warmth of the pulsing Soulbond and to the cool power of my wolf. Whereas the Soulbond was linking me to Johnathan, my wolf *was* me, a part of me. It was a deeper, stronger bond than anything external could ever be. We were *one*, and I called upon her to guide me, to show me the way.

Where do we go? Help me…

I let my wolf in, more than I had on any night except for during the Wild Moons, where she took charge. Where would *she* go if she were free and without the Soulbond?

North.

My feet turned on their own. Away from the edge of the river. Deeper into the forest. Into the unknown.

"That way," I whispered, lifting a finger and pointing. "We go that way."

Aaron followed my finger.

"Looks good to me," he said, whistling to his team, which had stopped far enough ahead to still be in sight but not able to listen. Then, he pointed.

We headed off again, and I hoped like hell I wasn't going crazy, that we actually *would* find something out there.

I followed, growing more uneasy with every step.

CHAPTER THIRTY-SIX

"How far do you think we came today?" I asked Aaron softly while I stared into the fire, mesmerized by the flickering lights of the flames.

"Eight, maybe ten miles," he said.

I blinked. "That's it? We hiked for nearly eight hours."

"Through the forest," he pointed out. "Going up and down hills. Backtracking around that gorge added an hour as well. When you're not moving in a straight line, it takes a lot longer. We probably walked closer to fifteen."

"Oh," I said. "That makes more sense. I guess."

I wasn't really used to this kind of expedition, and it was showing. I didn't ask any more questions that would betray my ignorance. Aaron had been right to call me out on my bluster. This was nothing like living in the country. If it weren't for his team, I would never have made it this far on my own.

My wolf tugged at me, and I glanced upward toward the sky through the canopy of trees. Above, the moon loomed into view, the cloudless skies giving us a beautiful view.

"It's so much brighter out here," I remarked as my wolf stirred again, empowered by that silver orb. Tomorrow night the Wild Moon would be here, and she would be stronger than ever. Until then, however, I was in control still.

That didn't stop her from feeling active tonight. She was like me, frustrated and confused by what we were feeling. Aaron helped to calm it, which is why we were perched on a fallen log, as close to him as we could get without being in his embrace.

If this keeps getting worse the closer the Wild Moon gets, then that just might be where I end up.

The Soulbond and my wolf were a mirror of one another. With only one night to go, I was having a hard time ignoring it. Especially with Johnathan growing closer. I could practically feel him gaining on us with each passing hour. I wondered if he was in his wolf form. That would let him pace us as he saw fit. Watching. Waiting.

But beyond him was that other pull. The unknown.

"Are you okay?" Aaron asked gently.

I needed to do a better job containing my inner turmoil.

"I'm fine," I said, trying to ignore the blatant lie we both knew I was telling.

For a moment, I almost leaned into him to rest my head on his shoulder. I caught myself in time, stiffening my spine to sit straight instead. This was impossible! I needed to be as close to Aaron as possible these days to keep my head clear, but the more time I spent near him, the harder it was to resist the call of my body.

I was being torn in multiple directions, and nothing I'd learned growing up as a wolf shifter had prepared me for something like *this*.

Looking up, I inhaled sharply. Aaron was staring at me. His eyes were brighter than I'd ever seen them before. The moon's silvery glow was catching the blue, giving it a ghostly twist. My throat was dry.

My body craved to be touched. The Wild Moon was always the hardest time of the month to be single. Hormones ran wild during it to help promote female fertility to keep the pack growing.

Right now, I was dealing with those effects while seated next to a man I *knew* could sate all my desires and more. It was obvious, from the way he walked to the curl of his lips. Aaron was an Alpha predator of his own, and a not-insignificant part of me welcomed him, wishing I could replace Johnathan with him.

Even now, as we locked eyes, neither speaking, my throat drier than the Sahara, I could picture how magical it would be to let him have me. Finally, a man who could sate my basest desires by railing me absolutely silly.

If this is what it's like now, how the hell am I going to resist him tomorrow under the full moon?

There was only one answer to that, one solution I could think of that wouldn't result in me giving away the entire existence of my species and perhaps killing some of the team in the process when I shifted and lost control.

I was going to have to be very far away from the camp. Which meant far from Aaron's protection as well. If Johnathan were out here, following us into the wild, I would be exposed. Vulnerable.

"Dani," Aaron said, tearing his gaze away. "We need to talk."

Gulp. "About what?" I asked hoarsely.

Was this it? Was he going to finally acknowledge whatever it was I could feel between us? Perhaps he would lead me out into the forest and take me as his own there, surrounded by the wild. I burned warm between my legs, unable to contain my desires.

"Who is it?"

"Who is what?" I asked, not caring if my words didn't make sense.

My brain was a steaming pile of mush thanks to those eyes, and I impatiently waited for him to get the hint and kiss me already. I no longer cared about his team, about what they might hear or think. I only had the *need*.

“We’re being followed,” he said quietly.

Ice entered his eyes and washed over me like the water of a cold shower, bringing me back from my fantasies of getting laid and plunking me down into reality. Aaron knew. He *knew*. But how?

“How can you know that?” I asked.

“Because,” he said, his eyes flicking around the campfire, “my team is very good at what they do.”

I followed his gaze, noting with surprise that none of his men were sitting looking at the fire. They had their backs to it, staring out into the forest. They were watching. I hadn’t heard Aaron say a thing. They were doing it on their own.

How did I miss that?

At some point, I’d become so wrapped up in myself I’d failed to notice the change in the team.

Johnathan. It had to be Johnathan. These men were used to being in the wilderness. They could sense when something was off. I had a cheat code in terms of my Soulbond, but it was also a blinder. I couldn’t see past it. I couldn’t focus enough on everything else to gain a sense of the world around me. The drums were too strong.

"Who is it?" I asked, wondering if he suspected I was aware of it.

"I'm not sure," he admitted.

He was telling the truth. I was sure of it. That meant he didn't know it was because of me that someone had come out here. *Probably multiple someones. Johnathan wouldn't have come alone. Would he?*

Unless he, too, was being driven by the Soulbond, like me.

"I was hoping you would know," Aaron added when I didn't say anything.

"I don't," I whispered, not sure of what else to say.

"Then, if you don't know who it is, you won't mind if my team takes care of it," Aaron said.

It was a test. He was trying to get me to admit to knowing.

"Deal with it?" I asked, taking the third option open to me, besides admitting or denying any further knowledge. "You mean kill whoever it is, don't you?"

Why did he want to kill whoever it was? Even if I *was* being followed, why would he care? There was no way Aaron could know I was more than just the daughter of a human explorer. So, why immediately choose violence?

Aaron didn't reply. He just looked at me, his face immobile, like it was carved from granite.

He wasn't bothered at all by the idea of violence.

"Why? Are we being pursued by enemies? Do we even have enemies?" I pushed when nobody responded. "I don't have any enemies. How do I know these aren't *your* enemies following us?"

"Exactly," Aaron said tersely. "We don't know that."

That opened my eyes a bit. "Wait. You seriously have enemies, people that would follow you out here, that you'd just up and kill? Without questions?"

Aaron stared stonily, not responding.

"Who the *fuck* are you?" I asked, getting a sick feeling in my stomach. "There's no way you're just treasure hunters. There's more. Are you some sort of mercenary group? Did you drag me into your issues? And why the hell would my father work with you?"

Sighing, Aaron stood. "There's a lot you have to learn yet, Danielle. Now stay seated."

I swallowed nervously. He'd never talked to me like this before. Aaron had always been kind. Calm. Sure, he'd roped me into being his unpaid thug, but he'd always been *nice* about it. This was an entirely different side to him.

One that I didn't like.

"Fred," Aaron said quietly. "Handle it."

Fred stood, and I realized for the first time that he was holding a weapon in his hands.

"Where the hell did that come from?" I yelped. The semi-automatic rifle was far too large to have been the bulge hiding under his shirt I'd seen earlier.

The other members of Aaron's team had procured weapons from somewhere as well, a mixture of rifles and wicked-looking pistols, and in Pieter's tiny hands, a sawed-off shotgun.

"Sit down," Aaron barked as I got to my feet, thinking I should try and stop them.

"What are they going to do?" I asked, still standing.

"They're going to make sure we're safe," Aaron said as the other five members of his team disappeared into the wilderness without a word. "Now, sit *down*."

"No," I said, worried sick for whoever was out there.

I hated Johnathan, his father, too, but I didn't want to see them gunned down in an orgy of blood and death. Not to mention, if they heard Aaron's men coming, the blood spilled wouldn't be that of the shifters. It would be his team. And then, they would come for us next.

Aaron stood, getting in my face. "You are safe, Dani. We're not going to hurt you. Now sit down."

"Call them off!" I shouted, not backing away. "Now!"

"You know who's out there, don't you?" he asked.

"No," I said, not sure why I was sticking with that lie.

Because to tell the truth would mean revealing the secret of what you really are. You can't do that.

"Then my men will continue to ensure our safety," Aaron said coldly.

He didn't like being lied to, but I had no choice. I couldn't just tell him we were being followed by a man who could sense me, thanks to our link, granted to us by the animal that lived inside us. I had to clamp down and hope that Johnathan and whoever he was with decided to avoid trouble instead of seeking out a fight.

I really hope you left your father behind, John. Because he wouldn't see the logic in retreating.

"This is insane," I hissed. "You're insane. I can't believe I trusted you. I want to–"

CHAPTER THIRTY-SEVEN

I blinked, and I was somewhere else.

Somewhere familiar, but certainly not the forest in the valley northeast of Kellar. There were no trees here. No green growth underfoot. No fire. There was nothing.

I was back in the Wasteland, as I'd come to think of it.

"Come *on!*" I shouted angrily. "What is wrong with me? I wasn't sleeping! I was wide awake, damn you. This shouldn't be possible!"

There was no response as usual. I closed my eyes, waiting for the presence of Mr. Mysterious, the giant sex hulk I met on previous journey here. But he must have been busy because nothing happened. There was no change. It was just me.

Eventually, I opened my eyes, deciding maybe

it was better if I didn't blind myself in an unknown land. So far, Mr. Mysterious had come across as friendly, but I really didn't know a damn thing about him, other than that my father had found a drawing of him somewhere. But that wasn't helpful without a name.

I was on top of that same hill I'd climbed my previous visit. In the distance, the giant stone wall and gates rose high into the sky, towering over the bleak, blackened landscape. They were the only non-flat objects around, besides the little hillock upon which I stood.

"Fine," I said. "If I'm stuck here, having a waking hallucination–is it even a hallucination if I'm fully aware I'm having it?–then I may as well go exploring."

As I stared down the hill toward the gates, my boots crunched their way through the brittle landscape, rock crumbling to dust with each step, compressing an inch or two. Looking back, I could easily see my path. It wouldn't be hard to retrace my steps to my starting point.

I walked for what felt like an hour, maybe two, toward the gates, but they never seemed to grow any larger. How big were they? They must be huge.

And what was going on back in the valley? Was Johnathan okay? Was I still standing face to face with Aaron? While I walked, I pondered how time might pass back there. Was this all happening in the blink of an eye? Maybe Aaron didn't even know something was up.

Even as I thought about him, I felt it. The change around me.

"So, you *are* here," I said, turning my head slightly to the side to speak behind me, even as I continued trudging toward the gates in the distance.

"How are you here?" the same smooth bass voice asked. "What are you doing here?"

"I'm not," I said cheerily, clomping along, step after step. "This is a dream. Except now I'm having one while I'm awake, which is really creepy, I have to admit. So, maybe it's not a dream anymore. It's a hallucination. I'm probably going crazy. That's what it is. I should see a shrink. Maybe they can give me some pills, so I stop coming here. Not that I won't miss our fantastic conversations and your complete and total lack of telling me anything helpful about yourself or this place."

Something poked me in the arm hard enough to make me stumble.

"Not a dream," Mr. Mysterious rumbled, moving up next to me with utter stealth. "You feel real enough to me."

I noticed he didn't leave any tracks in the ground like I did. *Definitely a dream.*

"Well, duh," I drawled. "My dream. I control it.

That's why it feels like you really poked me. A part of my subconscious is creating that to try and fool me."

"I am not part of your dream," he rumbled, looking down at me, his long black hair falling forward over his shoulders.

"Then, who are you?" I asked. "Because it seems like you're just some mega-hunk I dreamed up."

I was conveniently ignoring the fact that I'd seen the picture of him in my father's journal. There was an explanation for that, too, though. If he'd ever copied that picture somewhere, somewhere that I'd seen it, then it could just as easily have been in my subconscious waiting to come out.

It was a stretch, but what else was I supposed to think?

As usual, he didn't respond to me. Just stared down from way up high, making me feel small.

"Exactly," I said. "You're Mr. Mysterious and nothing more."

I started walking again. He moved to block me.

"Really?" I said. "Dream, remember?" I kept walking, telling myself I was going to walk through him or that he was going to move.

I rebounded off his chest. His very hard chest.

"Ow!" I yelped, clutching at my nose.

Mr. Mysterious stood there, unmoving, waiting.

"Okay, well, that didn't work out as planned." Pondering the situation, I nodded, stepped *around* him, and kept going. That worked.

"Where are you going?" he asked, falling in step next to me.

"There's no place like home," I said dryly. "I'm pretty sure if I dig past these crunchy rocks, I'll find some yellow somewhere. Which means... shouldn't you be wearing a pointy hat and cackling? Let me hear you cackle."

"No."

"You're no fun," I said with a falsely dramatic sigh. Shaking my head, I continued.

"It's not safe to go this way," the hunky hulk told me.

"Look around you, bub," I said, not slowing. "There's nothing but blackness, crunchy rock, that hill, and those gates. I've been to the hill already. Twice, in fact. It's time I visited somewhere new. I need change. It's good for you. Otherwise, you end up an old crotchety...whatever you are."

Mr. Unknown looked at the ground for a moment, then back at me. "You shouldn't be here."

"Tell me something I *don't* know," I said. "I don't *want* to be here. I don't know how I'm here. But I didn't choose this dream, hallucination, whatever it is."

"Not a dream."

"Fine. What is it then?" I asked, crossing my arms. "Oh, wait, let me guess. You're just going to stay silent."

"Danger is everywhere here."

Now *that* got my attention. Danger everywhere? I hadn't picked up on that. Other than the bleak sense of foreboding that a place as lifeless as this must have, it seemed perfectly normal. The danger was back in the real world, as far as I could tell.

"Danger?" I asked.

He nodded.

"From what?"

More silence, but I swear the depths of his eyes grew a little bluer. Not that I knew what that meant.

"Is the danger getting worse?"

He nodded.

"What can I do?" I asked.

"Nothing," he said without hesitation.

"You sure know how to make a gal feel helpful. So, if I can't help, then why am I here?"

"I don't know," he said, shaking his oversized head, sending his hair flying.

"Some scholar you are," I muttered.

"We must go," he said.

We? That was a new one. Since when had I

been included in his calculations?

"Go where?"

Mr. Mysterious looked away, back the way we came, and his face tightened visibly, tugging at his features. He was worried.

"We've been here too long. We must go. Come."

He reached out to grab me and–

My eyes flew open, and I sat up with a start, breathing heavily.

I was back in normal land. In my tent. My head whipped around sharply enough to give me a cramp as I heard sounds. But it was only Aaron, sleeping soundly next to me.

How the hell did I get back in here? Did Aaron bring me to bed? What happened to me?

Questions filled my brain, but even as I tried to reach out toward Aaron, to shake him awake, sleep rose up like a giant blanket, drawing me down. I yawned, my eyes drooping heavily.

No. I wasn't going to let this happen. I had questions! What had happened to me? What about the rest of his team? Were they back? Where had they gone!

I had just enough energy to search out my Soulbond. It was pulsing inside me. Still there. Johnathan was alive, but the drumming was weaker.

Driven off. They must have driven him off...

CHAPTER THIRTY-EIGHT

I awoke with a start.

The tent was empty. I started to scramble out of it when I realized I was only wearing underwear.

Pause.

Forcing myself to slow down, I got fully dressed, *then* I exited the tent, standing up slowly, taking everything in.

The team was all around, doing their usual morning routines.

Fred was sitting off by himself, silent, contemplating, sipping a cup of coffee while he pondered life, the universe, and everything in between. As usual, Alexi was already packed and looked like he was eager to get started.

A quick glance at the sun told me why.

"How long was I out?" I asked, noting it had to

be approaching noon already.

"All morning," Aaron said with a smile. "You must have been tired yesterday. When you crawled into bed, you were out in seconds."

He came into view as he spoke, keeping his back to the rest of his team. The look on his face implored me to go along with what he was saying.

"Yeah. I guess yesterday really tuckered me out," I said awkwardly. "Sorry, guys, I'm sure you're all bored out of your minds. Someone could have woken me."

"I told them not to," Aaron explained. "You're paying the bills, so you set the pace."

"Right," I said slowly. "But I'm only paying the bills for a few more days, aren't I?"

"Six, by my count," Aaron said.

"Six. So, that's another two days in and four for the way out, if my math checks out."

I didn't receive a response, which told me I was on the right track. Two days. Well, the Wild Moon was tonight, so if we didn't find anything, I suspected I wasn't going to care much past it.

"What happens if we find something?" I asked suddenly, curious. "If we *do* find the ancient city my father was looking for?"

"That depends," Aaron said cagily. "If we find anything worthwhile that can pay the bills, my team will stay."

I frowned. "Your team? What about you?"

"I'm not as concerned about the money as they are," he said.

"So, you'll stay for free?" I asked, surprised.

Aaron laughed. "I'm not a charity worker. But if there are interesting things to be learned, then I'll stay."

"Got it," I said, mulling that over.

Interesting. Aaron wasn't there just for the money. I wondered then why his fee had been so high. To pay for his team and gear, I supposed. But he was just as interested in the knowledge, it seemed. Which was fair. After years working for my father, who was probably rather limited in what he told Aaron, he would know that whatever was out here, there was probably something of value to it. And he wanted in. That seemed fair.

"Now that you're up, if you're feeling good, maybe we should get moving?" Aaron suggested a moment later.

There was no mention of the night before. No mention of his men running off either. All of them had returned, I could see, none looking the worse for wear. So, either they hadn't encountered anything, or the other team had been on the losing end.

"Yeah, let's do that," I said slowly, still trying to regain my mental footing.

We worked in silence to break camp, and then, at a pointed direction from me, we set out again, heading almost due north, guided by nothing more than the pull from a part of me I couldn't identify.

I made sure to fall in step next to Aaron.

"First things first," I hissed. "Did you strip me down last night?"

He shrugged. "You were overheating. It was necessary. I did what any person charged with keeping you alive and in good health would do. I didn't peek if that's what you're worried about. Not that you aren't attractive enough to want to, but I'm a professional."

"You're such a creep, even while being a nice person," I muttered.

Aaron chuckled. "You're welcome, by the way. For taking care of you after you went out."

I winced. "What *did* happen to me?"

He was silent for a moment as we walked. "I'm not sure. You were angry and talking to me all at once, and then suddenly your eyes rolled up into your head, and you collapsed. If it hadn't been for the fact that I needed to catch you, I'd have said you were swooning over me the way you fell and started moaning."

"*Moaning*?" I groaned. "What? You're joking, aren't you?"

Silence.

I looked up to see his mouth twitching violently.

"Asshole," I growled, shaking my head.

"You made no sound at all," Aaron continued. "Just like you'd fallen unconscious. Except you were growing very hot. I pulled you away from the fire, but that didn't seem to do anything. So, I stripped you and laid you on the ground until I heard the team returning. Then, I put you in the tent."

"Thank you," I said. "That was voyeuristically kind of you."

For whatever reason, knowing Aaron had seen my underwear-clad body didn't seem to bother me much. Perhaps it had something to do with all the times I'd imagined him ripping my underwear off me. I wasn't sure, but that *might* have something to do with it. But I wasn't telling.

"I'm still on payroll," Aaron said. "I believe in earning my money, even if I was paid it upfront."

"How noble," I said, switching topics. "How come you didn't listen to my orders last night then? You just sent your death squad out there to kill people."

"Nobody died last night," Aaron said. "But I had to ensure we were safe. That you were safe and without distraction."

It had worked. Although I could feel it growing stronger as we walked, it was clear that Aaron's men had driven Johnathan back, creating more distance between us. For now, hiking in Aaron's shadow, I could remain mostly calm and focused on whatever it was drawing me north.

I was glad Johnathan was still in control of himself, choosing to retreat instead of taking on Aaron's team. The last thing I wanted was to be responsible for bloodshed. Which was why I was going to go tonight. Away from the camp, luring Johnathan away from them. Keep them safe.

It was the least I could do.

We walked north through the afternoon sun. I was thankful for the forest in this part of the valley because the canopy blocked enough light to ensure we weren't roasted. When we crossed a meadow, it beat down upon us, a brutally warm day for late May.

Fred and Dave weren't so happy. Their gear had them sweating. Even Aaron seemed warm, despite the leafy cover.

"Do your men want to stop for a break?" I asked as the day wore on.

"We're getting close to dinner," Aaron said with a shrug. "We're fine."

"Are you sure?"

He smiled. "You've been driving a hard pace. Do you really want to stop now?"

No. I didn't. Whatever was here, it was growing stronger. The longer we walked, the more I could feel it. *Something* was here, and I wanted to get there. That wasn't all, though. Behind us, I could feel Johnathan getting closer. The drums in my head were breaking through Aaron's dead zone once more.

I knew if I didn't keep going, that if we stopped and I sat, the pull to turn back could potentially prove too strong to ignore. Even now, I could feel my shoulder trying to pull me back.

"We continue," I said, pointing ahead at the ridge we had been approaching. "Let's climb this, then see where we're at."

Aaron nodded, and we set off again. The Soulbond pushed aside for the time being. It didn't like that. With each foot I put forward, each step higher up the ridge, it pushed harder. My wolf whimpered inside me, and the call of whatever was in front of us wavered and faded.

No, I told her. *We're not giving up. Not now. Got it? That Soulbond is bad news. We're ignoring it.*

She shivered, and I could feel her being pulled back by a force stronger than herself.

"No," I repeated, gritting my teeth and forcing my legs forward. "Not happening."

"Dani?" Aaron asked, but I shouldered him aside, bulling my way up the side of this ridge.

"We're so damn close. I am *not* going back to that asshole now just because you're *weak!*" I shouted, elbowing Dave out of my way.

Alexi took one look at me as I came and stepped aside before I made him move.

I continued my charge up the ridge while my wolf went berserk inside me. She could no longer handle being separated from her Soulmate. We had to go back. *She* had to go back.

But I wouldn't let her.

Growling, I pushed onward, legs churning as tunnel vision narrowed the world around me to the path ahead. Getting to the top of the ridge was all that mattered! I had to get there. I had to show myself that I could do it. That no sissy wannabe-Alpha from my hometown was stronger than me.

I could choose my *own* destiny. And it did not involve Johnathan.

The slope increased as I got nearer to the top, and I fell to all fours, moving in an ungainly climb that had my wolf cringing at its awkwardness. She could do so much better.

"No!" I cried as she surged forward unexpectedly, taking advantage of my mind being torn in half by the unknown call in front of me and the driving force of the Soulbond behind.

I reached the top of the ridge at the same moment she started to burst free. Resisting as hard as I could, I pushed forward. Another step.

"Dani!" Aaron called from behind me. "Dani, wait!"

I didn't stop and went right over the top–and fell straight down the far side, the sheer face of it surprising me. Distracted as I fought off my wolf, there was no stopping us from going over.

We fell ten feet or more. My foot got caught on something as we went down, and I flipped over.

There was just enough time to scream before I smashed my face into a rock at the bottom.

CHAPTER THIRTY-NINE

When I awoke, it was too late. The Wild Moon had arrived.

I was in my tent, with a bandage pressed to my forehead. Getting to my feet, I crawled out of my sleeping bag, searching for the exit.

"Whoa," I mumbled as the world spun a bit.

My wolf howled inside me. She was on edge. I didn't have long. I had to get away from Aaron and his team to ensure they remained safe.

Uncaring of what they might see, I tore my way from the tent. I was greeted by the sight of Aaron and his team shooting to their feet from where they sat around a campfire. Night was here, and above me, the full moon was almost in the sky. I had mere minutes, if that.

"Dani?" Aaron asked, holding out a hand to

hold back his team.

I looked at him, then turned and started going the other way. I had to reach the bush. I pulled my shirt off as I went, uncaring of the scratches from the trees as I ducked past one.

A hand closed around my wrist, spinning me around.

"*Dani,*" Aaron said, staring at me, his eyes bright and blue, even in the dark.

I stared at my wrist. Holy *fuck,* that was hot. I yanked him in close, ready to kiss him, when something stopped me.

Overhead, the Wild Moon burst over the horizon, and the change came.

"*Stay away from me,*" I snarled inhumanly, shoving him away from me.

Aaron stumbled backward and fell, a look of shock on his face as I used more strength than perhaps I should have.

There was no time. I ran, tearing at the waistband of my pants and underwear, leaving them loose. My sports bra came over my head, nearly pulling fur with it as I started to change.

Somewhere behind me, I could hear Aaron barking commands, but I didn't have the wherewithal to pay attention to whatever he was saying.

It was *time,* and my wolf was pushing free with a vengeance. My body screamed with pain as she tore free, agony nearly causing us to black-out as we merged, the scream becoming a howl at the moon. We were one once more. Two minds melded.

From nearby, the howl was echoed by another wolf.

Run, we thought, bursting into a long lope that covered ground faster than any human could ever begin to keep up with. We went on and on, thankfully headed away from Aaron and the campfire. For whatever reason, we didn't want to go back there.

Scents by the thousands entered our brain, instantly catalogued. We passed within a few dozen feet of a weak doe. *No challenge.* The droppings of a grizzly whose territory we'd entered warned us to stay alert. A mouse darted by ahead, too fast even for us. A rabbit burst from cover, heading the opposite direction, but we didn't give chase to that. Something else was calling to us, even as an owl swooped by a hundred yards to the west of us, its scent brought to us by the gentle breeze.

Mate.

The thought filtered through us as another howl echoed from nearby.

It was him, we realized. Our Soulmate. The Soulbond was stronger than ever under the Wild Moon, and though we longed to run free and stretch our legs, we couldn't help but be intrigued by this call. A second, fainter call from the north reached out to us, snagging our interest as well.

We paused, intrigued by this new call. It was different from our Soulbond. That was warm and golden and a sense of completeness. This new call was cool and purple and spoke of power. Something we understood well. The strongest ruled.

Pawing at the ground, we whimpered with indecision. What should we do? Where should we go? For so long, we'd waited for the Wild Moon and the Soulbond, to fulfill that calling denied to us by that pesky two-legged part of us.

But now, this new scent tickled our nostrils, urging us to come to it. To find out what it promised. We were curious. We wanted to explore. The Wild Moon would last for hours. We could find our mate under the silver light later.

Turning north, we ran onward, spurred by some unknown sense of urgency. We *had* to get to whatever it was.

We crested a ridge with ease and ran downward, the trees thinning. We reached a meadow filled with wildflowers and tall grasses, swaying gently under the breeze, silver moonlight giving the open space an ethereal glow.

Two steps into the meadow, we came to a halt, looking around warily. Something was off. Testing the air, we scented what it was.

Mate!

Taking a few steps forward, we hopped onto a rocky outcropping, surveying the area around us.

Ahead, between us and our goal, six wolves stood, waiting. Watching.

One of them was Johnathan, and we howled at the moon with joy. Our mate was here! We could be Soulbound at last and together explore this new power. Together we could rule, as it should be.

We took one step forward, and I launched an all-out attack on my wolf. We split, our minds tearing as I struggled to fight her. To convince her that something was *wrong*. That it wasn't what it seemed.

I lost the first battle as we hopped down from the rock, trotting forward a few steps, but my frantic efforts were gaining ground. I had the stronger willpower. My wolf was powered by the Wild Moon, nothing more. I could break it. I could break her.

I had no other choice.

Throwing all my defiant, stubborn, angry will at her, I slapped my wolf's personality right in the end of her sensitive snout. She yelped, and the hammer blow I got in return was worse than any punches I'd taken in the ring. It left me reeling, and we moved forward some more, slow paces.

This is wrong! I shouted the words mentally. *He's not here for you or us. Look at him. He hasn't howled back. He hasn't come forward. It's a trap!*

My wolf didn't believe me. She wanted to go to him. To nuzzle snouts and enjoy the warmth of the evening underneath the wild moon. Together. A pair. She wanted to forge the Soulbond.

Look around. This isn't what you think, I screamed, even as my wolf looked up to the sky, drinking in the power of the Wild Moon.

We merged once more, but even as we did, something was different. The struggle to tear us away from our Soulmate had given us time to think, to look. We watched the other wolves, our mate's pack. We saw the way their claws dug into the dirt. Their eyes were focused on us with preternatural intensity.

The focus of everyone was on us. But they were wary. Prepared. Our two-legged mind was right. This wasn't a welcome party.

It was a trap.

Even as we thought it, the wolves began to fan out, blocking our path northward. They weren't going to join us, we knew now. They were here to stop us.

CHAPTER FORTY

The giant black beast at the center, his fur the opposite of ours, darkness to our light, the one who should be our mate, bared his teeth and growled.

We were shocked. He had bared his teeth. At *us*. A challenge to his *mate*. Angrily, we snapped at him, making our displeasure known. It was clear now he'd somehow fought the Soulbond. Was actively denying it. How, we didn't know, but it didn't matter. We couldn't let it matter.

If we stayed, we would be in danger. At his mercy, and judging by the snarling, snapping threats from the rest of his pack, there wouldn't be much mercy at all. Just death.

They were here to kill us, nothing more. We knew we couldn't take on all six, not together. They were bigger and stronger than us.

Run.

We're not sure where the thought came from, but it was a smart one. It was the only idea we had. With the power of the Wild Moon behind us, we would run for our lives. It was our only hope.

Fixing our mate with one final glare, we turned and bolted. Not back the way we had come. The humans we traveled with, *they* hadn't snarled at us. Hadn't threatened us. If they had, we would have torn them to shreds. We knew we could. They were no match for us. Not tonight.

So, we ran east, where the Wild Moon was high in the sky, making its journey across the heavens. Like the very wind itself, we ran, swift and eager, surging forward with all the speed we could muster.

Behind us, our mate howled, and they gave chase.

We snorted with laughter. There was no way they could catch us. Too fleet of foot we were as we raced onward, paws digging into the dirt, clumps occasionally thrown into the air behind us. We were leaving a track that couldn't be missed, but there was no other choice. To move with stealth would rob us of desperately needed speed.

Besides, with the Soulbond, our mate would find us anywhere. We couldn't escape him. It would be a chase, for all eternity, us running for our lives, him behind us, that giant sable-furred mongrel. Only, if he caught us, we would no longer enjoy a life of happiness together. He wanted us dead.

We'd like to see him try.

On we ran, the pack behind us. Our ears told us that our pursuers were getting strung out. Space was developing between them. Only our mate could keep pace, the others fell behind bit by bit. We knew we couldn't outrun him. But perhaps if we ran long enough, hard enough, we could find time to settle our differences.

Privately.

The moon continued to rise, falling off to our right flank as we headed north.

North?

We didn't recall deciding to turn north. Yet, we were. Our course had changed. At some point, we had stopped running *from* our mate and had begun following the call ahead of us. That elusive power, its call so different from that of our Soulbond. It pulled at us, summoning us.

Our claws dug deeper. We ran on, somehow finding another gear as we slipped between trees, dodged bushes, and leaped over fallen trunks.

We were going to find what called to us. No matter what else happened, we were going to discover what it was. Before our mate tried to kill us.

All at once, we burst from the edge of the forest, the thick undergrowth at its edge concealing the end of the trees until we were out in the open, running down what appeared to be a path. It ran straight and true.

Like a street.

I came skidding back to my senses, the meld snapping us apart as I directed the massive wolf's head to drift from side to side, giving me a better idea of what I was looking at.

We were on a road. It had to be. A road, or path, something that had been *built*. The stones there, to my left. Those had been worked. Right angle corners like that, built over multiple levels, weren't natural. Tools had done this. Intelligent minds.

My wolf let me hear it at that last comment, but I was too stunned by what I saw as we ran onward to notice.

People had *lived* here.

Behind me, Johnathan howled. I ran down the boulevard, noting that it headed straight at the face of the mountain ahead of us, a sheer vertical cliff rising high, towering over the remains of what could only be Shuldar. The lost city of shifters.

This had to be it. I'd found it. Finally!

It wasn't all for nothing, Dad.

Of course, it might still be if I didn't survive the night. Behind me, I could hear Johnathan closing. I couldn't slow now. Otherwise, he'd catch up. So together, with my wolf guiding us, we ran onward. In the open, though, our advantage of agility was negated. He was bigger, faster, and we couldn't outrun him.

Nor were we going to make it to the source of the calling first. He was going to catch us before we got there. I needed to do something else.

With our mate now snapping at our heels, I told her to turn. We skidded around a corner onto a more overgrown path, a side street perhaps, and raced onward, claws scraping across stone. We listened as Johnathan grew closer and closer. He was right behind us now, only a few lengths back.

My wolf abruptly darted us to the side, and I only belatedly reacted as his jaws swept through where our leg had been. The move cost us time, however, and Johnathan came up on our side and slammed into us.

We tumbled and rolled, crashing through a brick wall. A wall! This had been a building. People had lived here, built this place!

I had no time to appreciate it, however, since Johnathan appeared at the entrance, his yellow eyes glowing in the darkness. I looked up to see a tree growing thick overhead, acting as a makeshift roof.

The giant wolf came forward, taking a step as we got to our feet. This was it. There was no time left. We had to fight.

Bracing ourselves, we snarled at him. Told him

we hated him. That he was a coward.

Johnathan bared his teeth and took a step toward us just as the floor shook beneath us.

Reacting faster than us for once, Johnathan scrambled backward as the ground around us collapsed, dropping our small form while he stayed high.

We landed among the rubble, and I tore my brain free from the meld again, looking around frantically. We weren't injured from the fall, and I got up to all fours. We were in a tunnel. I wasn't sure if it were natural or manmade, but I could see both sides of it.

Above me, Johnathan growled and jumped down to an outcropping. He was still coming after us. That bastard!

Picking an option, I bolted down the tunnel entrance, claws scrabbling around wildly on the hard floor. It was tough to pick up much traction, but it didn't matter. I'd gone perhaps twenty feet when I nearly ran into a cave-in, my wolf eyes having a hard time seeing with the lack of light this deep in.

I turned and ran back, narrowly evading Johnathan as he leaped the last twenty feet down to the ground, jaws snapping for us. The other tunnel went on for some time, and for a moment, I thought we were going to escape.

I rounded a corner and accelerated, heading

for–

Without warning, I smashed face-first into an unseen barrier, coming to an abrupt and very painful stop. My wolf body collapsed to the floor, yelping in pain.

Behind us, Johnathan came around the corner, his deep rumble filling the hallway. I backed up as he came toward me, saliva dripping from his jaws. I locked eyes with him, and what I saw terrified me.

He's lost his mind, I realized when intelligence didn't stare back at me. The thing wasn't Johnathan. It was a feral beast. With only one mission.

Kill me.

He took a step forward, and I backed up, but I couldn't go anywhere. The invisible barrier blocked my path. It was a dead end.

Literally.

CHAPTER FORTY-ONE

Desperately, I tried to push through the barrier. I fought with all my might, straining against it as claws slowly click-clacked their way toward me.

I didn't want to die here. Nor did I want to fight him. I couldn't submit to it either. Meanwhile, my wolf was frantic, searching for some solution. She still wanted to throw herself at him, accept the Soulbond and live the life we dreamed of growing up. But just by looking at him, she knew that this wolf wasn't going to let us live. We would never have that life.

For different reasons, we both knew we had to get away from him. In this, we were on the same page at long last. The irony of that wasn't lost on me. That when it was too late, we were able to work together.

We shoved harder as terror overtook us, a

wave of never-ending fear as our doom approached us, stalking us, *torturing* us with his slow approach. It gave us nothing but time to contemplate our end as we dug our claws deep into the ground, straining.

There! It gave an inch, compressing ever so slightly. I swear I had felt it give on this latest push.

I still couldn't see what was stopping us, though. The tunnel was clear ahead, but we simply could not pass. It was blank. Like an invisible wall. After that first inch, nothing happened. It was like pushing against steel.

Hopeless.

Which meant escape was no longer an option. We were going to have to stand. And fight. I bowed out to my wolf at this, opting to ride in the back seat of our mind while she took control. If we were going to have *any* hope of escaping with our lives and our fur intact, it would be because of her.

Not that I held much hope. I'd shifted precisely *once* outside of the now nine Wild Moons that had passed since my twenty-first birthday and my first Soulshift. Johnathan, on the other hand, had been shifting for nearly two years. He and his wolf were much more in tune with one another.

But I had to try. *We* had to try.

As we turned, an icy spike of fear choked off any sound we might have made. He was less than ten feet away, a huge, furred form, fangs out, saliva dripping from them as he snarled and growled.

We can't win in a straight fight. We need to surprise him. Do something he won't be ready for. Submit!

I sent the idea to my wolf, telling her to let go. To bow down to the junior Alpha and truly submit. To open herself to him.

She resisted. If we did that, she wouldn't come back. He would overwhelm her with his Alpha power, and she would be as good as dead. A puppet to him.

I'll protect you, I said, reaching out to shield her mind with my own, a layer of defense.

It was our only hope.

My wolf didn't like it, but I wasn't sure how we had any other choice. It was this and probably die or don't do this and *definitely* die. Any chance was a good one right now.

So, she obeyed. She pressed down to the ground, meek and willful, opening herself up to his power. The Alpha's command flooded us, and I groaned mentally at the strain as it battered our shared mind like a typhoon raging against us.

My wolf retreated behind the mental shield I'd erected, whimpering and hurt.

But alive.

I had no idea how I was doing what I was, but it worked. Johnathan came to a stop, three feet in front of us, relaxed and confident that he could do with us as he pleased. He snarled and came for our neck.

Releasing the shield, my wolf sprang back to herself and surged through the body. We purged it of the foreign power, and my wolf went on the attack. She lunged at him, going for his neck, trying to end the fight in one swift move.

It was the wrong move. He was too strong. His jaws came around in a flash, and hot pain erupted down our side as his teeth sank deep. We yelped and rolled, paws coming up and tearing at his side as we fought to break free. It didn't help. Johnathan's grip was too strong.

With a blinding display of power, he hauled us around and let go, tossing us back down the hallway until our rump bumped up against the barrier. We got to our feet, blood dripping down our right flank.

Johnathan was done playing. He came toward us, step by step, waiting for us to attack. We did, darting to our right, shielding our wounded side, and going for the empty space in an attempt to get past him.

We went down in a heap together, the pair of us rolling, yipping, and snarling. Blood flowed from a dozen cuts on us, and our fur was rapidly becoming drenched in our lifeforce.

At one point, we took a paw to the snout, ripping part of it open. Retreating in pain, we returned to the barrier, breathing hard, exhausted from the fighting, our flanks heaving, foam dripping from our mouth. We were beaten. We could barely stand up, the blinding agony and pain rendering us nearly unconscious.

Our right paw gave way, and we leaned on the barrier, pressing our side to it–

And we fell right through it, landing in a heap, rolling to our feet.

Johnathan snarled and charged, and we backed away, rock crunching underfoot, only to watch as he slammed face-first into the invisible, impenetrable barrier.

The barrier through which we just passed.

CHAPTER FORTY-TWO

We stared in shock, our snout mere inches from the snarling, yellowed teeth of Johnathan's muzzle. Yet, for all his might, he and his midnight-furred beast could not break through. The barrier separated us, with him on one side and us on the other.

But there was still a chance he could come through. We would have to take advantage of our head start.

Turning slowly, we limped our way up the tunnel, flanks still rising and falling quickly. It was a short walk, leading us out onto a ledge underneath the starry sky. Turning back, we could still see Johnathan pacing along the edge of the invisible barrier. His eyes stared at us with helpless fury, promising more pain if he made it through.

We looked up at the sky, a feeling of ease washing over us as we sat weakly, nearly falling over again. There was a beauty in the sparkling skyscape, the stars twinkling against the unknown darkness beyond. A vastness that was incomprehensible.

"How did you do that?"

We turned to see Johnathan standing on two legs, naked, his chest still heaving from the exertion of our fight.

Shaking our head at him, we looked back up at the sky. There was no moon in sight here. Was that why we felt so at ease? The Wild Moon had somehow passed by us during the flight through the underground tunnels and our fight. How much time had passed? It seemed like a lot. Too much, even.

"Get back here, Dani," Johnathan snapped. "We have a lot to talk about."

We sneezed at him, expressing our disdain for that statement. Talking was the last thing he wanted to do, and we weren't stupid enough to fall for it. Even now, naked and walking around so ungainly on his two legs, we could see he was prepared for more violence. A predator's body language was unmistakable to another's.

"How did you get through this? Let me through."

Staring at him, we huffed a breath. The truth was, we had no idea. We'd simply been leaning against it one moment and falling through it the next. Like it wasn't there. It had vanished for us, but we couldn't explain why.

Nor were we going to shift back to explain that to him. Firstly, he didn't deserve that from us, not after what he'd tried. Secondly, we felt comfortable in this form. Safer, in a place we didn't know.

"This won't last," Johnathan threatened. "I *will* find you again."

We looked at Johnathan, our head tilting to the side as we searched for him in our core. For the bond that would let him track us anywhere we went.

Our eyes went wide. It was gone! Somehow, the barrier had cut the connection between us, relieving us of that horrible, horrid drumming that had filled our mind and soul with its incessant whispering to accept him as our mate.

That was the peace we felt. The sense of calm and relief that had washed over us mere seconds after falling through the barrier. It was the blocking of our Soulbond.

Blocking? Or elimination?

We didn't know. But this, we knew, this was what we wanted now. And forever. No more calling from within, no more pushing us to be with someone else. We desired freedom most of all. Choice.

"If you come back now, peacefully," Johnathan said from his side of the barrier, "I might be able to help you. To protect you from my father. But you *have* to come back through now. I'll make sure my father lets us be together."

Looking around, we surveyed our little tunnel exit. There didn't *seem* to be anyone else there. We couldn't sense anything. It felt safe...

I pulled away from the meld, taking control once more, forcing my body through the shift. Gritting my teeth, I held back any pained sounds. Normal shifting was hard enough, but the wounds on my body carried from one form to the other, and now I had my mind alone to block the pain instead of the two of us working together.

It *hurt*.

The rest of Johnathan's pack chose that moment to come trotting around the corner. Several of them made appreciative noises at seeing my nude form. I opened my mouth to say something, but to my utter surprise, Johnathan beat them to it.

He whirled on his pack and kicked the nearest one in the snout before grabbing the next by the scruff and slamming him hard to the ground. It was the most Alpha, dominant thing I'd ever seen him do, and a part of me wished he could have been like that *from the start.*

It was too late for such gestures now.

"I'm not going back with you," I said once his attention returned to me. "I'm sorry I stole the Idol of Amunlea, but I needed the money, and that was the only way to get it in time. It wasn't anything personal."

Johnathan nodded. "My father did not take it well."

"What *does* your father take well except for complete and utter obedience?"

His eyes narrowed defensively. "My father expects his pack to respect him."

I laughed. "Your father demands loyalty. A good leader works hard to earn it. Your father is a cowardly tyrant. There's no other way to describe him. Respect is *earned*, Johnathan, not demanded. I'm sorry to hear you say that."

"Regardless, if you come back through and go to him with me, I can soothe him over," Johnathan said, declining to respond to my points about his father.

I eyed the other wolves, none of whom looked very inclined to permit me to come through peacefully. They all had violence about them. Even if I knew *how* to cross over, if I did, they would go for the kill before letting me go back to Seguin.

In fact, I can probably never go home again after what I've done. Never see Jo or my old boss, Frannie. That life is gone now, torn away from me, like my parents.

"Listen carefully, Johnathan," I said, trying to sound tougher than I felt, given I was naked and half covered in my own blood. "I am not going with you. I am not coming back. Not now, not ever. I need you to understand that."

"In that case," Johnathan said. "I have orders to kill you."

I laughed, the sound sending stabbing pains through my side. "No *shit*."

He growled at me.

"I'm pretty sure you had those orders no matter what. Or, if you didn't, one of *them* did," I accused, pointing at his little pack of enforcers.

Johnathan looked surprised, glancing at the other wolves, none of whom would meet his eye.

I laughed. Take that, you asshole. Enjoy knowing I was right, that dear old Dad was plotting and conspiring behind your back because he didn't think you were good enough. Didn't think you were *strong* enough to carry out his orders. I'm sure that lack of trust won't hurt your relationship.

Johnathan snarled wordlessly at his pack, demanding answers, but none of them responded. All of them stared at me, unmoving.

No, I realized as Johnathan turned back around, letting me read the expression on his face. They were staring *past* me.

Because I wasn't alone anymore.

CHAPTER FORTY-THREE

One moment there was nothing, and the next, his presence slammed into and past me.

Before I could turn, I watched as blue fire appeared between Johnathan and me, rising from the floor until it obscured the other side from view, an opaque wall of blue energy that stayed in perfect position.

Grimacing, I turned slowly, fervently wishing for some clothes and a magic potion that would restore me to health. If it *wasn't* who I thought it might be, then I was in deep, deep trouble.

It wasn't.

"Uh, hi," I said, desperately trying to cover up as I stared at the enormous creature staring at me.

It had to be over eight feet tall. Blue fire burned all over his body, but most forcefully from his eyes. They were twin orbs of swirling flame focused entirely on me and my completely and utterly exposed skin. The flames flickered in and out over his body, that heavy mass of muscle that glistened in the ghostly white light of this place.

He was dressed in nothing but a pair of gray sweatpants, that had *no* business fitting someone of his size, and a pair of dark black boots. Nothing over his waist, revealing a delicious V-line that disappeared into the edge of his sweats. It was far too sexy a sight to be considered anything less than a turn-on.

With his looks came his *presence*, a sense of power and demand that made me shiver. I pressed the ends of my nipples into my arm as I desperately tried to stay covered up in front of... whoever this was.

He stared at me, unspeaking for a long time. The thick, heavy silence was broken only by my labored breathing as I struggled not to moan at the heavenly sight before me.

I had no idea who this Giant Sex Machine was, but my body wanted him something *bad*, and worst of all, even my wolf was begging me to throw myself at him. Which was entirely weird because I had no idea if he was going to help me or eat me. And not in the good way. For all I knew, this creature could quite literally burn me in his fire to a nice medium-rare and have Dani-strips for dinner and leftovers.

Though the more I focused on him, the more I realized I didn't *feel* in danger. He was giving off mega-power vibes something fierce, but nothing else. Certainly not the terror I felt when I'd been staring down Johnathan and his pack.

At some point, his mouth started moving, but I only heard a dull roar in my ears, nothing more. I couldn't focus on anything but him. My body was ready. Right here, right now, and that should have scared me, how easily he could have what he wanted from me, but it didn't.

It just excited me more.

His lips moved some more. I watched them, wondering what they would feel like on me. Would they burn, like the fire that covered him from head to toe? Or would they be as pleasant to the touch as they were to look at? Like everything else about him.

"Pardon?" I hear myself say when his mouth stopped moving.

I just wanted to watch him talk. I was so wrapped up in it I could probably masturbate to it. Which said a lot about my dreadfully nonexistent sex life, I'm afraid.

"Who are you?"

This time the fire-man's question came through enough that I could understand him. I stared back, trying to discern more facial features through the hue of fire that covered him, but it was nigh impossible.

"Who are *you*?" I asked back instead of answering his question.

"Why are you here?" he repeated. "Who are you?"

I shook my head. "Who are you? *Where* am I?"

Behind us, a third voice entered the conversation. Well, more a sound than anything. Growling rumbled through the tunnel. Turning, I saw the flames dulling over the barrier, Johnathan's face visible from the other side.

He had both hands planted on the barrier, and I realized with a laugh that he was trying to impose his will on this…man. Being. Creature.

I laughed harder. It was pathetic to watch. Whoever the being was, he was a thousand times more alpha and impressive than Johnathan could *ever* be. And he'd done nothing but speak to me. It wasn't even a contest.

When I looked at Johnathan, I could admit he was a handsome male. Tall, good facial structure, muscular. He was not hard on the eyes. But I viewed it in a dispassionate, detached, almost clinical manner.

Whereas when I looked at the newcomer, I wanted to *submit* to him, stranger or not. I practically ached for him to bend me over right there in the tunnel entrance or force me to my knees. I wanted to be *his*, even having no idea who or what he was. My body was on fire simply from his presence.

There could not have been a starker contrast between those who *expected* submission and those who *earned* it. Giant Sex Machine was an Alpha, a dominant force of nature, who earned submission by sheer presence.

Johnathan was an angry shifter who had never truly learned to become an adult. I would never look at him the same.

"*Leave her alone*," Johnathan barked through the barrier as he managed to gain enough space to talk. His voice was strained with effort, though. I didn't know how he was shoving the fire aside, but in a battle of wills, if Giant Sex Machine focused on him, Johnathan would lose in a nanosecond.

"Stop it," I said to Johnathan. "You can't fight him."

"Like hell I can't. She's *mine*, you asshole!" Johnathan snarled. "Remove this barrier and face me yourself. Coward."

I gasped and darted to the side of the tunnel as the giant man-thing's eyes flared so bright with blue flame that it lit up the entire tunnel and forced me to shield my eyes.

"Stop it, Johnathan," I snapped angrily as the fire faded.

"No. This coward won't face me because he's

afraid I would win," Johnathan said tautly, staring at the giant behind me.

"Yeah, I don't think that's it," I said, looking over my shoulder as the stranger hauled back a fist and casually punched a boulder out of the wall, hammering at an outcropping until a piece of rock the size of my torso fell into his hands.

He hefted it casually and then, with surprising speed and grace for someone his size, hurled it so fast past my head the air screamed. Johnathan had no time to duck aside, but it didn't matter because the rock shattered into a thousand pieces against the barrier.

The creature grunted, a sound that was almost…surprised? I wasn't sure, but that seemed like the best description. Perhaps mixed with some disappointment, too.

"What were you expecting to happen?" I asked the giant.

"Just that," he says, and this time I definitely picked up disappointment. "Though, I'd hoped otherwise."

I looked at Johnathan, who otherwise would have been pummeled with the rock.

"Yeah, me, too," I agreed. "That would have been nice."

He looked at me, forced to crane his neck way down. The fire still obscured everything above his lips, with only those blue eyes burning brightly enough for me to separate them from the rest of his face.

"What now?" I asked. "Do you kill me? Is that your next objective?"

That got me a strange look.

"No," the fire-being said. "Now, we go from here."

"We do? Where do we–*Oh*," I gasped as he reached down and threw me over his shoulder.

I had to stifle an unprompted moan at the sudden move, his muscles and dominance once more setting off an arousal in me that I couldn't seem to get under control.

Then, we *poofed*.

CHAPTER FORTY-FOUR

The arousal died the second we snapped back into reality.

"Oh, god," I moaned, wriggling desperately to get out of his grip as my stomach roiled and heaved.

Falling to the floor, I dry retched, begging myself furiously not to puke in front of the giant fire-sex-man-thing. I didn't want that embarrassment. My wolf agreed, but she did nothing to help, simply content to watch and admire the Alpha, ready to do exactly as he said, whenever he said it.

She'd already decided whom to submit to.

Moments later, my stomach settled so quickly I nearly lost control from the swiftness of it.

"What the *fuck* was that?" I swore, leaping to my feet. "Vir's Oath, man, you can't just *poof* people like that without warning."

I wanted to get really good and mad at my captor, to show him my fury, but it was hard when I only came to his shoulders. I'm no wimp in the height department, but this guy was *massive*, towering above me without even trying. There was no way I was intimidating him.

His fire faded with my fury, however, revealing the face of my abductor at last. I looked up–all the way up–and gasped.

"*Holy fuck!*" I shouted, backing away in stunned amazement. "You? *You're* fiery demon thing?"

"I'm no demon," Mr. Mysterious rumbled.

It was him. The man from my dreams. Tall, handsome, dark hair spilling to his shoulders, and eyes of a blue so rich it defied comprehension. Just like everything else about him.

"It's you," I said, feeling slightly faint. "You're here. You came. From my dreams. Now you're here."

"Actually, you've got it somewhat wrong," he said.

I raised an eyebrow. "Come again?"

"I didn't come to you," he corrected. "You came to me. To my world."

"Your world?" I said, voice failing me on the last syllable. "Where *are* we? This isn't my dream."

Giant Sex Machine shook his head, sending that beautiful, shiny hair of his flying. "I was never in your dreams. You came here. Visited."

"And now I'm here for real," I said, trying to comprehend what he was telling me.

"Yes."

"And it's you. You're the same person?" I was going in logic circles, but I didn't care. I think those sorts of things are excused when you're transported to another world.

"Yes."

"But why? How?" I asked. "I don't understand."

"Neither do I," he said, looking troubled. "But your presence will have attracted attention."

I recalled the empty, desolate nature of his world. "Attention? From whom? There's nobody else out there."

Dream Man, or was it Dreamy Man? I didn't know yet, didn't respond to my question. Apparently, some secrets were still his to keep.

"Where are we anyway?"

"A safe place," he rumbled, waving a hand around.

I really focused on the room we were in. I'd been so overwhelmed by everything that had happened that I hadn't really processed any of it.

We were in the center of a circular room, standing on a stone platform. There were faint lines written in the rock below us, which I figured must be some sort of runes, which allowed him to do that stomach-churning *poof* trick. Three wooden bridges, perhaps eight feet long, arced up and over a flowing river of water that split around the platform.

A variety of plants grew along the banks, adding flowers and color to the room. The walls and ceiling were rock, which meant, I assumed, we were underground. I continued turning.

"Oh, *wow*," I said, suitably impressed at the roaring fire in the middle of a semi-circle of seats and couches, all of which were laid out in front of two long walls full of books, meeting at a sharp corner. "Now *that* is a private library. Damn."

"I'm glad you approve," Mr. Mysterious said with a chuckle.

It was the first positive sound I'd heard from him. Maybe he wasn't going to kill me for intruding on his solitude after all.

"Absolutely," I said, noting an area near the reading chairs filled with more personal items. Some tokens, statuettes, paintings, and even a giant tapestry that hung from the rock wall and marked the outer edge of his lair, for lack of a better word.

Across the underground river, there was an area filled with what could only be workout equipment. Weights, dummies holding weapons, things of that nature. I'm not sure why he needed that, considering he could shoot fire and use his fists to carve rock, but I wasn't about to ask.

"Shit, where were you a week ago?" I said, staring at the next area. It was piled high with gold coins and bars while the firelight flickered off items that reflected blue, green, even red. Precious stones, they had to be. Rubies, emeralds, sapphires.

It wasn't all treasure, though. Rows of weapons lay racked against the wall. Swords, spears, suits of armor, whose origins I didn't recognize, and more. Some of it didn't even look human.

I had to admit, his lair was impressive and had a sense of grandeur about it, despite its welcoming, and almost cozy, feeling. Somehow, he managed to combine it all.

"Where *is* this place?" I repeated.

"It's safe," he assured me. "Somewhere you can rest. And recover."

"Recover?" I asked, tearing my gaze away from the library to stare back at Mr. Mysterious.

"From your wounds?" he said, pointing at my side.

I glanced down at my side, all at once reminded that I'd been badly wounded in my fight with Johnathan. Somehow, the adrenaline of being kidnapped and brought here had pushed the pain to the back of my mind, distracting me from its ache.

Not anymore. It came rushing back, and I gritted my teeth. "Right. That."

Which came with *another* realization. I was still naked. And I'd been standing here. In his presence. Without a care. Letting him get a full look at my completely naked body.

I clapped my hands to my body, trying to hide my tits from him while I crossed my leg in front of the other, desperate to try and regain some sort of decency. The fact that I was half-streaked in blood didn't do much.

"Do you have a shower?" I asked, eager to get the blood off me first and foremost.

Mr. Mysterious shrugged and pointed to the back corner, where water fell from an unseen crack in the wall, the start of the river.

"Right," I said, noting that it was completely exposed. Of course it was. "You don't have anything, um, more *private*, do you?"

"Why would I?"

I sighed. "Of course not."

"Why does it matter? The water will clean you." He frowned at me, his lips compressing into a line.

"Because I'm *naked*," I said, stressing the last word.

"That hasn't bothered you until now."

"Well, until now, I was kind of trying not to puke, then busy trying to figure out what the hell is going on. It...didn't seem like a priority," I said weakly.

It was easier to say that than it was to explain how my hormones were driving me wild, begging me to throw myself at this beautiful sex god and beg him to take me, touch me, do whatever he wanted to me.

He'd probably enjoy doing it with me covered in blood. He wouldn't understand how that grosses me out.

"You are confusing," he said.

"We humans tend to get like that sometimes," I agreed, still covering myself as best I could. "You'd know, except you aren't human, are you?"

The unflinching stare I got as an answer was all I needed to know.

"Fine, whatever," I said. "Do you have any clothes at least?"

"They'll be big."

"Yeah, I figured that," I said. "It would be creepy if you somehow had my size on hand, just waiting."

"I will get them for you," he said, heading over the third bridge without another word and disappearing behind a rock wall I just realized wasn't the outer wall. It must be where his sleeping chamber was.

He does sleep, doesn't he?

Taking advantage of the momentary privacy, I rushed over to the waterfall shower and plunged underneath it, ignoring the pulling at my wounds. My shifter healing would take care of those soon enough.

"EYAAHHHHH!" I shrieked, darting away from the absolutely frigid water.

"What's wrong?"

I jumped as Mr. Mysterious was abruptly at my side, concern lighting his eyes.

"Are you hurt? Did something happen?"

I shook my head.

"What's wrong then? Why did you scream like that?"

I shuffled my arms to keep my now glass-cutter-like tits covered and pointed. "C-C-Cold."

Mr. Mysterious wasn't impressed with my answer. "I thought you were in danger."

"Hypothermia is a danger," I pointed out.

"You're so delicate."

"Listen, mister whoever you are, not all of us can burn fire to keep warm, okay? So, I'm not invincible, like you. That's not the end of the world. Now, does this warm up at all?"

He grunted, walked over to where the water fell from the wall and placed a hand in the opening, so that the water rushed over his fingers.

"There."

I frowned. The water didn't look any different. Carefully, I tested it with my foot. It was perfectly warm, on the edge of being scalding hot without doing actual damage. Just the way I liked it.

"Thank you," I said and waited.

He didn't move.

"You can go now," I said, eager to clean off and get dressed.

"The water will cool if I stop heating it," he said, staring at me.

"You've got to be kidding," I moaned.

"Why would I do that?"

"I didn't–never mind," I said, exasperated.

Did it really matter? He'd seen me naked already. What did it matter if he saw a little more? It was either that or stay covered in my blood. Glaring at him, I hopped under the water and started to clean. I did ensure that my ass was the only thing he got a really good look at. It was the best I could do to maintain decency in the situation.

I definitely did *not* get disappointed when he didn't reach into the water and pull me back against him. Not at all.

Get a hold of yourself. Why does the touch of every male seem to inflame your fucking vag? You need to be more in control of yourself. Don't let them control you.

But that's what I wanted. Ever since my Soulbond had formed, I'd been a slobbering, slathering fool any time a hot man wanted a piece of me. It was like their attention reduced me to nothing, driving back women's rights a hundred years or more. And I *liked* it.

Aaron, this non-human sexual something–I lacked words to properly describe him and what he did to my body simply by looking at me.

I showered quickly and got dressed, hoping the big, baggy clothes would help calm things down. I didn't feel sexy in them at all. In fact, I had to work not to trip over the legs since there was so much extra material. I must have looked like a clown. Thankfully, there were no mirrors to give me a visual I'd never forget.

"It's time you give me some answers," I said in as firm a voice as I could, carefully plunking myself down in a seat in front of the fire so I could bask in its warmth.

"Such as?"

"Who are you?" I asked. "I think you owe me at least a name if you're going to just up and take me like this."

The frown I got back was legendary in its seriousness.

"I'm not like that. I am not going to take you. That is not why I brought you here."

My jaw fell open in a mixture of disappointment and disbelief at how he could misinterpret my comments.

Assuming he did so on accident, and not on purpose, to try and put me at ease.

"Not what I meant," I said, sighing internally. Rejected by another man. The only one who seemed to actively want me had gone from wanting me as his mate to trying to kill me.

What's a girl got to do to be loved properly? Why was it so difficult?

Unsure of how to handle his misdirection style of conversation, I got myself right back up and wandered past the fire to peruse his selection of books. My fingers dragged along the spines. I recognized the names of maybe one in fifty of the books I passed. Most of them were rare or sounded rare.

"Hey!" I said as a familiar title stood out to me. "I know this one. I've read this one."

I pulled out Froller's *The Ancients,* smiling as I reminisced about the books of old.

"My dad got me hooked on these, you know. All about the ancient shifter mythology. He was big into it, loved to talk about it."

I'd long since stopped thinking of my parents as "the people who raised me." I'd started to think of them that way shortly after my Soulshift, when I still wondered if they had lied to me on purpose and didn't care for me, but I'd moved on.

I knew the love I'd felt was real, that they had thought of me as their daughter.

Frig, I miss you guys. I'm sorry, Dad. I was trying to follow your clues, but things...things got weird. I'll figure out a way. I'll find you, wherever you went. I promise.

"What?" I asked when I finally snapped out of my reverie to see Hunky McHunkster staring at me.

"Mythology?" he asked.

"Yeah, you know. Legends, lore. That sort of thing. Stuff that isn't actually real, but people used to believe was?"

To my surprise, Mr. Mysterious' shoulders slumped. "Is that what we've become?"

I frowned. "We? What is this *we* business?"

"Page seventeen," he rasped, the strength gone from his voice. "Turn to page seventeen."

"Ooookay," I said, doing as he said and looking at the page and the depiction of the god Vir, Champion to Amunlea. "Now what do I–*Holy shit.*"

Mr. Mysterious was standing in front of me. At some point, while I'd flipped pages, he'd approached. But gone was the long hair, blue eyes, and sharp facial features of a sex god.

The picture on the page now stared back at me.

Except it was alive.

CHAPTER FORTY-FIVE

"No," I whispered. "That's not possible. It can't be."

The face of a wolf stared back at me. Giant yellow eyes stared down the snout. Horns of blue fire curved up from the top of its head. The rest of his body was the same, minus the wings of darkened *something* I saw fold in against his back. Whatever it was, it wasn't feathers.

One hand–human, like everything from the shoulders down–was reaching out to the side, a long golden spear gripped firmly in his oversized fingers.

"Impossible. It's not real," I said. "This isn't real. I'm dreaming. You don't exist. None of you exist."

The warrior-wolf hybrid faded, replaced by the face of the sexy shirtless man in sweatpants I'd come to recognize.

No, I corrected, *the sexy shirtless god.*

"I assure you," the god said, speaking to me directly. "I am quite real."

He spoke. To me. A god, a freaking *god*, was speaking to me.

"I need to sit down," I said, snapping the book closed and staggering past Mr. Mysterious and gently finding my way into a sitting position.

He wasn't Mr. Mysterious to me any longer, I noted in a distant corner of my mind. I knew his name now. I knew who he was.

"You're Vir," I whispered as if saying it louder would make it any less true. "I've read about you. You were the Champion of Amunlea. Empress of the Gods. You were–"

I stopped speaking abruptly. If he was real…

"She's not here, is she?" I hissed, looking around suddenly.

"No," Vir said quietly. "No, she is not."

I laughed once. My side ached from the sound. "This is supposed to be fake. It's all just legends of people we worshipped in the past. You're not a real person. You can't be. I have to be dreaming. Maybe Johnathan slammed my head to the ground, and I don't realize it. If I'd hit my head any differently, I'd probably have thought you were Zeus or Hades or something. Just as made up."

Vir snorted.

"What?" I asked, surprised by the outburst.

"Oh, nothing. I'll just be sure to tell Hades he doesn't exist the next time I see him." Vir tapped his chin. "Though, I suppose it's been a few thousand years already, so it might be a while yet before he gets word."

My jaw fell open so hard it popped. I winced in pain.

"Are you okay?"

I shook my head. "No, I'm not. I just found out that *gods* are real. That you're real."

And I wanted him to fuck me earlier. Ha. Now that *would have been an interesting experience, I'm sure.*

"I'm sorry if this is a lot to take in," Vir said gently.

I giggled, hating how hysterical I sounded. It was warranted, though, wasn't it? Who *wouldn't* be feeling a little unstable?

"So, Hades is real, too? They're all real? What about the Roman gods? Mars, Jupiter?"

Vir nodded.

"Oh, dear," I said. "I don't feel so good."

The room was spinning gently around me as my mind raced to try and adapt to all the new information it was getting, rewriting thousands of years of history, not to mention everything I knew about the world.

"Dani?" Vir said, my voice sounding like heaven coming from his lips. "Dani, are you okay?"

I swooned. Or fainted. Probably fainted, but swooned has such a better sound to it, so that's how I prefer to think of it. Either way, all the information was too much, and I passed out. I have no idea for how long.

When I came to, I was lying in a bed. A very comfortable bed. I stretched my arms and my legs out but no matter how far I reached, I couldn't find the edge. It was a very *large* bed. Which could only mean one thing.

I was sleeping in a god's bed. I blacked out again. This time when I came to, Vir was nearby, sitting on a chair. The copy of Froller's *The Ancients* was in his hands. It looked like a pocketbook when he held it, his hands were so large.

"It's been some time since I've read this," he said, noting I was awake. "Lots of interesting stuff about my kin I'd forgotten."

I frowned. How could he have forgotten about his kin? That was weird. But I guess when you're immortal, that happens.

"How long was I out?" I asked.

"A few minutes," he said. "Nothing more. You should relax, though. You need to rest. You were hurt worse than you thought in that fight."

"Maybe," I said, but I didn't struggle to get up. The bed was sinfully comfortable, which was befitting of a god, I decided. "But I have so many questions. I can't sleep."

Vir closed the book and turned to look at me, his eyes boring into mine. "Ask them," he said, a smile tugging at one side of his mouth.

"Where am I?" I asked.

"My lair," he said. "A safe spot."

"I don't understand."

"I know," he said with a nod, his voice not *quite* condescending. "But you will. Once you're stronger. When you've recovered."

"Was the place I saw in my dreams real?" I asked, staring at him. "The place with the giant stone wall and the gates?"

Vir just stared at me. I doubted I was going to get an answer to that one just yet.

When you're stronger, I thought to myself, mocking his voice.

Vir quirked an eyebrow, and I panicked. He's a god. Could he read my mind? Did he know I had just been making fun of him?

No further reactions or comments came, so perhaps he'd just read something on my face.

"Good talk," was all I ended up saying. "While it lasted."

Vir shrugged. "My turn."

"Your turn for what?" I asked. "You're a god. What do you need to wait your turn for?"

"Information," he said. "I want to know how you got here."

I sighed. "I told you the truth back at the tunnel," I said. "I don't *know*. Just like I don't know how I got here in my dreams either."

Vir grunted. "When you're ready to talk, so am I."

"I *am* ready to talk, you kidnapping sonofabitch," I snapped, forgetting for a moment I was talking to a being who could quite literally erase me from the face of the Earth with little more than a snap of his fingers. "I don't *know* how I got here. Probably the same way everyone else does. They go through the barrier."

His eyes burned brighter, but when he spoke, his voice was quiet. "Nobody goes through the barrier."

I faltered, my anger vaporizing. "Nobody?"

"Nobody," he repeated. "Until you."

CHAPTER FORTY-SIX

I blinked awake blearily.

What the hell? When had I fallen asleep? Angrily, I turned my head to the side, looking for Vir, demanding answers. We'd been talking about the barrier, and he'd told me nobody but me came through, and then suddenly I was awake. That reeked of god-interference, and I didn't like it.

He wasn't around, though, not that I could sense. For the time being, I was alone.

Taking advantage of that privacy, I carefully sat up in bed and pulled up the oversized sweatshirt, doing my best to keep the girls covered. I inspected my side, noting that the healing was kicking in.

It was going to be gross for a day or so before the fresh, pink skin that I could see forming at the center took over, but I wouldn't be weak for long. Some food, another period of rest, and I would be right as rain. Physically, at least. My mental psyche was another matter entirely.

Gods. Honest to goodness *gods*.

I climbed across a mile of covers and sheets to finally reach the edge of the Vir-sized bed. There was no way I could rest any longer. Not in bed, at least. Maybe I wasn't up for another brawl with Johnathan, but I could walk around the god-lair at least. That wasn't very taxing. Besides, I had too much mental energy to sit still.

Grasping at the waistband of the sweats, so they didn't fall mid-stride, I walked out from the partitioned sleeping chamber and back into the main part of his lair.

"How long was I out?" I asked, spotting Vir over by the hearth fire in the library section.

He was busy staring into the flames. Normal flames, I noted, yellows, oranges and reds. None of his blue.

"As long as you needed to be," he said. "Time works differently here. It would be impossible for me to quantify it to you in ways you would understand."

"Oh," I squeaked. "Right. And, um, just to clarify for me. *Where* are we? And what is that place with the gates? What is going on here?"

Silence.

Vir continued to stare into the flames. I watched and waited for a response. He'd heard me, I was right next to him, but his attention was on the flames. Following his gaze, I, too, stared into them for a long time, trying to spot whatever it was he could see, but it must not have been for mortal eyes because all I saw was the fire.

"We are in the Direen. All of what you have seen is of it."

When Vir finally spoke, I jumped, having been so used to the silence, the sound of his whisper was more akin to thunder.

"I know that name," I said quietly. My father's teachings were coming back to me. All the stories, the ancient legends, and histories of the gods. The Direen was spoken of often and described in great detail.

"I'm not surprised," he said.

"The Direen is supposed to be the Paradise of the Gods," I said.

"Yes."

I had so many questions, but of them all, one rose closer to the surface than all others before.

"Then why does it look so...dead? Not here, but out there. It's not very paradise-like. Unless you have some sort of twisted sense of what paradise means."

"No," he said, still staring into the flames.

"It's not. It hasn't been that way for a thousand years."

The pain in his voice crushed my very soul. I gasped, tears falling abruptly from my eyes. It hurt. Physically hurt me just to hear him speak of it. I cried out as his agony washed through me. Humans aren't made to handle that sort of pain, and I fell to one knee.

It passed, but still, Vir stared into the flames, unseeing, or uncaring, of what his power had done to me. Slowly, I got to my feet, trying to compose myself.

"I don't understand, Vir," I said once I found my voice.

He turned to me, still shirtless, still sexy, but somehow haunted by what he'd seen in the flames. "I know."

"Help me understand?"

Vir nodded and reached out, taking me by the waist. I had just long enough to notice that his touch was warm and that his hand fit around my waist in interesting ways before we blurred up through the rock and were standing on a hill.

I leaned on him. "Warning, dude. A warning, please. For my sanity," I gasped.

"Sorry," Vir said, sounding truly apologetic. "It's been so long since I've dealt with a human. I forget your kind cannot handle the travel very well."

"If I had a moment to prepare myself, it might be different," I said, glaring at him.

We were outside again, I noticed, seeing the starscape above us. It was the same one I'd been greeted with every time I dreamt of Vir.

In fact, we were on the same hill I arrived on. There, in the distance, the giant stone gates rose, the wall on either side leading off into the distance farther than I could see.

Rock crunched under my bare feet as I did a quick circle, confirming we were where I thought we were.

"Why bring me here?" I asked, the gates looming over us even at this distance, dark and foreboding. I couldn't stop staring at them. What was their purpose? Who had built them?

"Once, a long time ago, this place was nothing but white, pink, and gold," he said. "Light was everywhere, and everything was shiny. Perfect. Beautiful."

"A paradise," I said quietly.

"Yes," Vir replied. "Precisely."

"But not anymore."

He shook his head. "Those gates used to stand open. Always. Everyone was welcome here, beings from all realms. I used to spar with Hades and Horus, among others, every decade or so. Our battles were legendary."

I watched Vir's face as he talked, seeing the

shine of his eyes, the twitch of his lips, as he relived memories that had to be millennia old. I couldn't begin to comprehend.

"Trees," he added. "There were trees everywhere. Giant ones hundreds of feet tall lined the road."

He gestured from the gates, pointing to the east to a line of smaller hills in the distance I'd never noticed before. I wondered what had once been there.

It was impossible to picture what he was describing. The world I looked upon now was the complete opposite of what Vir described. Dark, always so dark, covered in blackened rock.

"What *happened*?" I asked in a hushed whisper. "Everything is so bleak. And crunchy. The rock is so messed up."

Vir looked down at our feet. "That is not rock upon which you walk," he explained.

"It's not? What is it?" I asked, taking a step, more non-rock crunching underfoot.

"Bone."

I gagged. "*What*?" I hissed, staring at my feet. Then around me.

"Layer upon layer of bone." His words were hard. Angry even.

"So many," I whispered. "Whose bones? There weren't that many shifter gods. Not to cover this much space."

Vir shook his head. "We don't leave bones when we die."

I swallowed nervously, remembering his warning at the tunnel about how our presence would have attracted attention. "Vir," I said, my voice shaking, "who *does* leave the bones?"

"They do," he said.

"They?"

"The enemy," he said with a shrug. "The ones that come from beyond the Gates. From another realm."

"Which realm do they come from?" I asked.

It's not like I was an expert on other realms or anything. Until this morning, I'd thought Earth was the *only* realm. Now I knew that not only were the shifter gods real, but so were the ancient Greek gods, the ancient Roman gods, even the Egyptians seemed to be represented with his mention of Horus.

That left a *lot* of possibilities, and I was going to go out on a limb and say there were probably others I'd never heard of.

Vir opened his mouth to answer. Simultaneously, his eyes locked on to something in the distance, and his body tightened.

"We must go," he said quietly. "We've lingered for too long."

"What happens if we linger?" I asked, nervous anticipation filling my chest. I had a suspicion what his answer would be.

"They'll come," Vir said. "For both of us. You have to go. I can only hide you here for so long."

He picked me up, careful to avoid my wounded side, though it barely hurt anymore.

"Wait!" I yelped, suddenly realizing what he was going to do. We were going to poof again. "Wait-wait-wait!"

Vir didn't wait.

CHAPTER FORTY-SEVEN

This time, I lost the battle.

Seconds after we reappeared, I emptied what little there was in my stomach all over the ground.

"Sorry," I croaked. "But you've really got to learn to warn me before you do that. This is all your fault."

"You have to go."

No apology, no remorse, nothing but stony dismissal from Vir.

"I just got here," I said. "Shouldn't we try to figure out why before you dismiss me?"

He lifted a finger and pointed. "You have to go. *Now*."

I looked at where he was pointing.

We weren't back in his lair like I'd suspected but instead were at the entrance to a tunnel, much like, if not the same one, I'd emerged from. Back when I was young and naïve and thought gods were nothing but stories and fairytales.

"The barrier," I said, unsettled at the thought.

Vir nodded. "I'll fight them off for as long as I can, but I cannot risk getting trapped when the warriors arrive."

"Warriors?" I croaked, vastly unsettled at the way Vir, a freaking *god*, didn't want to combat these foes. How dangerous were they?

"Get through the barrier, Dani. Now, before it's too late."

I swallowed nervously but nodded, making my way slowly down the tunnel, hands out in front of me, shuffling forward so I didn't slam face-first into the barrier.

Frustrated by our slow pace, Vir thrust a hand out, and blue fire leaped forward, highlighting the barrier for me, perhaps twenty feet ahead.

"Thanks," I muttered, moving swiftly to its edge, my fingers brushing against the invisible wall that blocked my path.

I grunted and *pushed* against it, determined to do as Vir asked. If he said it was dangerous, I had no reason to doubt him. The faster I got through the barrier, the sooner he could escape without drawing the so-far unseen invaders after him.

Like before, however, the barrier didn't give. I pushed, and it shrugged my strength off. Setting my feet, I leaned into it, trying to get more leverage to push my way through the wall.

"Vir, this isn't going to work," I said, doubt entering my mind. "I don't know how to do this."

"You must," he said. "You made it here. That means you got through the barrier."

"I *know*," I ground out. "That doesn't mean I have any idea *how*, Vir. It just sort of happened. I was also in the middle of a fight with my stupid ex."

"Your Soulbound mate, yes."

I stared at the giant god. "You *know* about that?"

He stared at me.

"Right. God and all that," I muttered, spinning a finger in the air. "Must be nice."

Vir chuckled. "It has its perks sometimes."

I nodded. "Vir, if you're so knowing, can you tell me *what* the barrier is? Why is it there? Why can nobody get through, not even you?"

Watching a freaking *god* look troubled and unsettled was not an experience a mortal should ever feel comfortable with. Even when they were as sexy as Vir, the uncertainty he was showing was enough to leave me terrified. I much preferred the Alpha, all-knowing version of him better. It instilled confidence in me that this look did not.

"It protects the Earth," he said quietly.

I didn't have to know from what. It was quite obvious he was referring to the unseen enemy whose bones literally covered the ground around us.

"I don't understand. I mean, I get that it's a barrier that protects Earth. But where did it come from?"

Vin stared at me stonily. Some secrets were apparently not for human knowledge.

"What happened when it went up?" I asked.

"All contact with Earth was lost," he said. "There was no way in, no way out."

I thought about that for a moment. Vir had said the Direen had been a wasteland for a thousand years.

"That was why you became myth and legend," I said quietly. "We didn't turn from you. Nor did you abandon us. The city of Shuldar, the one on the other side of the barrier. It was built here because of this passage between Earth and the Direen, wasn't it?"

Vir nodded.

"And when the barrier went up, nobody understood what happened. But without gods, they eventually denied your existence and the city lost its importance."

"I would assume that's true," Vir said. "I was rather busy, though."

"But why the barrier?" I asked. "Why couldn't

you and the other shifter gods stop them?"

Vir's eyes looked down. "We tried," he said quietly.

"Where are they now?" I asked, fearing the answer.

The giant god turned and walked back to the tunnel entrance. He lifted an arm and pointed at the nearest hill, similar to the one I appeared on in my dreams.

"Lorana," he said, naming the shifter god of the shift.

His arm swung to another hill. "Irr."

"The god of death," I whispered.

Another hill. "Mino."

And another. "Terrano."

I stared, aghast, as his arm swung across the horizon.

"Rase. Shax. Kline."

"They're dead," I whispered. "All of them?"

Vir nodded.

There was one god he hadn't mentioned, I realized at the end, swinging to face him.

"What about Amunlea? Your empress? She's supposed to be the most powerful of all of you."

Vir turned without speaking, stalking back down the tunnel. "Come, it is time you left. We don't have long. We shouldn't have wasted this time."

I hurried after him, the fire-ringed barrier staring at me. Taunting me.

"Are you sure you'll be okay if I go?" I asked. "It must be…lonely here."

"It is for the best," Vir said, tilting his head at the barrier. "Now, go through."

"What about Johnathan and the others?" I asked quietly. "If I go through, they'll kill me. They're probably waiting."

"They're gone," Vir said. "Besides, they *might* kill you. The enemy will."

I opened my mouth to protest, but he cut me off.

"And eat you, I might add."

"Ew. Gross." I stormed up to the barrier, tracing its outline, feeling for a weakness, a point with give. Anything.

"Hurry," Vir said.

I looked over my shoulder to see that Giant Sex God was gone. In his place stood Vir, Champion of Amunlea. The golden spear he gripped in his right hand was easily as tall as I was, probably closer to seven feet long. The wolf head sitting atop his broad shoulders glowed with blue fire, while foot-long horns sprouted from the top of his head.

Golden armor appeared from thin air, draping his shoulders, secured around his torso. Bracers of some unknown dark metal protected his arms. I noticed a dagger strapped to his side.

No, not a dagger. A sword. It just looks like a dagger on him.

"Get moving, Danielle Wetter," the Champion of Amunlea growled, his voice powerful enough to shake the cavern, pebbles and rock dust falling down.

I swallowed nervously. Less than ten feet behind me, a god was preparing to go to war. Somehow, I felt like this wasn't something humans were supposed to be a part of. The power he contained was shimmering the very air around us.

"I'm trying," I said, refocusing my efforts, pushing against the barrier, willing it to let me through. "Trust me. I'm trying."

A ghostly wail filtered down the tunnel.

"We are out of time," the Champion growled. "They are here."

I was nearly knocked to the ground as Vir strode to the tunnel entrance to meet the enemy in battle. Each step released power, its energy washing over me.

Clearly, he was holding back when it was just the two of us.

A mighty roar filled the tunnel, nearly bursting my eardrums. I screamed.

"Let me through!" I shrieked, my wolf howling her agreement.

Nothing was happening.

Looking over my shoulder, I saw Vir battling the enemy. His spear moved so fast it appeared like a golden wall in front of him. Bits and pieces of whatever he was fighting sprayed around him, the spear spinning so swiftly everything was chopped into fine bits that adhered to the tunnel exterior.

"You must go!" Vir said. "Now that they've found us, the warriors will be here soon."

"I'm trying!" I shouted.

"Try harder!" he bellowed. "Or we both die!"

CHAPTER FORTY-EIGHT

"No pressure," I told myself, gritting my teeth. "Just get through this impenetrable barrier, or you'll be responsible for the death of the last shifter god in existence. Not the sort of story to tell your grandkids."

I won't be having any grandkids if I don't get through. Because I'll be dead right alongside him. Probably a fitting punishment.

Heaving my entire weight against the barrier, I struggled to gain ground. It was harder than rock. Unmoving. I snatched up a nearby rock and, gripping it in both hands, lifted it over my head and brought it down on the barrier.

The impact shattered the rock, but its impact *did* reveal a ghostly blue dome, showing me the barrier for the first time, not just Vir's outline of it. Though, I had no idea how I could use that information.

Maybe brute strength isn't the answer. How did you get through it last time?

That was easy. I'd fallen through it. Hurt and wounded in the fight, my wolf's leg had given out on me. I had tried to lean on the barrier to keep me on my feet, but instead of the solid wall, it had simply vanished, letting me through.

The sounds of combat up the tunnel grew louder.

Part of me was grateful that only I had made it through the barrier. Not Johnathan, and certainly not Aaron. It was good I'd left him and his team behind. Hopefully, they were okay, having ditched me and headed back for the city. With the time I'd spent in Vir's lair, their contract was up. I'd have to send word to him if I made it through, let him know I'd survived.

Unless Johnathan had gone after him.

That would be just like that asshole.

Angrily, I shoved against the barrier again. Someone needed to teach Johnathan a lesson, show him he couldn't just do whatever he wanted to whoever he wanted. Him and his asshole of a father. Maybe I couldn't stop them, but I had a better shot of success against them than I did against whatever had killed Vir's brethren.

"Hurry!" Vir grunted, his voice closer now.

I risked a look over my shoulder to see him backing down the tunnel. Following him was a mass of shadow and darkness, hiding the enemy from my sight. I could hear them, though. Ghostly wails filled my ears, a near nonstop sound, paired with the whistling scream of Vir's spear as it sliced through the closest ranks, splattering them all over the walls.

"I'm trying!" I hollered back. "It's not working."

"Once you're through, I can vanish," Vir said. "If the warriors aren't here, they won't track me. Once you're safely through, I'll go."

"Easier said than done!" I shouted.

From the tunnel entrance came a horrifying bellow that could not have come from a human throat.

"Vir," I said uneasily. "What was that?"

"A warrior," he said calmly. "Go."

I shook my head. "Vir, I'm not getting through. You have to go."

He turned to look at me, his face clouded by blue flame, but I could still see the shock written on it.

"Go," I said. "Before the warrior gets down here. Disappear and be safe. There's no sense in *both* of us dying."

The golden spear continued to weave its impenetrable wall in front of Vir, even with his head turned.

"Danielle Wetter," he ground out. "You are the

first person or being to come through in millennia. I am *not* going to just let you die without figuring out how you did that."

I sighed. "Well, then, I guess both our stubborn asses are dying then. Good job. Unless you can poof us out of here?"

Vir shook his head. "If I do, they'll track me."

"It might buy us some time," I pointed out. "Enough time to figure out how I get through."

"It won't matter," Vir explained. "I can only go from here to my lair. I can't go to another place. If they find the lair, then I am exposed and nowhere will be safe. We die there, we die here. It's how the others fell."

"Crap," I muttered.

"Either you go, or we die," he said, turning back to face the wall of shadowed darkness.

That was when the first creature slipped past, narrowly escaping the golden spear by flattening itself against the wall and pushing past as his head turned.

I shouted and, without a second thought, charged the creature as it lunged at Vir's back. I took it to the ground before hauling back with a fist and punching its lumpy, misshapen head. It wailed at the blow, so I hit it again and again.

Claws tried to scratch my stomach, but they got tangled up in Vir's oversized clothing, and the creature couldn't generate any force. Eventually, my blows cracked whatever it had for a skull, and it lay still.

I got to my feet and backed away until my shoulders pressed flat against the barrier.

Farther down the tunnel, a much deeper shade of black entered the mass of shadows attacking Vir. It formed into a tall bipedal creature, though I could not see much detail beyond that. Even the creature I'd killed was hard to describe, shrouded in darkness still.

What *were* these things?

"I take it that's a warrior?" I asked, trying to sound calm as the dark shape came toward us.

"Correct," Vir said.

"Can you handle it?"

"Yes," he said with that same calm assurance.

"Good. Hurry up and do so," I said.

"Creatures will get through."

"Yeah," I said with far more confidence than I felt, shaking myself out of his clothing. "I know. Let them come."

Okay. Time to earn your keep, I called to my wolf, lifting the mental chains her that kept her restrained within my mind.

The she-bitch from hell charged forward, and my body shifted with a speed I was unaccustomed to. We howled in pain as bones changed and reknit, dropping us to all fours while we took on our true form.

We lunged at the first creature to make it past Vir as he focused on the warrior. Our speed surprised it, and we tore its throat out with ease, rebounding off it and ripping the leg out from another. Free from our constraints, we fought as one, jaws and claws tearing the enemy apart as fast as we could.

They came even faster, their sheer number driving us back. Vir had dispatched one warrior and now another, but other shapes were entering the tunnel as more warriors came.

We fought as hard as we could. Black blood dripped from our jaws, our vision dimmed with red, both from the blood blocking our vision but also from rage. We didn't want to die, and that pissed us off.

A wave of blue fire lit up a warrior, and Vir slammed his spear through the throat of another, buying us a momentary reprieve even as the mass of smaller creatures came forward on all fours in a wave of darkness.

We stared at them, trying to pick out individual details, but it was all happening too fast to get a real picture of *what* we were fighting. They walked on four legs, but everything about them was so dark it was hard to grasp more specifics than that. They had a head and possibly a tail, we didn't know.

But they died, and that was all that mattered.

On and on we fought until one of the warriors pierced Vir's defenses, rocking him back.

We howled and went to his aid. The warrior's pitch-black blade swept down at me. We ducked under it, hitting it low in the feet, disrupting its balance. It flailed its arms, and a golden spear took it in the chest. Snarling in victory, we went after the second warrior, but before we could get to it, heat blossomed on our flank.

A moment later, pain slammed into our brain as we registered the hit of the third warrior, its blade gouging a deep line in our side.

Vir bellowed his rage and launched a new attack. Blue flame burned the minor creatures, forcing them back. They raced up the tunnel, leaving just us and the two warriors.

Launching ourselves at the leftmost warrior, the one who had cut us, we snapped and feinted at his feet, keeping him occupied while Vir dealt with the other. We feinted left, went right, only that was a feint, too, and we went back left.

The warrior was waiting, and its blade sliced a gouge down our chest, flinging us back until we smacked a shoulder against the barrier and hit the ground, disoriented by the blow.

Nearby, Vir howled and tried to come to our aid. He took a blow in the process that sent him stumbling. A warrior lifted its blade and went to deliver the killing blow.

We slammed into its feet, using our body as a battering ram. It kicked us. Hard. We bounced and rolled past Vir, who was wrestling with the other warrior. I shifted back, my wolf having had enough.

"Get out of here, Vir," I groaned, climbing to my knees, my back to the barrier.

He kicked the warrior off him, sending it flying across the chamber, momentarily creating space between the final warrior and us.

"I won't let you die here," he growled, but I could see he knew the truth.

We were both dead.

I reached out and took his hand, not sure why. "I'm sorry," I said.

He stared at our intertwined fingers. "Why did–"

The last warrior came charging in. Vir blocked him with his spear, but with only one hand to hold it, he fell back into me as the warrior pushed. I was pushed back against the barrier, my back making contact–

And we fell through it, hitting the ground on the other side.

All three of us.

CHAPTER FORTY-NINE

I howled in instant agony as the full force of my Soulbond slammed back into me with incomprehensible savagery.

Scratching, clawing at my face, I tried to deal with the brutal wake-up call as I rolled on the ground screaming while my head tried to tear itself in half.

GO TO HIM. He is yours. You are his.

The message repeated itself over and over again. Some part of me knew I had to ignore it, I had to shove it aside, there was a very good reason for it, but I'd forgotten what it was. The only thing I wanted now was to be with him. To find Johnathan. Only he could set me free from this pain.

My wolf was trying to tear herself free of my control, and as we fought, my body changed back and forth repeatedly, hair growing and shrinking all over me, and I'm sure other things did too.

"Danielle Wetter! Get up!" a voice boomed.

The Alpha call slammed into me like a hurricane, momentarily pushing back the thundering call of my Soulbond as it sought complete control over me. I gasped. That brief reprieve nearly enough to make me cry. Never had I experienced sensations like this in my life. It was too much. I couldn't handle it. *No one* could.

"Better," the voice grunted, the command in it calmer. "Now get over here, ugh, and help me."

I looked up to see Vir battling the warrior that had come through the barrier with us. He was still dressed as the Champion, but something about him was...different.

The fire, I realized abruptly. His fire had gone out. The horns were gone as well. The rest of him was still there, but not the fire. And he seemed... diminished. The warrior was pressing him back, and the golden spear still spun but without the whirring scream it'd had before.

He was slower and without his fire. And the warrior was winning.

All at once, I had something to focus on. If I didn't help Vir, the warrior would dispatch him and then me before I could even get to Johnathan. So, I *had* to help him. It was the only way, I told myself.

Struggling to my feet, naked and in pain, my

front and back carved up from the onyx-black blade the warriors wielded, I searched the tunnel for something, *anything*, that might help me.

I couldn't find a thing. All I had was myself.

"Guess it'll have to be enough," I said, and without thinking about what I was going to do, I flung myself on the warrior's back.

It was a good thing I didn't take the time to think it over because what was left of my sanity would have screamed at me for doing something so absolutely *stupid*. I was way out of the warrior's league, even when healed. What was I thinking by trying to overpower it in my current state?

My attack caught the creature completely unaware, however, and it stumbled. I was tall and willowy, and most people didn't think that could amount to much. But when you're nearly six feet tall yourself, small or not, you've still got a certain amount of mass to throw around.

I threw mine hard, locking my arms around what I hoped was its neck and hauling back tightly, using my legs to grab onto its waist like some sort of spider monkey. My shrieks filled the tunnel while I wailed on its head with my fists and elbows, trying desperately to crack its tough skeleton.

The creature reached back with one hand to pull me off, but I batted its arms aside and continued my fight. Vir pressed forward, ensuring it had to focus on him with its weapon.

I found some openings in the darkness that was its body and immediately shoved my fingers in them, scratching, clawing, and driving them as deep as I could. The creature's roar must have burst an eardrum, it was so loud, but I didn't stop to check. I held on for dear life.

Then we were falling. I landed on top.

"Off!" Vir commanded, and I was rolling away before I had fully processed what he'd said.

The golden spear plunged through the creature's back, and at last, it lay still.

Gasping for air, I stayed hunched over. Closer to Vir, I was able to remain in control, the agony in my head reduced to migraine level but staying just shy of debilitating. I didn't know how much longer I could go on like this, but for now, I had the energy to keep fighting.

"They watch us," Vir said.

I looked up, then followed his gaze to the barrier. Warriors stood on the other side, shrouded in darkness but clearly staring in our direction.

"Let them," I said, chest heaving as I tried to come down from the post-fight high. "They can't harm us here. Not now."

"Perhaps," Vir said, turning to face me.

"I'm sorry," I whispered, the lack of flames evident. "I didn't mean to pull you through with me. I don't even know *how* I did it. I just sort of *did.*

Then you were here, too, and now you…you're not on fire."

"Yes," Vir said. "The barrier seems to have robbed me of my godhood."

"Oh, no," I whispered.

"It's okay," he said. "This was how it used to be. Back when the path between Earth and the Direen was open and traversable. To bring my full powers to Earth…that would be very bad indeed. Earth is the realm of mortals. Gods do not belong here. Not in full."

"You're still strong, though," I said. "And still… beastly."

"It would seem not all my powers are gone," Vir agreed. As he spoke, he changed, the fearsome visage of the Champion fading, replaced with human-Vir.

He shrunk as he did, though my eyes never really noticed it happening. One moment he was nine, ten feet tall—I didn't have a measuring stick handy—the next he *only* towered over me by half a foot or so.

Seeing him this way, watching him now, had an unexpected side effect. The heavy beating of drums in my head was kept at bay. It wasn't gone, it would never go away, but I didn't need to roll around on the floor and claw my face anymore.

It was like the effect of being around Aaron but stronger. Perhaps a true Alpha dulled the call of the Soulbond somehow? I didn't know.

"I don't suppose you were left with the powers of clothing," I muttered, once more naked in front of him.

I almost covered up, but it hardly seemed to matter. This man, this *god*, had seen more of my titties than anyone, even my ex. What was some more at this point?

"Sorry." Vir shook his head, then stopped suddenly, his face lighting up. "But wait. I have an idea."

All at once, he was giant again. I yelped and backed away, the sudden transition catching me by surprise.

"Careful with that! You'll hurt someone."

"No, I won't," Vir rumbled, reaching down.

"What are you doing?" I asked.

He tore off a strip of his gray sweat pants and handed it to me. Then he tore a longer part off the other side and tossed it to me. When he shrunk back to human size, I was ready this time, though I was still holding the two pieces of clothing.

"There you go," he said. "Put them on."

"On?" I asked, looking at them.

"Tube top and skirt," he said. "Best I can do on short notice."

"You have got to be–fine," I said, doing as he

suggested.

Shockingly, they fit. Not well, and any abrupt movement was likely to send the top down to my waist, and I didn't have underwear on, but it would work for the moment. In times like this, there was little room to be picky.

"Okay, come on," I said. "Let's get out of here before Johnathan or his friends notice I'm back —"

With my mind shifting gears and considering escape, I finally had the time to look around. We were in a cavern. Not a tunnel.

"Vir," I said slowly.

"Yes?"

"Where are we?" I asked calmly as the drumming in my head grew stronger once more. "This isn't where I went through."

"Another exit," Vir asked. "What's wrong?"

By now, I was holding my head, the pain threatening to make me delirious.

"My Soulbond," I hissed as it stabbed deep into my skull. "I've denied it too long. I feel like I'm being torn in two, Vir. Part of me is pulling me to him."

I lifted a hand to point, not that it mattered.

"A part of you?" Vir said. "Not all of you?"

"No," I whispered, eyes closed as I tried not to scream. "Another part of me is guiding me that way."

I pointed off to one side, a hundred or so degree angle away from Johnathan. "But that one doesn't hurt. It just...pulls at me. If that makes any sense."

Vir stared in the direction I'd pointed. "Yes," he said quietly. "It does."

"What is wrong with me?" I whimpered.

"I'm not sure," Vir said, his gaze traveling to me, watching me curiously.

"Great." I stood up, the room spinning slightly from the pain in my skull. "We should get going then. Before they find us. If I can feel him now, then Johnathan will be coming for me, and I won't be of much use to you against him or his little gang. Maybe if we build enough of a lead, we can catch up to my guide. Together, we could probably hold Johnathan off long enough to get out of here."

"Your guide?" Vir asked.

I shrugged. "Yeah. I hired a guy and his team to lead me out here. To follow my dad's journal. He was looking for Shuldar, you know. Had been for years. He's the reason I'm here. He went missing."

I was babbling now, talking about anything I could think of to try and distract myself.

"Who is your guide?"

"You'd like him," I said with a laugh. "Tall, stubborn, and annoyingly mysterious, kinda like you. Calls himself Aaron Greiss. I dunno who he is. Tall, really pale, blue eyes way lighter than yours. Almost unnaturally so."

Vir's lips twitched. "I'll be damned," he rumbled. "Blond hair? Sharp facial features, smooth sweeping cheekbones? Walks like a predator? Exudes sex?"

My jaw dropped open. "You *know* him?"

Vir shrugged. "We should go find him. Come on. I'll lead the way."

"Better hurry," I said, shoving aside the million questions I had.

"Why?"

"Because," I said tightly as we crossed the cavern and entered the tunnel. I blinked as my eyes adjusted to the pitch black of the tunnel. "My head is hurting worse. He's nearby, and he won't be alone."

Up ahead, Vir grunted.

"Vir?" I called, rushing forward as I heard something hit the ground. "Vir, are you okay?"

I nearly tripped and fell over something. I reached down, my eyes adjusting at the same time, and I realized it was Vir. He had a huge bump on his forehead.

"He's quite close by," a menacing voice said from behind me. "But I'm closer. Time's up, little wolf. My patience with you is at an end."

Then, something struck me in the back of the

head.

CHAPTER FIFTY

There was no dreamland visit this time.

One moment I was awake, kneeling over Vir's unconscious body, and the next, I was shooting back to awareness fueled by a headache vicious enough to give a god pause.

"You know," I growled through the anger rising in me. "I am getting *really* sick and tired of being knocked out. Do you people not realize that brain damage is a thing?"

When there was no response, I tried to sit up. My head was on fire, and I was nearly blinking back tears. I could feel Johnathan around somewhere. It was his father, Lars, who had appeared in the tunnel out of nowhere, but my Soulbond pulsed with my mate's nearness. They were both close.

Closer than I thought.

I got halfway up into a sitting position before I could go no farther, the bonds on my chest and wrists holding me down. I thrashed and tried to get free, but I couldn't. Grunting, I strained, trying to pull my wrists apart, using all my shifter strength.

"Don't bother," a familiar voice said from nearby in low tones. "You won't rip them."

"Vir?" I called.

"Yes. They're silver bonds. Your strength means nothing to them."

I groaned, lying back down on the cold stone, using its cool touch to soothe my aching head. My vision was returning now, and it dropped into the lowlights. There was light emanating from somewhere, but I couldn't see from what. Still, it allowed me to look over and see Vir.

He was trussed up on top of a slab of stone. Glancing down at myself, I could see I was likely on a similar stone, pedestal-like spot.

"Where are we?" I asked. "Any ideas?"

An unfamiliar sensation fluttered through my chest. I glanced to my left, but no one was there.

But something is, I realized. That was the direction I was being pulled in. The one with its purple power. In my imagination at least.

Whatever it was, it was close by now.

"We're in Shuldar," Vir said. "The true Shuldar."

"What? What do you mean? I found Shuldar," I said. "I ran down a street, I know it. You're telling me that wasn't it?"

"It was," Vir said. "In a way. But the true Shuldar resided *below* the surface. Only a few places were aboveground."

"Oh." I felt slightly cheated. "So, where I came through the barrier?"

"That was in my temple."

I worked my jaw a few times. "Right. Of course you have a temple. You're a god and all that."

I groaned in pain as my Soulbond kicked it up a notch.

"He's close," I said. "I can feel it. I can feel both of them. Whatever that other thing is, Vir, it's close. I can barely concentrate. Oh, god, it hurts so much."

Tears were falling down my face now, and I couldn't wipe them. They ran down my temples and into my hair as I stared up at the ceiling.

"You must hold on, Dani," Vir urged.

"I'm trying," I whispered. "I don't know how much longer I can hang on."

Vir was silent while I fought my mental battle. The thundering in my temples went on and on, a ceaseless assault on senses. My stomach was upset, threatening to be sick, though I hadn't eaten in who knew how long at that point. My limbs were practically shaking. I wanted to claw my eyes out.

Anything that would stop the hurt. Anything. I even considered giving in. Accepting Johnathan. I could do it. I could. It would be sad, but anything was better than the pain. By now, I swore I could feel each individual step as he grew closer, the drums hammering in time with his footsteps, or so it felt.

"He's close," I heard myself say. "Close to… wherever we are."

"We're in the temple of Terrano," Vir supplied helpfully. "One of many scattered throughout the city."

I went still, a cold fear sweeping over me.

"Terrano? You're sure?" I asked.

There was no reply.

"Of course, you're sure. God. He was your brother, I guess. Of course you'd know. Right. Good. Okay. Um, correct me if I'm wrong, but wasn't Terrano the god of rituals? I didn't know much about him, but I'm pretty sure I'm right about that."

"Yes," Vir said.

We weren't on pedestals then. Rather, we were on altars.

Sacrificial alters.

They stood in the center of the rectangular room. A trough ran between them, up past my head, where it dropped into a deep depression in the ground. A bowl, I realized, to collect the blood.

Above the bowl was a raised altar with two

doorways set into the wall behind it. Wrenching my head around, I spied stone slabs set in rows leading back to a large, double-wide doorway that must be the entrance for the audience. The doors above my head would have been where the priests entered.

The walls were adorned with carvings, but my eyes hurt too badly from the pounding of the Soulbond to focus on them in any detail. But I could see enough. Vir was right. We were in the ritual room. Probably.

"Okay, that could just be a coincidence, right?"

"Could be," Vir agreed, but he didn't sound positive.

"Shit. What can you tell me about his rituals?" I asked, not sure I wanted to know.

"The more blood, the stronger the ritual you could enact," Vir said, somewhat disgusted. "Terrano would bless people like that. A sacrifice would garner special attention."

"Crap. What ritual do you think they're after?"

"I don't know," Vir said. "But I don't particularly want to find out."

"Me neither," I said, my heart racing as fast as the pounding in my head. "We need to get out of here. Like now."

Vir said something, but my head chose that moment to go into overdrive. I thrashed against the bonds, a thin wail escaping my tightly clenched teeth. The Soulbond. It was coming. It was *coming!*

"Can you break us free?" I struggled to say, my words broken and choppy. I was nearly out of time.

"No," Vir said. "They were smart and prepared. Silver works on gods as well. I am as helpless as you."

A third voice broke in. "Guess it's a good thing for your grumpy, old godly ass, then, that she isn't helpless, isn't it?"

My head turned so fast my muscles locked up on me.

"Aaron?" I gasped.

CHAPTER FIFTY-ONE

"I am not grumpy," Vir said.

"*Right,*" Aaron drawled. "What about–"

"Now is not the time for that," Vir snapped, cutting Aaron off.

Aaron just grinned and winked at me. "Time to get you out of here before the big dick shows up."

"Okay," I said, confusion cutting through the pain. "But what are you doing here? And how do you know him?"

"I'm doing my job," Aaron said as he flicked out a knife and went to work sawing the metal-thread bonds. "Remember? You hired me to guide you and keep you safe."

"This isn't exactly what I meant by that second part," I said.

"I know," he whispered, keeping his voice

down, hinting I should do the same. "But I'm a man of my word."

"That's very noble of you," I said, truly touched by his dedication. He had quite literally just saved my life. And Vir's, too, most likely.

"I felt guilty because I overcharged you by twenty percent."

I snorted. "That makes more sense. But how are you here? How the hell did you find us?"

"We went after you," he said, "when you ran out of the campsite. Followed you from a distance. There was a good amount of wolves after you. We weren't ready for that many."

I had *so* many questions. How was he ready for *any* shifters? And how did he know Vir? There were a lot of conclusions to be drawn there, but there didn't seem time for that.

"Anyway," Aaron said as he continued to saw away at my bonds, the silver resistant to being cut. "We stuck around the area. Dave monitored things with some of his techy gadgets, one of those drones or whatever. There was a commotion a few hours back, and we started moving in. Found this giant underground place and just sort of followed from a distance."

"I see," I said, gritting my teeth against another fresh, blinding stab of pain. "I don't believe you."

"Good thing it doesn't matter. Are you okay?"

he asked as I tried to shake off the pain.

I'm pretty sure I only made it worse.

"I'll be fine," I lied, struggling to see through the constant parade of tears down my face. "Where's the rest of your team?"

At that moment, a tremendous angry bellow filtered through the temple. It could have been my agony-riddled brain, but I swear it sounded like there was a bit of pain mixed in with the anger.

"That answer your question?" Aaron said, sawing faster with the knife.

I stared at him. "You sent your team after *Lars*?" I asked incredulously. "You know he's an A–"

"A huge asshole who deserves all they're giving him and more?" Aaron finished. "Yes. You're right on all accounts."

"Your team is that good?" I asked, closing my eyes as my wolf swirled inside me, circling, eager to get out.

"The best," Aaron said. "I don't go anywhere without them."

My dad must *have known that. He must have known what they were. But why did he link up with them? Why did he bring them along? And why did he want me to meet Aaron?*

There were so many questions that needed answering. I turned my head to Aaron, wanting to pull out some much-needed information, but at that moment, my wolf went berserk.

I screamed, back arching high into the sky as the she-bitch inside me fought with all her strength to escape. Hairs on my arm lengthened. Then shrank. She wasn't getting me without a fight. My fingers curved into claws and then back to human-sized once more. My face jutted forward and then back.

Something slapped me across the face.

Eyes snapping open, I glared furiously at Aaron.

"Get a hold of yourself," he hissed, slurring his consonants slightly. "I didn't go through all of this just to lose you now, she-wolf."

I harnessed the rage inside me, from myself and my wolf at being slapped so casually, and poured it all into my control. I took her anger and stripped it from her, robbing her of strength.

She calmed, ever so slightly.

The bonds parted around my wrists at long last. I reached down to untangle my feet, to free them, while Aaron started cutting them.

"Damn silver," I hissed, the metal braids icy cold to the touch as I pulled at them.

With both of us working at them, it took much less time to free my feet. I slid off the ritual slab with an audible sigh of relief and hurried over to Vir's altar.

"No," Aaron said. "I'll handle him."

"What am I supposed to do?" I snapped back. "I'm not helpless."

Aaron and Vir spoke at the same time. "You need to go."

"Go *where*?" I demanded angrily. "I don't know where I am or where to go."

There was a clattering of noise from the door. I crouched, prepared to spring at whoever came through the front entrance. Sparing a quick glance, I noted the rear entrance of the rectangular room was dark and empty still. That was probably where I would escape.

The first shape came through the huge entryway at the front of the temple, and I nearly leaped.

"Dave!" I hissed, rising from my crouch as the rest of Aaron's team came in, all of them toting guns. They were armed to the teeth!

"We're out," Dave said, tossing his gun to the side. "One minute, maybe less. They're all still up."

"Very well," Aaron acknowledged. "You distract as many as you can. We'll handle as many as we can."

He looked down at Vir. "Assuming you've still got anything left in you," he added with a chuckle.

Vir's answering growl shook the room.

"I'd say he's still in the fight, wouldn't you?" Aaron said cheerily. "Just like old times."

"Yeah," Vir said, muscles flexing. The bonds around his wrists tore with a shrieking *snap* of overstressed metal. "*Just* like old times."

I opened my mouth to laugh, but it turned into a gut-wrenching cry of pain as my head erupted in fresh agony beyond my ability to control. My knees gave out, and I fell to the ground, narrowly getting one hand down in time to avoid smashing my face on the stone floor. A moment later, a familiar shape stepped into the opening of the temple chamber.

Johnathan.

My wolf strained toward him. To run at him, giving ourselves to him. *Anything* that would end the incredible pain in our head. My tears stained the floor as I stayed still, unable to move while I fought against that call.

"*We can't,*" I sobbed to my wolf, my body wracked by guilt, grief, and agony. "*If we go, we'll lose ourselves. Our parents. We'll be alone.*"

But we'll have him, the voice inside me countered. *He'll take care of us. Love us. He'll be our partner.*

"He wants to kill us!" I snarled through the sobs.

Claws clacked against stone as four-legged shapes appeared at Johnathan's sides.

"You," Johnathan rumbled ominously, lifting a finger to point at Aaron. "Who are you?"

"None of your damn business, son," Aaron said coldly. "Now, turn around before you regret it."

Another much larger wolf stalked into the room. Midnight black, it blended into the oddly lit room with ease, but there was no mistaking who *that* was. His power rolled off him in waves.

Lars.

CHAPTER FIFTY-TWO

The Seguin pack Alpha snarled at me, and my wolf tried to flop over and submit instantly.

"*No*," I growled, forcing myself to not only not submit, but to get back on my feet. I swayed unsteadily, but I got there.

Take that, asshole, I thought as Lars' yellow eyes filled with wild rage at my defiance of his call.

"Go," Aaron said. "We'll hold them off."

I stared at him in a mixture of horror and disbelief. "You can't be serious."

"It's in our contract," he said, rolling his neck. "Besides, it's been some time since I taught some upstart wolf pups their place."

I turned to Vir, who was now on his feet. He hadn't assumed the form of the Champion yet, but he looked ready for battle, nonetheless. His eyes were blue and focused on me. Though he didn't speak, the calm, single nod he gave me told me all I needed.

"Where do I go?" I asked, unsure what to do as the two sides stood arrayed against one another, waiting for the other side to move first.

Vir tilted his head slightly, and some fire entered his eyes.

"Follow the call," he whispered.

The call. He didn't mean my Soulbond, but rather that *other* part of me. The one drawn elsewhere. To something still unknown but definitely nearby. With the surge of the Soulbond's power due to Johnathan's proximity, I'd all but forgotten about it.

I frowned accusingly at myself. It was trying to obscure that call, to *make* me ignore it, so I'd focus on the Soulbond instead. Insidious. I hated the Soulbond. I wanted it gone. If I could rip it from me, I would. But I couldn't.

"Go," Vir urged as Lars snarled again.

I staggered, barely able to resist.

"Okay," I said, looking at the team and Vir, all of whom were prepared to sacrifice themselves if necessary, so I could get away. "I'm sorry."

"Go!" Vir barked, his voice strong, commanding, without being arrogant.

A true Alpha.

I turned and ran from the ritual chamber as the wolves from my pack behind me went apeshit at Lars' call. I winced as a wolf yelped in pain, and then a human voice roared in agony as well.

Coward. That's what I was, I told myself as I went out of the chamber and down the darkened hallway, fighting my wolf's urge to go back, her desires mixing with my Soulbond to form a potent drag on my efforts to follow the *other* part of me instead. Each step was a battle, but as I picked up speed, it grew easier.

A lifetime of stubbornness had helped me get to this point, and I wasn't about to give in to some magical link that wanted to make me become a passive, submissive mate to a deranged lunatic's son. *Hell no* to that.

I followed the tunnels, blinding listening to that other part of me, letting it hopefully guide me to where I wanted to be. Where I *needed* to be.

Claws scraped on the stone behind me, somewhere in the distance.

Someone was after me. Fear pierced my chest, spurring me on, moving me faster. I didn't want to know who it was or what they were going to do if they caught me. But wolves were fast, and my only advantage was the staggering amount of turns the corridors made.

I raced onward until the hallway abruptly spilled me out into what could only be described as what Vir had called the *true* Shuldar. The underground city of shifters.

The cavern was enormous. It must occupy most of the mountain itself. Silver light cascaded down from somewhere, likely the moon itself, giving the city a ghostly feel that was strangely comforting. I was underground in a giant den, but also still running under the moon, in a way.

I followed the call, taking a hard right and running down a street between stone buildings. Dozens of them. Shuldar was *huge*. Thousands of shifters must have lived here. Unlike the surface, most of these buildings were still mostly intact. Some had caved in or crumbled, but most still stood.

It was amazing. Everything my father and I had ever dreamed of and more. I wanted to stop and marvel at it, to admire and inspect everything. There was so much *history* here, of our people. So much that we had lost over the years.

But I couldn't. Behind me, I could feel the pounding of my Soulbond as Johnathan came after me. It could only be him. Nobody else could have that agonizing, debilitating effect on me.

He chased me through the city as I headed for one end of it. The buildings stopped, giving way to row upon row of giant statues set into the wall on either side of me. I recognized some of them, including one that could only be Vir, instantly recognizable with his wolf's head and giant spear.

I noted the horns were oddly missing, though, and I wondered if they were a new addition or if he'd only revealed them to me.

Behind me, Johnathan snarled. Glancing over my shoulder, I saw he was closing on me fast, the straightaway between the statues of the shifter gods giving him an open line. His wolf bounded forward in great leaps even as I ran on.

My Soulbond drummed hard in my head until I was wiping away blood from my nose, my ears going deaf as pain filled me to the bursting point. I felt my throat stripped raw from screaming, but *still*, I ran on. Whatever was calling me, it was ahead. I was almost there.

I was practically running blind now, my vision graying. I clipped my shoulder off something as I ducked into the opening at the end of the field of gods, following the call inside me. Fresh pain, *real* pain, helped clear my mind for just a moment, but then it was gone, wiped away by the demands of the Soulbond as it renewed its assault on my mind.

Johnathan came in hot on my tail, and I knew it was a toss-up as to whether he would simply tear my throat out or shift back and mount me there, against my will, to help seal the bond. His wolf was in a frenzy like mine, and I doubted he could control himself much better than I could.

We'd denied the bond for too long. It was driving us insane.

I emerged into a large, domed room. It was dark, so dark I could only make out the barest hint of detail. One thing I could see clearly, however, was that there was no other exit.

I was trapped.

Johnathan stalked into the room after me. I stood there, breathing hard. This was it, dammit! I could feel it. I was here. It was right *here*, all around me. This was where I was being called to!

Fearfully, I reached out, trying to figure out what it was that was calling me to this spot, that had driven me to run from people I respected, to leave them to die, just to come *here* of all places.

Where nothing happened.

"Damn you!" I sobbed, falling to my knees as Johnathan came to a stop a dozen or so feet behind me. "Why? What is this place? Why won't you help me!"

My pleas went unanswered. The only sound was Johnathan's growl.

"Fuck you," I said, turning to spit at him. "Go ahead and try to kill me. Because I will *never* submit to you."

The black-furred wolf snarled, saliva dripping from his yellowed canines, and in a blur, he came at me.

I rolled aside, but I was too slow. My forearm was suddenly covered in warmth as hot blood ran from the wound his teeth had torn in my shoulder.

Gritting my teeth, I turned to face him as blood covered my forearm.

I wasn't about to die on my knees. Fuck that. I put my hands on the ground to push myself to my feet.

Around me, the room came alive.

CHAPTER FIFTY-THREE

Purple energy cascaded out from where I knelt.

It ran out in a circle, racing through runes on the floor and up the walls, carving an intricate pattern up to the center of the room, which was right above me.

The thing that had called to me had called to that energy. It reached out, and as the entire room cackled with brilliant violet light, it surged back down and *into* me.

If I'd thought I was being torn in two earlier, I didn't know a thing about pain. That was like stubbing my toe compared to the sheer blinding agony that filled every part of my body, burning every pain receptor and nerve ending I possessed.

I screamed until my throat bled. My eyes were bleeding. I tasted more blood on my lips as it trickled from my nose.

Nearby, I somehow saw motion. It was Johnathan, his wolf staring at me, mouth open in shock.

"*You*," I said, my voice reverberating with astounding strength, filling the room.

This was *his fault*. I wanted him to feel my pain. To share in my hurt.

Without thinking, I thrust a hand at him. Purple lightning coursed out from my hand, slamming into him and hurling the giant wolf across the room until he crunched against the wall.

I slowly turned my palm to face me, staring at it. Well, *that* was new.

Getting to my feet, I wavered. My wolf was howling, struggling to get free, the energy pouring through me hurting her, too. The room blurred, and I lost consciousness for a moment. When I regained it, the pain returned with stunning rapidity. I screamed some more.

My senses were flickering in and out of human and wolf, overwhelming me. I abruptly shifted into wolf form and then back in less than two seconds. My body wasn't designed for that, and I curled up on my side, altering between whimpering and screaming as energy continued to pour into me and then out of me, lighting up the room with its purple glow.

I heard more noise from somewhere behind me. Rolling over, I lashed out, more lighting slamming into the wall just next to the opening.

Vir skidded to a halt, the blast having missed him by less than a foot. He stared at me. I could see the shock on his face.

"HELP ME!" I screamed, the sound shaking the entire room. *"HELP ME, DAMN YOU!"*

Vir raced to my side. "How? How can I help? How are you doing this?"

His voice was like a whisper on the wind, barely audible over the howling storm of energy around me and inside me.

"I DON'T KNOW," I wailed, my cry like that of a banshee. Even Vir had to shield his ears. A god. *"I CAN'T STOP IT. I CAN'T. I DON'T KNOW. THE BOND IS TOO STRONG! PLEASE."*

My mind was destroying itself, the two powers warring for control over me. I scratched and clawed at my face, trying to dig in, to let the pain out. To free them both. I saw blood on my fingertips, but I didn't care. I had to stop it. I had to free myself.

Vir grunted, and abruptly, the energy seemed to calm. But not the pain inside me. It went on. And on. And on.

"Please, Vir," I sobbed, able to speak without screaming for a moment even as the throbbing built anew. "You have to end it. You have to help me."

"What are you saying, Dani?" the shifter god asked.

I locked eyes with him.

"You have to kill me, Vir," I pleaded. "It's the only way. I can't do this. The Soulbond is tearing me apart. I don't *want* to be mated to him."

Vir swallowed, his gaze heavy. "No," he said.

I wailed, energy filling my hand as I prepared to strike at him for denying me my release.

"There is another way," Vir said, taking my hand calmly and pushing it to the ground.

"What?" I whispered. There was no way he could have heard that quiet plea over the cackle and howling of the energy I'd somehow released in the room, but he responded anyway.

"I can sever the link."

I stared at him, stunned. That was possible? It was a thing?

"You can?"

He nodded.

The Soulbond sensed what he was talking about, and I found myself dragging my body toward Johnathan.

"DO IT!" I screamed as more purple energy rose to combat the Soulbond. I could feel my body breaking apart. It wouldn't be long before the energy, the golden Soulbond or the purple of this

new power, started to pour through my skin, quite literally shredding me to pieces.

Vir hesitated. "If I do this," he said. "You will never love."

"I DON'T CARE!" My voice shook the chamber once more.

"You will be alone," he said heavily. "Forever."

I looked at him, my eyes snapping open. "I'm already alone," I whispered. "I have no family. No mate. I have nothing."

Vir stared at me sadly.

"Please!" I wailed. "I would rather *die* than be with him. He's everything I hate."

Nearby, Johnathan got to his feet. I could sense his every move. I felt his muscles. It was killing me.

"Please," I whispered.

A loud, powerful roar from outside the chamber filled me with more dread. Lars was coming. He was almost here.

"Okay," Vir said.

Then, he reached out and worked the energy. It responded to him. He absorbed some of it and grew swiftly in size. His wolf's head reappeared, as did his weapon of war, the spear.

Reaching out, he touched me with that same worked energy. A line of golden brilliance appeared, rising from my chest into the air and running across the room to where it plunged deep into Johnathan's chest. Linking us. It glowed so brightly it fought back the purple energy.

"*Cut it!*" I cried as my wolf started pushing through my skin, taking over.

I couldn't resist any longer. We were going to mate with Johnathan. We were going to end our torment.

The building was shaking around us as my fur lightened, my hands and feet reshaping themselves into paws. The pain of the shift was nothing compared to the agony in the rest of me.

"I'm sorry," Vir said quietly, and the tip of his spear came up and through the golden line.

Severing it.

CHAPTER FIFTY-FOUR

Peace.

The feeling flooded me instantly as the golden bond split apart, the ends of it beginning to blacken even as the force of the spear slicing them sent the two ends fluttering up into the air.

Pain receded next. Giving me some clarity. I could see the room again, still lit by the bursting, crackling energy that was still being absorbed by me, somehow.

What was this place? What did it mean?

My attention was focused on the very Soulbond itself. I hadn't realized it was an *actual* thing. A tangible line between the two of us, but now, as I watched the blackness work its way toward me, the entire thing happening in slow motion, I knew without a doubt I'd made the right choice.

A life of loneliness was better than the alternative. This was what I'd needed to do.

I watched the line die, waiting for it to reach me.

Finally.

Once it did, I would have no hope of ever having a mate again. And I would be *free*. At last. Of everyone. Of everything.

It continued to shrivel, and I heard myself exhale in relief.

It was over. At long last, my fight was over.

Johnathan. Lars. Whatever Aaron was. Vir. Even the temple and the energy still swirling around. *None* of that mattered to me now as I watched the line darken and turn to dust.

"*NO!*" Johnathan, now back in his human form, bellowed as he lunged at me, his hand grasping for the still yellow part of the bond.

He was going to try and reattach them! I watched it happen, horrified. I put my hands up, trying to block him, to affect the bond, but my arms passed through it.

But Johnathan came on anyway. He took two steps and leaped toward me.

I screamed.

At the last second, Vir jumped between us, intercepting Johnathan. Stopping him short of his goal. But the impact sent Vir stumbling backward. Toward me. I watched, stunned and terrified, as the still golden part of my Soulbond plunged deep into Vir's back.

And grew bright.

To Be Continued...

Thank you for reading The Wild Moon. If you enjoyed it, please consider leaving a review so that others might enjoy the adventure as well.

The Story Continues in:

As Darkness Falls (Soulbound Shifters Book 2)

OTHER BOOKS BY RILEY STORM

Thanks for checking out my other books!

Below you can find all my novels, divided up by series. The brackets indicate which of my worlds the series is written in. So dig in!

-Riley

Soulbound Shifters (Soulbound Shifters #1)

The Wild Moon

As Darkness Falls

Fate Unbound

Blood & Fangs (Soulbound Shifters #2)

Soulbitten

Blood Letter

Queen of Darkness

Shattered Wolf (Soulbound Shifters #3)

Under a Cursed Moon

The 'Ex'-Mate Hunt

Dragons of Mount Aterna (Five Peaks #1)

A Mate to Treasure

A Mate to Believe In

A Mate to Protect

A Mate to Embrace

Dragons of Mount Teres (Five Peaks #2)

In a Dragon's Mind

In a Dragon's Heart

In a Dragon's Dream

In a Dragon's Soul

Dragons of Mount Valen (Five Peaks #3)

Her Dragon Guardian

Her Dragon Lord

Her Dragon Soulmate

Her Dragon Outcast

Dragons of Mount Atrox (Five Peaks #4)

Dragon's True Mate

Dragons' Second Chance Romance

Dragon's Fake Wedding Date

Dragon's Devotion

Dragons of Mount Rixa (Five Peaks #5)

Dragon Claimed

Dragon Loved

Dragon Bound

Dragon Savior

Storm Dragons (Winterspell Academy)

Stolen by the Dragon

Trapped by the Dragon

Dragon's Chosen Mate

High House Ursa (Plymouth Falls #1)

Bearing Secrets

Furever Loyal

Mated to the Enemy

Shifting Alliances

Blood Bearon

High House Canis (Plymouth Falls #2)

Savage Love

Blood Mate

Moonlight Bride

Shadow's Howl

Royal Alpha

High House Draconis (Plymouth Falls #3)

Fire Dragons Bride

Mated to the Water Dragon

Ice Dragon's Caress

Earth Dragon's Kiss

Claimed by the Dragon King

ABOUT THE AUTHOR

Riley Storm

Riley is one of those early morning people you love to hate, because she swears she doesn't need caffeine, even though the coffee-maker is connected to her smartphone. She lives in a three-story townhouse by the good graces of a tabby cat who rules the house, the couch, the table, well, basically everywhere. When she's not groveling for forgiveness for neglecting to pet her kitty enough, Riley is strapped into her writing chair coming up with crazy worlds where she can make her own decisions of when feeding time is and how much coffee can be drunk without her friends—of which she has three—holding yet another intervention that they threaten to post on the internet.

Find her on:

Website: *www.highhousepress.com*

On Facebook: *'Riley Storm Author'*

Printed in Great Britain
by Amazon